I0524354

It's a Kink Thing

UNKINKED

M.C. ROTH

Unkinked
ISBN # 978-1-80250-981-6
©Copyright M.C. Roth 2022
Cover Art by Kelly Martin ©Copyright September 2022
Interior text design by Claire Siemaszkiewicz
Pride Publishing

UNKINKED

Dedication

For Q

Chapter One

Derreck

Derreck killed his car's engine, letting his eyes fall shut as he leaned back against the leather seat. He could barely keep his eyes open as exhaustion pulled at him, sinking into his weary bones until his frame was thinly stretched.

The seat was comfortable enough that he could almost imagine himself drifting off to the sound of gentle ticking as the Mustang slowly cooled. The air conditioning faded, draining his hope for restful peace as sweat beaded on his forehead. Wiping it away, he let out one last sigh before he opened the door.

Even warmer air coated him as he stepped onto the pavement, his sweat drying under the sun almost instantly. A single shriveled maple on the street hung limp, its leaves barely managing to hold on as the sun baked them black. He rubbed his eyes as his shoes kicked up enough dust to blind an army within a few steps.

Stumbling on the curb, Derreck managed to catch himself on the lamp post that jutted out of the edge of the sidewalk. His palm burned as it touched the heated surface, a gasp pushing through his lips.

Usually it wouldn't bother him — the pain. It was a part of life that he could easily ignore or twist into something much better — but not when he'd gone weeks without a decent night's sleep.

He'd thrown himself into his work, pulling more hours than anyone else, all to avoid the enthralling eyes of the sub that haunted his dreams. *If only it had worked.*

"Are you okay?"

He turned toward the voice as it trickled into his thoughts. The street was empty. Even the plant that hung from the lamp post was nothing more than a few dried twigs and a bunch of dehydrated pansies. He paused, raising his hand to block his eyes from the sun's glare.

The voice had sounded close, but he couldn't spy anyone as he looked around before noting the white door of his destination and the Office Depot across the street. *I must be worse off than I thought.*

There was usually no one to see him coming and going in this part of town, which was exactly how he liked it. There were a few other cars parked along the curb, and he recognized them all except the red Toyota next to him.

He huffed, ready to turn away, before something caught his eye. The Corolla's windows were down, the sun baking the exposed gray-cloth interior with heat waves escaping through the openings. It wasn't a car that should have had its windows down in a place with nobody around.

Derreck took a step toward the car before peering through the passenger window. In the driver's seat was a man who must've been one step away from heatstroke, especially with his black sweater that probably soaked up warmth that much quicker. The interior was tidy, except for a few empty bottles of water stacked on the passenger seat.

Derreck had chosen a baby-blue tank top and jeans himself, but he wished he could pull his tank over his head and dunk himself in the nearest swimming pool.

Leaning over the side of the car, Derreck touched the hood, hissing as heat lanced over his palm. *I am going to be useless tonight.* Shaking his hand, he leaned down to get a better look at the driver.

The driver was flushed, his face a healthy pink and his brown hair soaked with sweat so thick that it looked nearly back. His sweater clung to him, the fabric dark in almost every spot on his rail-thin body. The man gave Derreck a broad smile, sending a small wave as Derreck peered into the steaming interior.

"I didn't mean to startle you," said the man, leaning back in his seat and adjusting the strap over his chest. "I saw you stumble and wanted to make sure you were okay."

Okay? Derreck couldn't keep the disbelief off his face. He didn't even have the energy to turn the question back at the guy who was sweating his ass off in a car when it was sweltering, even in the shade. He didn't want to know.

"I'm good, thanks," said Derreck, slapping the top of the car as he turned away. *You should ask him if he's okay.* Derreck bit down on the urge as it rose behind his teeth. He had too much on his plate, and he couldn't take one more ounce of anyone else's shit before he exploded.

But how many times had he stopped things just before they had been about to go to shit? Too many to count.

"You waiting for someone?" Derreck asked, clenching his fists as he paused on the street. The sun soaked into his shoulders, fresh sweat gathering at the base of his neck. Sweet air conditioning was only a few steps away, but this man was so much worse off than him—sitting in his car...in a fucking sweater.

"Uh, yeah." The man looked up and down the street once before he settled his gaze on the familiar blank door that called to Derreck like the sweetest siren. Beyond those doors was relief and relaxation that couldn't be rivaled by anything else in the world. Too bad there wasn't a bed meant for just sleeping.

The door to the club Unkinked had never been labeled, which kept a lot of pointed fingers from finding it. This man seemed to know what was inside the same way Derreck did.

Someone's sub? The guy didn't look like a Dom, although looks were as deceiving as book covers. Derreck had seen twinky Doms control guys twice their size—putting them on their knees and making them beg usually did the trick.

Derreck had it easier. He looked his part of ruthless Dom, and no one in their right mind would ever ask him to be their sub. It would have been their last question with their own teeth in their head if they did.

He turned away, heading to the door and pressing his hand against the cool surface. He could already feel the stress draining from his body, seeping into the beams of the place where his mind and body felt safest. All he needed was a bit of play and he would be set for the next week. If it were good enough, the high might even last a bit longer and he would be able to catch a bit of sleep.

But his highs were becoming few and far between, and the last one had left him wanting—wanting to never step foot in his place of solace again, wanting to leave the lifestyle behind for good, wanting to be *vanilla*. He shuddered at the thought.

After pulling his key card from his pocket, he tapped it against the door's sensor, the light taking much too long to flip over to green before the lock slid back with a clunk. The security was necessary, as was the bouncer on the other side of the door and the dungeon master who was patrolling the club. It kept curious seekers from sneaking their way inside the place where people laid their hearts and souls out in the open.

He nodded at the unfamiliar bouncer, giving him a quick once-over before thoroughly dismissing him. Derreck didn't care if a sub was burly and thick or lean, because he'd long since mastered hitting a target with a touch of jiggle. But he couldn't pull the bouncer away from his duties.

The bouncer was the third fresh face he'd seen in as many months. The owner of Unkinked, Clint, must have been outsourcing his help for there to be so many unfamiliar faces—either that or maybe they got sick of hearing people fuck and not being able to join in.

Derreck let out a sigh as the cool air trickled over his skin, his sweat turning into goosebumps as the summer heat was sucked away. He let his eyes fall shut as he took a deep breath. Earth and mold that always clung to him gave way to sex and desire, dredging up memories in an instant. He had thousands of memories of Unkinked, and some of them were the best days and nights of his life.

The pull of desire lured him a step away from the door. The sharpness of vodka and rum tickled his nose as he stepped to the curtain. *Am I drinking tonight?* A drink meant no scene, and a scene was everything he needed.

There was a subtle staleness to the curtains as Derreck trailed his fingers over the fabric, finally opening his eyes. He pushed them aside, taking in every detail of the dark interior.

Three of the booths were occupied, all by Doms and subs whom he recognized. A few looked up as he entered, one sub blushing and looking back to the floor. Derreck kept his smirk to himself as he nodded to their Dom, Selina. She had allowed him to borrow her sub, after all. It hadn't been nearly as interesting as he had hoped, but he'd still cherished the submission.

The inside of the club was clean and still bright in the early hour—and was likely different than any newbie expected. There was a touch of nudity in the main area, as well as some rocking leather, but the best parts of the club were out of view. Hidden near the back was the entrance to the main stage and open play area, and tucked around the corner were nine private rooms that made even the most stoic Doms salivate.

From the entrance, though, it could have been any other club, with booths along the wall and a bottle-rich bar with wooden stools for those who wanted to socialize and grab a few drinks. The virgin menu was even more robust than the alcoholic one, catering to the couples who wanted to play.

He stepped to the bar, slipping into an unoccupied stool. Brennen was in the next stool over, bent over a shot glass that reeked of vodka and whiskey—a killer combination that Brennen usually stuck with. There were three more glasses strewn around him and his eyes were already glassy.

He wouldn't be playing, and he was a Dom anyway, which was something Derreck never tried to push. He had no desire to change a person's identity, whether it was Dom or sub. Both positions demanded respect.

"Hey, Derreck. It's a hot one today," said Brennen, looking up from his glass just long enough to ask.

Derreck grunted, tapping the bar top. His nails were still crusted with dirt and clay. No matter how hard he scrubbed, they never seemed to come clean. Even the potato scrubber from the discount store hadn't done the trick, although it had stung.

He leaned against the bar as another wave of exhaustion settled over him. The murmur of voices was almost enough to send him straight to sleep, and the ease that always settled over him in Unkinked had him even closer.

"You drinking tonight, Derreck?" asked Clint as he worked his way through the half-dozen others at the bar.

Clint had started Unkinked with his husband, and after his husband had passed, he had taken full responsibility to keep it going. Derreck couldn't imagine keeping the hours Clint did, along with bartending, organizing events and schedules, giving lessons in first-aid and the mountain of paperwork he must have.

Besides the bouncer and the volunteer dungeon master, Clint worked alone, although there were many subs who offered volunteer service as well.

Derreck blinked as he dropped his gaze to Clint's hips when they swayed with each sauntering step when he moved closer. He was attractive and strong, with a wicked smirk that had caught Derreck's eye more than once.

Nodding his head, he peered back over his shoulder. Clint was so far off limits that Derreck shouldn't have even been looking. *One drink. One drink before the fun starts.*

Clint gave him a quick smile before reaching for a bottle of Jameson. "The usual?"

Derreck shook his head, eyeing Clint up as he passed under the bar's light. Clint looked *tired* and from more than just lack of sleep. He looked the way Derreck had felt for the past few weeks. It was another thing that Derreck just didn't have the energy to fix.

Clint was his friend. Maybe not in a traditional sense, but Clint had been there for him more than once. In return, Derreck usually had his back. But it had been weeks since Derreck had stepped inside the bar. Things had obviously not changed while he had been trying to convince himself he could stay away.

"Give me a shot of Jäger." Derreck leaned his elbows on the bar top, sagging as he took in his surroundings. *Ask him if he's okay.* He looked back to Clint and to the tightness around his eyes. *Not here.*

"Must've been a shit day," said Clint as he set the bottle of Jameson down and reached for the Jägermeister instead. His grip was steady, and the liquid didn't slosh over the side as he poured Derreck his shot. *Maybe I'm just projecting.*

"Shit week," said Derreck, surprised that Clint didn't mention his absence. He shouldn't have been surprised. Clint was one of the most intuitive men he knew, and he must've seen the strain in Derreck's every movement.

Derreck's callused palms were red and blistered, his skin dry and still dirty-looking, despite his lengthy shower. His muscles burned, even as he raised his glass to his lips and tossed back the shot. The liquid seared a path down his throat, turning him inside out as it sank into him. It eased the ache in the rest of his body for an instant. A bit of rain would have gone so much further than the shot, though.

"You starting a tab?" Clint grabbed the empty shot glass, setting it on a tray beneath the lip of the bar.

"I'll stop at one." Derreck pushed off the stool, heading deeper into the club without looking back at Clint. If he'd stayed any longer, he would have had to ask Clint if he was okay. *Letting two people down in one day. Must be a record.* He grimaced as his gut throbbed with every movement. Jäger had probably been a poor choice.

He scoped out the bar a second time, slowing his stride until his stomach calmed. His gaze lingered on a couple—two subs—as they kissed over their table. *Kristie and Katie.* It was too bad that they weren't his type, because two subs *were* better than one. They needed a soft Dom, but he needed a sub to torture the fuck out of.

There were a few other couples, despite the early hour. After dark was when the real sadists started to emerge from the shadows, but the lifers didn't care what time of day it was. Derreck was a lifer, too, he supposed, and after more than fifteen years, he should have known that his life was nothing without kink.

He circled the bar area again. There was nothing happening on the main stage or open floor, and he had no desire to just *watch* if one of the kink room doors were open. He spied a Dom who was reclined in the seating area outside of the rooms, her sub at her feet with his head across her shoe. From the blissed-out look on his face, he was still floating.

Derreck needed something more than that. He needed them sobbing with euphoria in his arms after he fucked them up. It was the only way he was going to get a certain sub out of his thoughts.

He clenched his hands into fists, the calluses on his palms like pebbles over his skin. His hands could do a lot of damage to a person, then dig a grave on a moonlit Tuesday. The damage was always consensual, but the grave...not so much.

He slipped down the hallway of doors that led to kink rooms, which held more implements than any Dom or sub could ever ask for. He slid his hand over the engraved gold letters on his favorite room. *Impact.* Even the name made goosebumps burst over his skin and sent a shudder of need to his core. His cock stayed soft, as it usually did, except for those rare occasions when a sub managed to surpass his expectations.

Like Nav. He closed his eyes, letting his hand rest against the carved surface.

Nav had been introduced to him by a fellow Dom, and after their first scene together, he had gone straight home with his hands still aching from holding the flogger tight. Stepping in the shower, he had dropped his hand to his cock, jerking himself to hardness with Nav on his mind.

But Nav wasn't his in the loosest sense of the word, even though he still managed to haunt Derreck's dreams. Nav had safeworded during their second scene together, then had fled back to his true Dom, Trick. The call of *"yellow"* still sounded in his ears as if it had only been yesterday.

Sex was so rarely a part of life for Derreck, but during their first scene, he had watched Trick come as Nav had shot against the wall from Derreck's beating alone. He wouldn't have been a gay man if he hadn't felt *something*.

But Nav had belonged to Trick before the two of them had even realized it. Derreck had seen their looks and had chosen to ignore them, despite his better instincts. It had been a miscalculation that had added to his sleeplessness and had prompted him to steer clear of the club for weeks.

He gritted his teeth, turning away from the closed door and pushing his way down the hall.

He'd come to the club so he could forget his mistake and move the fuck on.

The private rooms were all closed as he passed them, tracing his fingertips over each name. *Play, Spoil, Calm, Wet.* He wasn't sure whether or not there were couples on the other side of each door, but the closed door meant that voyeurism was not welcome. *I'm not welcome.*

He circled back to the main area, sliding into an empty booth, despite invitations from several tables that he passed. He didn't pause for conversation, just tilted his head before he moved on to his own space. Rapping his knucks against the polished tabletop, he leaned back to survey the room once more.

17

There was no one for him yet, but he was patient. He could spend hours staring at the same spec of dirt, letting his mind drift until he was content. Sitting in a comfortable chair with the hum of music and the smell of sex in the air was paradise in comparison.

He looked up as the curtain to the entrance slid open and another couple stepped off the street and into his world. Derreck got a flash of the bouncer and a few others before the curtain fluttered back into place. The hum of conversation lulled against his eardrums.

His chest did *not* squeeze when he spotted Nav tucked under Trick's arm as they entered the club together. Trick's tanned hand glowed against Nav's pale, naked shoulder, a pair of tight boy shorts the only thing on Nav's body.

It wasn't that Derreck was jealous of his friend, but there was a certain longing at seeing Nav that summoned his darker side. It wasn't very often that Derreck could take himself in hand and come quickly, and a treat like Nav would have made any man salivate.

Trick spotted him first, nodding from across the room before he gripped the back of Nav's neck and pushed him to the ground.

Nav had come a long way since Derreck had last seen him. Dropping to his knees, Nav didn't seem to care how hard he struck the ground or how rough Trick jerked his head back by his hair. His eyes glazed over immediately, going deep without resistance. He was something *special*.

Derreck shifted in his seat, trying to ease the tension in his gut. Nav—*no, Trick's sub*—stayed on the ground as Trick strolled toward Derreck, giving him a smile as he approached.

"Derreck." Trick stopped at the edge of the booth, holding his hand out in an offering. Derreck took it, accepting the handshake at face value. Trick had grown a few calluses on his palm, the surface rougher than Derreck remembered. *Working his sub hard. Good.* Nav deserved someone who would put the effort in.

"Maverick." He squeezed once before he broke contact, smothering the urge to wipe his hand on his pants. Trick's sweat on his palm was like a raw nerve, his touch buzzing under Derreck's skin.

"My slut has something to say to you, if you are agreeable to it," said Trick, glancing back at Nav. Trick's eyes were hard, despite the languid way he moved. He traced the room, eyeing someone up as they moved from a booth to the bar, passing close to Nav. *Too close, apparently.* Trick clenched his fist, his jaw going tight.

Derreck paused, looking back at Trick's sub. Nav had lowered his eyes to the floor, unmoving, despite the way his knees had to have been aching on the hardwood. Perhaps he had done something to not deserve a pillow — or perhaps he preferred it like that.

Nav wasn't beautiful in a traditional sense — too pale and soft to meet the stereotypical desires of most men — but Derreck had seen first-hand how alluring he was after a scene. Derreck valued that more than any beauty.

He inclined his head, sliding his hand over the tabletop as he looked to Trick. "I'm agreeable." His voice sounded more strained than he would have liked, but he'd buried too many people in one week to feel normal. Trick gave him a sharp look, probably seeing straight through him. *I must look worse than I thought.*

Trick didn't say anything, though, which made him a better friend than Derreck gave him credit for. Instead, he called his sub over, Nav crawling on all fours with his head lowered as he approached.

Derreck slid his hand over the tabletop, Trick's sweat on his palm spreading over the surface until he could no longer feel the edge of it sinking into his skin. It left a streaky mess on the polished surface, his fingerprints blatant beneath the light.

Derreck looked up as Nav finally stopped his crawling and kneeled at his feet with his head bowed. His dark hair shone in the low light of the club, looking almost black against his pale skin. A purplish welt peeked through the waist band of his low-riding shorts and Derreck fought the urge to reach forward and press his fingertip to the bruise.

"Speak," said Derreck, keeping his voice quiet. Nav had a very particular brand of humiliation that he desired, and that brand name was *Trick*. Derreck was *nothing* to him.

"I wanted to apologize, Sir," said Nav, keeping his gaze pointed to the floor, despite his steady tone. "I was lying to myself, and to you, when I asked for a second scene. I should have never disrespected you, and I'm sorry for my behavior."

That…was unexpected. Derreck tilted his head, not fighting the smile that tugged at his lips. It was also a huge fucking relief. It had been a mistake, but maybe it hadn't been his alone.

A smidge of his exhaustion uncoiled, his lungs filling easier than they had in a long time.

"Forgiven," said Derreck, fighting the urge to keep his hands to himself for a second time. Trick, having no need to hold back, threaded his hand through Nav's hair, tugging him so he had to crawl a step closer.

"Thank you, Sir," said Nav, tension visibly draining from his body.

So good. Derreck turned his gaze away, swallowing down the words that started to rise. Nav was one of a kind, but Nav was not *his.*

"Clint will be joining us for our scene," said Trick, patting his sub on the top of his head. "You are welcome as well, of course."

Trick's eyes darkened as he looked at his sub, and it wasn't because of the low light. Derreck shook his head. That was not the type of torture he was after tonight. He had no desire to string himself along, gaze at Trick's sub and *imagine.*

"Slut, go get ready in our room. You know which one," said Trick. Nav scurried away on his hands and knees, the bottom of his ass cheeks peeking through the hem of his shorts. Another small bruise caught Derreck's eye and he licked his lips before forcing his gaze back to the table. Trick was staring at him, his eyes hard.

"You're my friend, Derreck, but I've never seen you this distant before — not with me, anyway. You haven't been here in weeks and tonight…you aren't yourself. I know you won't ask for help, so I'm offering it."

Shit. Am I really that obvious? He swallowed the lump in his throat that had formed as soon as he'd seen Nav walk through the curtain. "It's nothing. I just need to find myself a sub and let off some steam."

But will that be enough? It had been before, but Trick was right. He wasn't himself and hadn't been for some time. Even before Nav, things had been…*off.*

Trick hummed before looking around the bar. "There's only one sub who can take what you have to give right now. The offer stands. You can come, watch or get involved again if that's what you need. I'm sure Nav would be open to the idea, too. He's been kicking himself for weeks about what he did to you."

Not his fault. "He's good for you," said Derreck, turning his gaze back to the table. Maybe he wouldn't stop at one shot tonight. His stomach churned at the idea, goosebumps breaking out over his skin.

A smile cracked Trick's face, his blue eyes glowing with the glee and something more. Trick had never looked at his previous partner like that, but Derreck had always wondered how their partnership had lasted so long when their kinks hadn't aligned. *Compromise maybe?*

"He is. He's a good man and a good slut," said Trick.

"The best of both worlds," said Derreck, his voice flat. Maybe Trick was right. There was no one in the club who could take what he had to give. And on a Wednesday afternoon, that wasn't likely to change.

His patience snapped and exhaustion settled over him again like a weighted blanket. He stood abruptly, leaving Trick behind as he headed for the door. Hopefully, the blond would understand. He'd seen enough of Derreck to know when to take it personally and when not to.

Pushing the curtain aside, he grabbed the doorknob without acknowledging the bouncer who had jumped to his feet, sliding his cell phone back into his pocket. The bouncer opened his mouth once before snapping it shut, taking a step back as he looked at Derreck.

Stepping outside, the sun instantly soaked into his skin, blanketing him in warmth and urging sweat from his body in seconds. The sun had barely moved in the sky, blazing down with what must have been record-breaking heat.

He could barely feel his feet as he stumbled his way along the sidewalk to his car, stopping at the lamp post and leaning on it as he took a deep breath. The post seared through his shirt, heat bursting over his flesh until he thought he might erupt into flames. It did nothing to quell his exhaustion.

He'd never let it get quite that bad before, but he'd never stayed away so long, either. He hadn't wanted to face Trick or Nav or anyone else. He just wanted relief. The apology had given him a touch of respite but not enough to calm the restless energy in his core.

"You sure you're okay?"

Derreck looked up and his gaze followed the sound of the voice.

The guy was still sitting in his car, as if it hadn't been almost an hour. He had pushed up one sleeve of his sweater, one thin and delicate wrist exposed, but the rest of his upper body was still covered with thick, black material. The flush on his cheeks and the sweat in his hair told of how hot he must've been, but he was making no move to remove his sweater.

"Still waiting?" asked Derreck, looking back at the club entrance. None of the couples had been missing a third that he knew of. And no Dom would leave their sub in a hot car like he was some sort of oven-baked dog.

No responsible Dom, at least.

The man nodded, flicking his gaze to the door and back to Derreck quickly. His eyes had gone shiny, as if he was just managing to hold back tears. How long had he been there before Derreck had come to the club? How long would he wait?

It pulled at what few heartstrings Derreck had, but it also spoke to his Dominant side.

It pissed him the fuck off is what it did. He clenched his hands into fists, crossing his arms and staring down at the man in his car.

"Who are they? I'll go get them for you," said Derreck. There was no way he was walking away with this guy still sitting in his car as he got closer and closer to heatstroke.

"Oh." The man dropped his gaze, the pureness of his submission pulling Derreck deeper into the strange thrall. His cheeks flushed brighter, sweat beading under his eyes.

Perhaps it had been the wrong question. Some Doms insisted on titles, and Derreck would have no luck if the guy simply said 'Sir' or 'Master'.

"Describe what they look like," said Derreck, taking a deep breath to keep the anger out of his voice. He was definitely kicking someone's ass tonight—just not in the way he'd hoped.

"I—I don't know," said the man, his gaze still fixed on his lap. "I only have his name. Someone—a friend online—gave me his name and said that he might be able to help me. They said he comes to this club, but I can't get in without an invite."

"You can if you're a guest," said Derreck, letting out a sigh. This was just getting stranger and stranger. "Your friend can invite you as a guest, and you'll have a temporary pass."

"Oh, they aren't a member," he said, finally looking up, but only for a moment. "They went to an open house event here years ago, but they don't live in the city. I don't know anyone with a membership."

It was a conundrum that had always bothered Derreck. Privacy came with the price of inaccessibility and exclusivity, especially for subs who were heartbreakingly shy. He would still take his privacy, though. The one-and-done kinksters could fuck off.

He ran a hand over his scalp, scratching the short, tight curls. It was too fucking hot to think, and he had to get off the street before he passed out.

"What's the name, then? I can tell you if they are here," said Derreck. He *wouldn't* give away much, because if this guy was a stalker, which was quickly becoming a possibility, then he didn't want to encourage him.

"Oh, it's… Let me grab my phone. I have it in there." He fumbled with his pockets, finally sliding his phone out from the pouch in his sweater. Why the hell was he wearing so many layers? Derreck was getting warmer just looking at him. "I saved it in here, 'cause I'm terrible with names. The guy's name is Derreck."

Derreck almost choked on his spit when he heard his own name. Cocking his head to the side, he dragged his gaze up and down the guy's form one more time. His first impression had been pure madness, but he never was one to hold on to a first impression for long. He usually waited until the sixth before he really made up his mind.

The guy was in shorts and flip-flops, which Derreck hadn't noticed before. It couldn't have been great for driving, but at least he wasn't insane enough to wear long pants along with his sweater. His clothes were good quality but well worn, so he probably wasn't out to try to kidnap Derreck. He didn't stand a chance either way, unless he had a gun in his pocket.

The man fiddled with his thumbs as Derreck watched him, the chewed edge of his nail vibrant with fresh blood. All his nails were like that — bitten past the quick to the delicate pink flesh beneath.

"How did your friend say he could help you?" asked Derreck, eyeing the guy's cell phone. It was a new model, fresh out of the store with a custom case.

"I…" The man trailed off, bringing his thumb to his mouth and catching the vermillion edge with his teeth. A fresh droplet of blood oozed up, shining against his lip until he slowly dragged it away with his tongue.

"I heard he could hurt me," said the man, so quietly that Derreck had to strain to hear him. "I need someone to hurt me."

Pushing away from the post, Derreck circled around the car and pulled the door open with a jerk. The man's eyes went wide and he drew back, shrinking into his seat as Derreck loomed over the car.

"What's your name?" asked Derreck, lowering himself into a squat. It left the man with a slight height advantage, hopefully easing some of his fear that had sprung up. Derreck reached for the man's hand, pulling his thumb from his mouth. The flesh was burning beneath his palms, slick with sweat and clammy.

"Maddy," he said, letting out a sigh at the touch.

There was no buzzing under Derreck's skin or desire to wipe his fingers clean. It was the rare perfection that always seemed to elude Derreck when he needed it most.

"And why do you want me to hurt you, Maddy?" asked Derreck, watching as Maddy's eyes went wide with realization.

"So I don't hurt myself."

Chapter Two

Maddy

Oh God, this guy is Derreck? Maddy wanted to duck his head into his sweater to hide in shame like a frightened turtle, but it was too hot. It was so hot that he was surprised he was still alive. He wasn't sure if he had stopped sweating or if his clothes had just turned into soup at some point. *Am I the chicken or the noodle?*

Derreck's hands were cool against his own, sucking the warmth from his skin like a cure in a Final Fantasy game. His eyelids threatened to slide closed at the sheer bliss, but he couldn't stop staring.

Maddy was pale—like he'd never seen the sun because he lived like a vampire pale. Derreck's caramel skin looked like a cup of coffee with the perfect amount of cream next to his. It was almost *exotic*—which was probably a strange word to describe a man.

Did Derreck think he was insane? Maddy was almost certain that he should have checked himself into a hospital, but they probably wouldn't let him go...ever. He had one foot in the door there anyway, not that it helped.

He hadn't really known what his plan was, but he had been so desperate that it hadn't mattered. The heat and the blinding sun hadn't mattered. Three hours later and halfway to a steaming pork chop, when he'd been seconds from giving up, Derreck had found him...*like magic.*

Everything he knew about Derreck had sounded too good to be true, but he'd had no choice except to take the chance. It had been an impossible task to find someone on their first name alone, but Derreck was next to him, clutching his hand with a palm that felt like it was made of callus and blisters.

"Come with me," said Derreck, tugging his hand softly. "I'd like to take you inside so we can cool down. It's not healthy to be sitting in a car when it's so hot outside."

Maddy knew that, but he'd still done it. He'd gone through three water bottles and a bottle of Gatorade, but he still didn't have to pee. Every ounce of fluid was soaked into his hair and his clothes, the sweat doing nothing to cool him in the super-heated interior of his car. His university degrees had done little to prepare him for the reality of heatstroke.

Derreck steadied Maddy as he pulled himself out of the car, the world tilting as slightly cooler air touched the back of his neck and his exposed wrist. His tongue stuck to the roof of his mouth, and he longed for another drink of water, or apple juice, or really anything — except cranberry juice because *hell no.*

"I can go inside? In the club?" asked Maddy, steadying himself against Derreck's arm. What he grasped with his fingers could not have been a part of an actual person. He blinked, staring down at Derreck's bicep. Maddy could bench press a fifteen-gram pencil, but this guy?

Maybe Jennifer hadn't exaggerated. Maybe Derreck was everything she had said. Heatstroke was one-hundred-percent worth it if that were the case.

"Yes...as my guest."

His imagination burst to life as a thousand fantasies clambered for attention. There could be anything behind the door from a dungeon to a torture chamber. As long as it looked nothing like Grey's room in *Fifty Shades*, then he would be happy. Hell, he just hoped to get into the air conditioning. He was about three seconds away from frying his brain.

He could have sat in his car with the engine running and the air conditioning blasting, but he happened to enjoy living on a planet where he could still breathe. Burning that much fuel for his own comfort had not been an option.

Derreck tapped his key card against the tiny black box that Maddy had inspected earlier in the day. Maddy had knocked quietly hours ago, but no one had answered. He had thought about slipping in with another couple as they entered, but he had caught sight of the scary-looking bouncer just inside the door. Getting his ass kicked like that was not his poison.

Maddy took a·deep breath of cool air as the door swung wide. Months of anticipation peaked with the smell of alcohol and different perfumes. He was finally there — inside the building that he had dreamed about for years but had unknowingly craved for as long as he could remember.

The first time he had heard about kink, he had *known*. He had yearned for it worse than chocolate, coffee and cake combined. But it had taken even longer to discover the club that he had no way of getting into — longer still to find the name of the person who had a chance of helping him. *I won't forget it next time.*

Maddy eyed up the red curtains that looked like they had been stolen from the stage of an old gentlemen's club where the ladies danced in nylons and tutus. The bouncer looked even more terrifying up close, with more bulk than anything but still a fair amount of muscle.

"Can we get Maddy checked in as my guest?" Derreck's voice rumbled next to him, and Maddy realized that he was still clutching Derreck. His palm had slicked with sweat, soaking into Derreck's, but he hadn't pulled away.

Paperwork and waivers were something that Maddy had expected, and he filled them out, signing his name with a staggering flourish. He licked his dry lips, shivering as a sudden chill descended. Could he ask for a glass of water? Or was that somehow against the rules?

He'd read about different kinds of relationships in his extensive online research, steering clear of almost all the chat rooms for fear of being somehow turned away. There were some where a sub wasn't even allowed to eat or use the bathroom without their Dom's permission. Maddy could imagine that scenario, and he could also imagine himself telling his Dom to pound salt, as he pissed when he wanted to.

Maddy handed the papers back, looking to Derreck, who was waiting next to the curtain, completely still as he stared unwaveringly. Derreck reached for the curtain, pulling it aside and ushering him through.

A bar…was not what he had been expecting or what he needed. Jennifer had told him about a stage that had been set up during an open house she'd attended, where a Dom and sub had given a demonstration that Maddy had dreamed about. But there was nothing like that in the dimly lit club. There was only a bar and a few booths, with quiet music trickling along the edge of his hearing.

It was busy, and a few people glanced their way as Derreck stepped toward the bar. Maddy tugged his sleeve down over his wrist, shrinking back a step until he was just behind Derreck. Their gazes burned into him, seeing straight through his sweaty clothing. *Don't look at me.*

"Not what you expected?" asked Derreck, watching every move with dark eyes. *Where are the orgies? Where's the torture stuff?*

Maddy dropped his gaze to the scraped wooden floor, hoping that Derreck couldn't read his mind or see his disappointment. The floor was an old-style hardwood, which was strange for a bar because of how hard it must've been to keep clean. There were a few stains that looked to be permanent, but it was tidier than he would have expected.

But what had he been expecting? In his dreams he'd seen a Dom snorting cocaine off their bound sub's belly as another person fucked their throat. Maybe the drugs had been stretching it a bit, but what about the fucking? The threat of getting fucked was the reason that Maddy had taken so long to start looking for a kink club in the first place.

But seriously? Maybe it didn't make sense that he had expected cum to cover every surface. But where were the naked subs sitting at their Dom's feet drinking from a dog bowl filled with champagne? Okay…maybe his imagination had been a bit over the top.

"Just different. I didn't think it would be a bar," said Maddy, sliding onto a stool as Derreck leaned against the counter. The stool was softer than it looked, but the drunk man on his other side instantly had him on edge, even though he hadn't even looked Maddy's way.

"Don't get comfortable," said Derreck, before he turned to the barkeep. "Clint, give me two Sprites and set me up in a room. You know which one."

Clint eyed Maddy as he filled two glasses with ice. "This is last call for the next hour. Harold will be watching the bar, but he won't be serving." He typed something into a touchscreen computer before he slid the drinks toward Derreck. "Have fun. I know I will."

Maddy turned away, unable to bear the grin Clint sent his way. He was about two seconds away from sliding off his stool and bolting for the door. He wasn't here to have fun or have sex. Those were the last things he needed — that he craved.

Derreck grabbed the frosted glasses, turning away from the bar before walking toward the back end of the booths. He looked over his shoulder when Maddy didn't follow him.

"We can sit at a booth if you're more comfortable, but I thought you would prefer a private room to chat," said Derreck, his eyes almost black in the low light.

I didn't sit for three hours in a hot car to leave now. Maddy scrambled off his stool, trying to ignore the gazes that glared at him from all sides. How many people were watching him make a fool of himself?

Turning his head, he spotted a gray-haired man kneeling at the foot of a blond in one of the booths. He was fully clothed with his eyes shut in either sleep or bliss, his head resting in his Dom's lap.

Maddy's heart picked up, his stomach bubbling for the first time since coming through the door.

That was not what he was here for either, but neither was a *chat*. But he supposed he wouldn't be able to get past the chat. Derreck would have questions for him and probably assumed that Maddy had some as well. *I know exactly what I want.*

Maddy had been reading about kink since before it was legal for him to go into a bar. He knew about negotiation, limits and safewords and he would suffer through them if it got him what he wanted.

Derreck turned toward a hallway that had been hidden behind the last booth. To one side there was a closed curtain and a seating area off to his right, but beyond that was a corridor of doors, names etched into each one with cursive gold.

There looked to be about nine doors, but Derreck headed straight for one called *Impact*, tapping the same key card that he had used to unlock the front door.

Maddy's jaw nearly hit the floor as he stepped through the threshold, the door sliding shut behind him with a quiet whoosh. The room had the best lighting of any dungeon that had ever existed on television or in his imagination. His chest relaxed, and he took a deep breath.

This was what he had been expecting and craving.

The far wall was covered with an array of floggers, whips, canes and paddles that made his mouth water and goosebumps break out over his skin. There was a restraint bench in the middle of the room, as well as a standing cross on the far side. An ominous pair of manacles hung from the ceiling at a height that would put him on his tip toes.

Maddy took a step toward the wall of floggers, clenching his fist at his side to keep from reaching out. He had never touched one — only dreamed about them over and over. Saliva burst in his mouth, and he swallowed. The thick scent of leather with a touch of plastic was so strong that he swore he could taste it.

Derreck turned away from the wall, heading for a black couch set away from the implements. He pulled up a small side table and patted the seat next to him before he placed one glass of Sprite on the surface. Condensation dripped down the side of the glass, staining the top of the table dark.

"Is it okay to talk in here?" asked Derreck, resting his arm on the back of the couch. Maddy stared at the wall of torture, unable to look away. "You are looking a little shell-shocked. You have no obligation to stay, and you are free to go at any time if this isn't what you are looking for."

"It's better," said Maddy, slowly lowering himself into the seat next to Derreck. His shirt was clinging to his skin, and with the cool air of the club, he was quickly getting uncomfortable. A shiver trailed up his spine, and he let out a shudder.

"Is this what you had in mind when you asked me to hurt you?" asked Derreck, sliding one of the glasses over to Maddy.

Maddy brought it to his lips immediately, groaning as the carbonated sugar trickled down his throat. He swallowed past the threatening brain freeze, downing the entire glass. Swallowing the last few drops, he took a deep breath and set the empty glass back on the table.

He hid the burp behind his palm as it worked its way up his throat.

"Kind of," said Maddy, squinting at the implements as his head ached from the cold drink. "I've thought about a whip before, but I didn't know there were these many kinds of floggers. I've never been to a kink club."

The Internet had kept that from him, for the most part. He had been convinced that there were only a few kinds of implements that anyone actually used, and the rest were just for show.

Derreck inclined his head, pushing the second glass toward Maddy. "As my guest, I have a responsibility to make sure you follow the rules of the club. If you break them, you will never set foot in the club again — and good luck getting into any others in the city. Word travels fast in this world."

Wait…! There are more clubs? Where the fuck had they been all his life?

"You already signed off on them, but I need you to understand that in any scene, all parties involved must be consenting. Other than that, almost anything goes," said Derreck. "I don't do checklists or anything as tedious as that, but we will talk about limits after you ask me your questions."

Am I that obvious? "Where are all the naked people? I thought this was a sex club." The words left him without permission, but boy, did he want to know. There should have been an orgy out front, and where the fuck was the stage his friend had told him about?

"Did you consent to seeing a Dom or sub naked in the midst of play?" asked Derreck, a frown playing on his lips. He was rather intimidating while sitting, and his long limbs were thick and glowing with a hint of fresh sweat.

Maddy shook his head. He hadn't thought of it like that.

"There is an open play area for those who want to scene in front of others and for those who want to watch, but you won't see anything like that at the bar because you haven't consented. Drinking and drugs aren't permitted if there is going to be play. You can't consent if you are drunk or high. Do you understand?" Derreck took the empty glasses and set them to the side. His eyes weren't black as Maddy had originally thought, but almond brown with a few lighter brown flecks.

It was a lot to take in. Maddy had thought consent was only a sex thing, to be honest, and a simple yes or no question. *When did things get so complicated?*

"I don't want to screw up," said Maddy, fighting the urge to pull his damp sweater away from his body. If he screwed up, everything he had hoped for would disappear. *I can't let that happen.*

"I'll help you," said Derreck. "I'm not a Dom who won't let you speak or ask questions. You don't need to call me 'Master' or 'Sir', because I haven't done anything to earn those titles from you." Derreck rapped the table with his knuckles. "You'll need two safewords. One to stop everything, and one to slow down or ask questions if you need to."

Maddy let out a breath. He had been slightly worried that he was going to be gagged, bound and beaten, then tossed back out of the door with a smile and wave. Even if that appealed to him more than sex did, he wasn't sure if he wanted to be alone after the scene or not. Perhaps the Internet had been wrong about more than one thing.

"What are your limits?" Maddy asked. Jennifer had known Derreck's specialties but had known nothing of his limits. Apparently, limits were more important than kinks themselves. *Just another layer of keeping things consensual.*

"I'll only have one limit for today," said Derreck. "No sex. I won't fuck you, and you won't fuck me. Oral sex, or anything like a hand job is off the table unless one of us checks in during the scene."

Can relief give me an orgasm? It was the closest that Maddy had come to one in years. "Thank fuck," he said, letting his head fall into his hands. Sweat drenched his palms instantly and a shudder passed through his body.

Why had he waited until he was desperate before he had parked his ass outside the kink club? "I don't want to do any of those things," said Maddy, shaking his head. "I...I don't do sex." *Is that how I should put it?* He didn't do sex, and sex didn't do him. *Nope. Not happening.*

A small smile tugged at Derreck's lips, his dark eyes sparkling with mirth. "I think we are going to get along just fine, Maddy. What are your other limits? Or are you not sure."

"Nothing gross," said Maddy, eyeing up the empty glasses. His stomach was gurgling from too much too fast, so it was probably best to wait to ask for more, even if his mouth still felt bone-dry. "No poo-play or anything like that. And please don't spit on me. That will probably just make me puke, and if I puke once, I'm puking twice."

"Any problem with restraints, blindfolds, knives, choking?" Derreck listed off a few more and Maddy shook his head at each one.

Knives? Fuck yes! This was finally happening, and it was going to fix everything. *It has to.* If things kept going the way they had been, then Maddy was sure he would end up on the wrong side of barred windows. People didn't understand him or his addiction, and that terrified them.

"Anything else?" Derreck's voice pulled him out of his thoughts. Derreck looked so calm and detached, when Maddy was one step away from terrified. It was perfect. If Derreck had been afraid — afraid of Maddy — then Maddy wasn't sure what he would have done.

Maddy plucked at his sleeve, tugging it down until it covered his knuckles. "My shirt stays on. I don't care about my pants, but I'm never taking my shirt off, so don't ask."

And here comes the questions. "*Why are you wearing a sweater? What are you going to do when it gets cold?*" There were so many more out there that managed to piss Maddy off every time.

"Fair enough. Did you need anything else to eat or drink or are you ready to start?" asked Derreck, stacking the glasses before he wiped the table clean.

Wait. What? "Start...like now?" asked Maddy, tugging at his sleeve and gnawing his lip. He had expected to make some kind of appointment. "*Show up at nine p.m. tomorrow and I'll beat your ass. Make sure to bring a snack and an ice pack.*"

"Now," said Derreck, his smile gone. His voice had gone deep, and there was a furrow on his forehead. "Stand against that wall with your back to me and take your pants off. I'll start you off easy."

Maddy swallowed, his heart thudding as energy burned beneath his skin. He trembled but he wasn't afraid. It was finally happening, and he was so fucking ready.

Chapter Three

Derreck

Maddy's uncertainty fed the fire that was slowly building in Derreck's gut. Maddy was too cute — strange, but cute. A shirt had never been a deal breaker for Derreck and neither had a bit of atypical behavior. He wasn't one to judge on that front.

Unfortunately, he had no doubt that Maddy would be safewording by the second hit of the flogger, tears in his eyes as he begged Derreck to stop. Maddy was thin, with wide eyes that Derreck imagined would look even better with tears in them. *Innocent.*

As fun as it was to break someone in, Derreck knew it wouldn't be enough for him. But at least he'd managed to kill some of his spare time, and he'd gotten Maddy out of his car before he'd gone into a coma. Derreck's exhaustion had ebbed a bit while they spoke, and he almost felt like a human being again.

He strolled to the wall, taking his time to select his implement, even though he knew exactly which one he was going to use. Broad strips of soft leather would feel more like a thud than the sting of a narrower flogger, and the fibers were soft and non-irritating. It was the best thing that he had for a beginner, especially one who looked like he was putting on a brave face while begging to be hurt, when he really just needed a hug.

When he turned back to the wall, Maddy had stripped off his pants and boxers, leaving his pale ass exposed to the room. His ass was narrow with a tiny dimple on each cheek. He didn't look overly boney, but he certainly wouldn't jiggle with each strike. It was a perfect stretch of flesh, unmarked with untapped potential that Derreck could turn into absolute artwork.

If he were given the opportunity. He refused to get his hopes up.

"What's your safeword if you want to stop?" asked Derreck, slapping his hand a few times with the flogger to test its weight. He hadn't used one like it in a while, but it always came back to him. He hit it against his leg, waiting for the thud and sting to tear over his flesh. Mild, with a hint of a burn. *Perfect.*

"Pancakes," said Maddy, his voice trembling.

Derreck held back a snort. This was not going to last long. Would he even get one strike in? Maddy looked like he was ready to run for the door. "And if you want to slow down?"

"Teddy bear."

They were certainly unique words. Derreck moved in close as he readied himself to take the first strike. It wasn't just about hitting someone until they screamed or came. It was about making them really *feel*. Every little strap on the flogger was an extension of his hand, each one capable of pleasure and pain. It was his job to use it to its fullest—and all of it was nothing without Maddy's submission.

41

Derreck took pride in his workmanship.

The scent of male sweat and fear trickled across his nose, and he rolled his eyes. Maybe he would only get one strike in, but he was going to make it count. Maddy had come to him to *feel,* and Derreck wouldn't let him walk away empty.

"What are your safewords?" asked Maddy.

Derreck halted in surprise. He could count on one hand how many subs had asked him that. Maddy's voice had gone surprisingly steady, even as he leaned against the wall, his hands trembling.

"I use the traffic light system. Red for stop and yellow for slow down," said Derreck, drawing his arm back.

He struck before Maddy had acknowledged his reply, expecting him to yelp and cry out at the first strike. Whether he was ready for it or not didn't matter. One could never be ready for pain unless one craved it.

Maddy flinched, gripping the wall with his hands as he sucked in a breath. Derreck waited a beat to give Maddy a moment to safeword if he needed to. Three seconds came and went, and a smile tugged at Derreck's lips. *Perhaps I'll get two.* Derreck struck a second time, putting a touch more force behind the strike.

The flogger collided with Maddy's ass, spreading over his pale cheeks with a hundred tiny hits. Redness had seeped into the pale flesh from the first strike, glowing deeper as the second sank in. It was already breathtaking.

It wasn't often that Derreck got to play with someone so pale — their skin so responsive to his every whim.

Maddy widened his stance after the second strike, arching his back and pushing his ass into the hit.

Derreck licked his lips. It was the best non-verbal green light he could ask for.

Shoving his surprise to the side, Derreck delivered the next hit with more force than the first two combined. A blister tweaked against his palm, sending a zing down his arm.

His breath caught as Maddy twitched his hands against the wall. Derreck waited for Maddy's safeword to end it all, but it never came. Maddy hadn't even made a noise after his initial gasp. *A bit better than two.*

He knew not to judge anyone by their appearance, but Derreck couldn't help but be a bit shocked. Maddy looked so *frail.* The next strike slammed just below Maddy's ass cheek, licking across the sensitive skin and leaving reddened fingers behind.

Maddy didn't. Fucking. Move.

Derreck growled under his breath, his next hit so close to his full strength that he knew it would be brutal. *Nothing. Fucking beautiful.* He hit again, painting Maddy's ass until red started to blush to an even deeper burgundy.

Derreck grinned as his biceps started to ache, his breath coming in low pants. Adrenaline burst under his skin, giving him a high better than any drug. Even better was the picture before him.

"Teddy bear?"

Maddy's voice cut through his haze of madness and strength, halting Derreck's momentum like a brick wall. Derreck waited a moment before taking a deep breath and letting it out slowly. He gripped the handle of the flogger until it creaked. Perhaps it wasn't meant to be.

"Too much?" asked Derreck, tossing the flogger toward the couch to be cleaned later. The leather strands struck the cushion with a sparkling thump like a tiny firework.

"No, um." Maddy turned his head so he could look back at Derreck, his lip caught beneath his teeth. "I was just wondering if you could go harder, please? That one really doesn't hurt all that much."

Fuck yeah. Derreck let the smirk stretch across his lips as he paused to cherish those words. He could go so, *so* much harder.

"Sure," he said, keeping his voice even and calm. "Do you know if you would prefer another flogger — or maybe a whip or cane?" He strolled to the wall, strumming his fingers over a few implements. It wasn't often that he was able to step it up a notch, and even then, he couldn't go *too* far.

"You choose. Just something that hurts more, please."

Well, if he was going to be so fucking polite about it, who was Derreck to say no? He plucked a cane from the wall, gripping it in his palm. For such an unassuming thing, he could do a lot with it. He tested it against his thigh once before he carved it through the air, striking Maddy's blushing ass with a quiet *crack*.

Canes fucking hurt. No matter how soft he hit, there was always a sting. They were also so much better for the designs Derreck longed to paint on Maddy's skin. In the wrong hands, they could cause real damage, but Derreck wasn't inexperienced in any sense.

The first stripe blushed red, while the second sank in as a purple bruise. By the tenth, a thin strip of skin had raised into blisters that would ache for days.

He usually tried to keep himself from breaking skin, but Maddy arched back into every touch of the cane, seeming to crave the pain as much as Derreck did.

"Are you okay if I break skin?" Derreck asked, pausing his strikes to stretch out his arm. It had been a while since play had made him sweat.

"I thought you did already. But yeah, it's fine. I heal quickly," said Maddy, his voice steadier than Derreck had heard it so far. Most subs would be weeping, but Maddy seemed to get stronger with every passing moment.

Derreck strode closer to his sub before leaning against the wall next to him. Maddy's face had flushed again, and his eyes were half-lidded. His gaze was clear, though, and his breathing was steady. He glanced down to Maddy's soft cock that was resting between his legs. *Good.*

"Checking in. Did you want a break, or are you good to continue?" asked Derreck. His chest warmed as Maddy nodded, opening his eyes wide. His eyes were so, so fucking blue that Derreck could almost see the ocean in them.

"I'm good. It's good. Please keep going."

Such a good sub. Derreck kept his words to himself. He wasn't sure how Maddy would react to praise, and he didn't want to fuck it up for either of them.

Derreck took up the same position, before switching the cane to his dominant hand. He flexed his hand in a warm-up before tapping his thigh with the cane to double-check his strength. It seared through the thick material of his jeans.

Derreck held back on the next strike, but Maddy's skin still split, a tiny bead of blood welling up and trailing down his ass. Derreck knew that it wouldn't bleed much, but it would hurt like a motherfucker for a long time.

Maddy let out a soft breath at the strike, the noise so close to a moan that Derreck peeked between Maddy's spread thighs. Maddy's cock was still soft, the head hanging just past his sac, which had drawn tight to his body as his skin no doubt prickled.

Derreck grunted as he let the last blow fly. His arms burned, his chest aching for breath as sweat trailed down his skin. Maddy's ass had changed to a landscape of strikes and blows, the few spots of blood a dark rust against the purpling bruises. He was flying so high that he wasn't sure if he'd ever come down. He'd never seen anything so fucking beautiful in his life.

Maddy's eyes had glazed over once Derreck had broken skin. He looked so far away, his soft cock untouched and completely detached from the pain. For Derreck, it was almost like seeing himself in the mirror.

Some Doms and subs didn't understand why Derreck kept kink and sex in two very different compartments in his life. Derreck couldn't understand how they combined them into one harmonious masterpiece. He'd seen it a hundred times, but his cock rarely stirred at the sight of a flying sub.

Derreck tossed the cane toward the couch, letting it clatter to the floor as he went to Maddy. The closer he got, the more beautiful it became. Each touch had left its mark in a different way and Maddy? Maddy had taken every little bit and had asked for more.

Derreck brought his hand down on Maddy's bruised ass, drinking in the soft breath and low whine that pushed through Maddy's lips. Maddy burned under his palm, hotter than the summer sun or the fevered interior of Maddy's car.

"Fucking perfect," said Derreck, unable to stop himself. It was perfect, and he was in complete and utter control of himself for the first time in months. Adrenaline surged through his body, pushing all thoughts of sleep and worry from his mind. The bodies he'd buried faded to nothing, rolling off his shoulders like another dew drop.

Grasping Maddy's hand and tugging him away from the wall, Derreck led him to the couch, taking his weight as he stumbled. He slowly lowered Maddy to the couch ass-first, thinking better of draping him over his lap. Maddy smiled as he touched the cushion, letting out a groan and closing his eyes.

"What happens now?" asked Maddy, his voice wavering for the first time since the scene had begun. He dug his hands into the arm of the couch, clenching the fabric as Derreck slid next to him.

"Now, I take care of you," said Derreck, frowning as Maddy gripped tighter. He had to at least *try* to soothe Maddy. He had done so well for him, and Derreck couldn't stand to see him already pulling away.

Gripping Maddy by the shoulders, Derreck tugged him close until Maddy's head rested on his chest. Maddy's body snapped taut against him, his breath picking up as he opened his eyes.

"I won't touch you sexually, Maddy. I just need to hold you while we come down. I can put cream on your ass, if you'd like." The moments after a scene were one of the only times that Derreck could stand someone's touch. Even handshakes usually made his skin crawl, but he craved human contact when his high was falling. If he didn't get it, he fell too far too fast.

Derreck kept his grip loose, even when his instinct was telling him to hold Maddy tight. *Please don't run.* He couldn't take two runners back-to-back.

"No cream," said Maddy, shaking his head before burrowing against Derreck's chest. "I want it to hurt for a long time."

And fuck, if that didn't make Derreck's week.

Chapter Four

Derreck

Derreck heaped another shovel of dirt onto the pile next to him before he slammed the spade into the grass. After wiping the sweat from his brow, he guzzled half of his remaining coffee before dusting the grime from his hands. It clung to the hairs on each knuckle, caking under his nails and into each and every blister on his palm. He had tried every kind of exfoliating soap on the market, but his hands never came clean.

His pocket vibrated as a text came through, jingling his change and the bolt he'd found a foot into his dig. Reaching for his phone, he tapped his password instead of unlocking it with his fingerprint. With dirt in every crease, his fingerprint changed on a daily basis.

He'd kept an eye and ear glued to his phone, despite how many bodies he'd had to bury before dawn. The sound of the gentle vibration put a hell of a lot more sunshine into his day than the actual sun.

He glanced at the name on the display, and his heart thumped a touch faster. It was…strange, and unlike anything he'd felt after a scene — even an intense one like the one he'd experienced with Maddy.

He rubbed at his sternum, trying to ease the ache. He could have pushed himself too far. Coffee on an empty stomach never went over well, and digging was a motherfucker in the middle of a drought.

Even with the rock-hard ground and the extra blisters, he was still in better control than he had been in a long time. His mind was clean, with no clinging extra bits like the dirt under his fingernails.

Hey! Checking in with you to make sure you're okay. How r u feeling?

He snorted at the text from Maddy, shaking his head before leaning against the closest tree. He fucking *hated* trees. Even if they were beautiful, their roots were like icebergs, stretching everywhere underground and always ready to stop his progress at the most inopportune time.

Derreck typed out his reply before cleaning the dirt from the screen with the damp sleeve of his T-shirt.

Good. Really good. But I should be the one checking in with you. How is your ass this morning?

He couldn't help but wonder how the marks looked against Maddy's pale skin. He'd never been much of a 'morning after' kind of guy, but occasionally he would give in to the temptation, just to see his artwork. *Would it be weird to ask him for a picture? Probably.*

'Morning after' usually implied sex the night before. And he probably needed sex on the table to ask for pictures of someone's ass. Sex was…fine, but it wasn't in the cards.

His phone dinged a second later and his eyes went wide. It was a picture, not a text. His heart picked up as he opened it, not even thinking of the possible consequences. His remaining breath disappeared, sweat dripping from his temples as his body lit on fire.

Holy fuck. He bit his lip to cut off his groan. Maddy had sent a picture of his ass. Derreck hadn't even needed to ask.

Maddy must've taken the picture in the bathroom mirror because he was looking over his shoulder with a cheeky grin on his face. He wore a light gray sweater that stopped just a bit too low, obscuring some of the welts from view.

But the area that Derreck could see was beautiful enough to bring tears to his eyes. *Every color of the rainbow.* The grin left him in no doubt as to how Maddy was feeling. Derreck wasn't the only one still flying high.

His cock twitched unexpectedly as he stared at the picture, pushing against the zipper of his jeans. He peeked down at it, tilting his head before grabbing himself to adjust his length so it was more comfortable. Glancing around, he let out a sigh of relief that the coast was clear. If someone saw him standing over a partially dug grave with dirt up to his elbows as he groped himself, he would have big problems.

He forced his hand away, looking back to the picture. Despite the fuzzy quality from the indoor lights, Maddy had a certain allure that Derreck hadn't noticed when he'd first seen him in the car.

Overheating and sickly was not his type, but Maddy had tacked on his shyness and uncertainty, along with enough politeness to make any Dom proud. Having a higher pain tolerance than almost anyone he'd ever met definitely kicked Maddy up the scale a few notches.

But Maddy had hardly looked at him, and he had been so relieved when Derreck set sex as a hard limit. Derreck knew he had a good body – he could thank his job for that one – and his face wasn't half-bad, either. Guys usually looked at him with either desire or jealousy, but Maddy had hardly even seemed to notice anything besides his hands and arms. He'd caught Maddy staring at the calluses and blisters on his palms, along with his biceps every time he had flexed.

An arm guy? That didn't seem to fit, either. An arm guy would have gotten hard. Maddy could have been straight, or maybe he'd been so nervous that he hadn't even noticed what Derreck had to offer.

It didn't matter. Sex was off the table. One scene and Derreck was back on his feet, but there was no guarantee that Maddy would come back for more. Minimizing the picture, Derreck typed out a reply.

Looks good. I think I missed a spot. Seriously, though, I still have that cream if you need it.

Flicking back to the picture, Derreck saved it to the memory card on his phone before sending it to himself in an email. He would not be deleting that one in his lifetime, and when he got home, he was going to upload it into the cloud so he would never lose it.

There wasn't another living soul who would ever see it, either. It was for him – *just* for him. His phone vibrated as he sent the email.

No cream. This is the only thing that's going to get me through my week. I'm game any time you want a repeat. As long as you promise not to hold back next time. ;)

Derreck read Maddy's response, his breath catching as his cock throbbed, a drop of pre-cum soaking into his jeans. Maddy was dangerous — and getting more alluring by the second. Who cared if he was a touch different when he was so fucking perfect?

Same time next week, if you think you can take it. Text me if you start to feel off before then and I'll do the same.

He hit Send and powered his phone down before sliding it back into his pocket. Glaring up at the tree, he let out a breath as he tried to calm the situation in his pants. He was not going to start digging again until he went soft. He was into kink, but he was not cool with having a boner while he dug a fucking grave. The departed deserved better than that.

* * * *

Maddy

"Take a seat, Madison," said Mr. Jameson as he leaned back in his chair, steepling his chubby fingers. His office was the largest in the building, and he spent the majority of his time making sure everyone knew it. When he wasn't spinning in his seat, he paced the hallways, confronting his underlings about tiny details that didn't matter — like the way someone sat in their chair or how they had their computer screens laid out.

Maddy had overheard a few grumbling employees accuse Mr. Jameson of having a micropenis to go along with his micromanaging. If Maddy hadn't accidentally gotten an eyeful in the bathroom one day, he would have agreed. As it was, Mr. Jameson was slightly above the average for his ethnicity.

Maddy shook his head, trying not to get sidetracked too early in the conversation. It always confused him how people valued penis size over intellect.

"It's Maddy, sir," he said, struggling not to roll his eyes. His boss's lips turned down. "And I'd prefer to stand, if that's okay. I slipped on the sidewalk and landed on my tailbone last night." Maddy shoved his hands in his pockets, pulling his slacks tight over his ass. *Yes.* They were still there. It hadn't been a dream.

Maddy's gossiping coworkers were right about one thing. Mr. Jameson was not worth a pinch of respect. And he definitely didn't have the balls to intimidate Maddy into taking a seat.

Sitting was the last thing he needed to do with an audience. He could imagine himself groaning in bliss as he slid into the chair, letting his head fall back and his eyes flutter shut as the ache washed over him. He knew it would happen, because it was exactly what had happened every time he returned from the copier and slid into his chair at his own desk.

"As, you know, Madison, this is a professional office. Nicknames are not acceptable." Mr. Jameson slid his fingers together as he stared up at Maddy, his blue eyes watery and bloodshot. His slim tie looked like he'd borrowed it from a child's wardrobe, and his shoes were scuffed.

Professional. What a fucking joke. Employees gossiped at the water cooler and doodled on each other's desks as a joke. He didn't doubt that they passed each other notes about who was crushing on whom. Food frequently when missing, and the dishwasher seemed to exist in an invisible dimension where nothing ever got unloaded.

"Maddy is the name on my birth certificate. Is that good enough for you, sir?" Maddy failed to keep the edge out of his voice, holding his head high as his boss's gaze morphed into a glare. "It's also the name on all my employee information as well as my tax forms and passport. So, I would really appreciate it if you called me Maddy and not Madison." He would also really appreciate it if Mr. Jameson got to the point, but he couldn't see that happening any time soon.

"Do you know why you were asked to come to my office this morning?" Mr. Jameson continued as if Maddy was a mute.

It's high school all over again. Can't he just tell me so I can get back to class?

"No, sir," he said instead, glancing away before his eye started to twitch. Being pissed off did that to him, especially if he were busy.

Aww. He grinned as a cute picture that had been drawn with scribbled crayon caught his eye. He wasn't sure if it was supposed to be a cat or a cow, but that didn't matter. Kids were so adorable, even if those ones belonged to his asshole boss. Hopefully his wife wasn't as dull and condescending, or they would need more therapy than Maddy.

"It has come to my attention that you will be seeking another leave of absence, and I wanted to caution you on that. You've just returned from time off, and, as your employer, I cannot constantly grant you time off for your *vacations*." Mr. Jameson leaned forward, sliding his hands along his polished desk.

A boulder of ice dropped into Maddy's stomach as the color drained from his face. He staggered as goosebumps broke over his skin and his breath went ragged. Was the room spinning, or was it just him? He widened his stance as his knees went weak. He should have accepted the offer to sit.

Mr. Jameson continued to speak, but Maddy didn't hear a word, just a distant garble that resembled something close to human speech. He watched his boss's mouth open and close, shit pouring out that he would never be able to decipher.

Vacations? He looked down at his hands, watching them tremble before his eyes. He couldn't feel them — like they didn't even belong to him. He was a puppet, barely hanging onto his stings as his world came crashing down.

Every ounce of energy that Derreck had poured back into his body seeped away like he had severed his femoral artery.

He knew people talked about him behind his back and speculated on things that were none of their business, but to have his boss throw it back in his face? What was he even supposed to do with that? There was no way he could respond, not without saying something that would cost him his job.

Sweat gathered under the collar of his sweater that was suddenly too tight and too warm for the air-conditioned office. He tugged at it, but it sprang right back against his skin, closing tight around his throat until he could hardly breathe. His chest ached as a shudder racked his body.

What would Derreck think about his *leaves of absence*? Would Derreck ever lay a hand on him again? He'd been searching for so long for someone who could help him, but it already threatened to slip through his fingers. Kinksters were an accepting bunch, according to the Internet, but so much of what he'd read online had been wrong already.

"I-I have to go," said Maddy as he turned away, stumbling to the door. He grabbed the knob as his knees threatened to give out. The metal was freezing under his palm, branding his molten skin and pushing a quiet gasp from his lips.

"Do we have an understanding?" asked Mr. Jameson.

Maddy's escape came to a grinding halt as he peered through the glass beyond the door. People were staring over the tops of their cubicles, their gazes burning into his skin as he was laid bare before them. They were probably the same assholes who had started the rumors in the first place. People got their kicks from the most interesting activities.

"No, sir. We will have to continue our conversation later. I have a few things that I need to think about." Maddy's voice quivered like a nineteen-year-old virgin on prom night.

It took him three struggling attempts to open the door before he beelined directly to his office. He ducked his head, watching his feet as the back of his neck burned.

Grabbing for his phone, he slammed his office door and dialed the number that he'd memorized over the last five years. The phone hummed against his ear once before it went to voicemail. He cursed, running a hand through his hair and tugging the sweaty strands hard.

His therapist was probably on the other line, but that didn't ease the tension in his chest. His hands shook as he bit his lip hard enough to draw blood. He needed them. He needed somebody who would understand him.

"Fuck. Fuck." He ran the back of his hand across his lips, shuddering as blood from his lip streaked across his skin. He stared at it, goosebumps bursting over his skin as something else inside him reared its ugly head.

He redialed the number, nearly throwing his phone across the room as it went straight to voicemail a second time. His heart thudded in his chest. *I've been doing so well. Could one person fuck that all up for him? I'm stronger than this.*

Derreck. He could call Derreck. He would understand, or at the very least, his voice would take the edge off. Even the thought of his dark, grumbling consonants made Maddy's hair stand on end.

Maddy dropped down in his chair hard, his breath whooshing out of him as his ass screamed in protest. Fuck, it hurt…but he needed more.

He dialed the number, holding his tongue between his teeth. He wouldn't bite. He wouldn't draw blood, no matter how tempting it was.

The phone buzzed in his ear, each pause like the wait on death row.

There had to have been a reason that Derreck wasn't answering. He had to have had a job, even though he didn't seem like the kind of guy to be stuck in an office building.

Or maybe he saw Maddy's name and decided not to answer. Derreck didn't owe him anything.

Or he was with another sub. Someone who could give him what he needed, when Maddy obviously couldn't.

His panic spiraled with each ring, his chest going so tight that he wanted nothing more than to rip his sweater over his head so he could finally breathe. But they were watching him, their beady eyes peeking over their cubicles in a way that they probably thought was sneaky. They should have pressed their faces to the glass walls that surrounded him, then he would have been able to sell tickets to the freak show.

"Hello?" a garbled voice filled with sleep startled him from his gloom. He cursed as his phone slid from his grip, slamming face down onto the floor as he choked on his own spit.

"Oh shit," said Maddy as he reached for the phone and tried to catch his breath. The screen was thankfully unshattered, but it was also blank. He must've cut Derreck off when he'd dropped the phone.

He slumped in his chair as he slid his hand over the screen. He wasn't sure why Derreck was sleeping at ten o'clock in the morning, but he certainly hadn't sounded impressed about being woken up. It was just another thing he'd fucked up in the long line of fuck-ups.

His phone rang in his hand, Derreck's name lighting up the screen as he stared at it in disbelief. Trembling, he accepted the call and lifted the phone to his ear.

"Hello? Maddy?" All sounds of sleep had evaporated from Derreck's voice. Maddy pulled the phone away from his ear, staring as the timer climbed past ten seconds. What was he even going to say?

"Maddy, you okay? You've got me worried over here," said Derreck, his voice getting louder with each word. Perhaps it was his tone, or the sheer volume that compelled Maddy to press the phone back to his ear and answer.

"Hey, Derreck," he said, clicking his mouth shut again as he looked down at his desk. Phil Patterson was written at the top of the page under his fingertips. He knew that Phil would be fined at the very least, perhaps worse if he found more evidence. He always found more evidence.

"You sound down. What can I do?" asked Derreck, cutting straight to the point. Derreck seemed like a man of few words, but Maddy wondered if he would have preferred some small talk.

"I don't know," said Maddy, sliding the paper back into the folder on his desk. "I'm not feeling great right now. I tried to call my therapist, but they didn't answer."

Most people gave him a knowing look when he said he had a therapist. "*Oh, you're one of* those *people.*" Like mental illness or an addiction were on the same level as a hate crime.

"Okay," said Derreck, his voice even. "We can talk about it, or I can come to you."

"I..." Maddy's jaw seized up. Two options were a hell of a lot better than the thirty-thousand scenarios that stretched before him in his mind. But he couldn't even force himself to talk right now. How much could he not say before Derreck hung up on him?

"I'm coming your way now. What's your address?" There was a shuffling noise in the background and the phone burst with a second of static.

"I'm at work." Maddy struggled to get the words through his lips that seemed to have seized. Derreck was coming? He blinked, looking around his office. The world beyond the glass door and walls had blurred, the organized shelves within seemingly inconsequential.

"Where do you work?" asked Derreck, grunting as he did something on the other end.

It should have been an easy question, but the company name refused to come to him. He had worked in the same office for years, but it was gone. He looked down at a half-written address on an envelope that was partially covered by a sticky note. "Three-five-seven Main Street. I'll meet you at reception." Swallowing hard, he disconnected the line.

I can do this. His boss wasn't going to bring him down — not without some dire consequences.

With newfound strength, he rose from his chair, sliding the folder back into his drawer with the other ongoing investigations. Striding out of his office, he held his head high as he locked his door. One of his coworkers perked up as he passed her, but he ignored her questioning look, even as it burned against his skin.

"I have a brunch meeting," he said to no one in particular, his voice still a bit strangled. Let her spread those rumors and see how far she got.

He took the stairs, deciding to steer clear of the elevator that was bound to be packed with people arriving late to other floors. He was sweating and trembling by the time he reached the main floor, his hands clammy and numb.

At least he didn't cry — not since his sister's funeral. With more than ten years of living on the edge, feeling like he might combust at any moment, he didn't have a single tear to show for it. Some people might think he was strong for it, but he was much closer to desperate than he wanted to admit.

Pushing through the stairwell door, he took a deep breath of the bleach-tinted air of the reception area. There were a few stragglers stumbling through the revolving entrance doors and toward the elevator. None of them looked his way as he leaned against the wall, doing his best to blend in with the modern art sculpture.

The reception area was clean from its daily overnight scrubbing, and minimalist, besides the clunky art. The art itself had been donated, making it perfectly suited for a government building.

The star of the room sat behind the low desk to the side of the door, a *'please see next attendant'* sign in the middle of her desk. The receptionist herself was one of the grumpiest motherfuckers he'd ever met, and he absolutely loved her. She was also the only attendant, despite the sign.

She gave him a quick once-over as she spotted him leaning against the wall, barely looking up from her bowl of oatmeal. Her inattention was the reason that he loved her. He wasn't sure if she didn't give a crap or couldn't be bothered, but she never got involved in anyone's business.

She was also completely friendless in the company. There had been talk of firing her, but he had pulled his only strings to stand up for her, just so he could see her unsmiling face every morning and evening. If all else failed, at least she was consistent.

He touched his sternum as he pushed away from the wall, slipping through the door as the last straggler disappeared. The ache had gotten better, but it wasn't gone. It had been with him for most of his life, and there had only been one short time in recent memory that it had faded completely.

Sweltering heat descended on him like a swarm of hornets, sweat prickling on his skin as the air turned to water in his mouth. He couldn't believe how some animals survived the heat. At least *they* didn't draw the attention of onlookers like he did every time he tugged at the sleeves of his sweater.

He slumped his shoulders as he leaned back against the shaded red brick wall. Unlike some of the modern skyscrapers in the city, his office was a solid twelve-story brick building. It was over one-hundred-years old, according to the date stamped on the brick, and the foundation was probably stronger than most other buildings in the city. The only thing that had worn out completely was the bell to the clock that decorated the peaked roof.

The brick was like molten lava against his covered skin, even in the shaded bit he had chosen. Sweat dripped down his back, soaking into the waistband of his slacks. The ice in his belly hadn't melted in the least.

Vacations. How could they think that? He glared at a woman across the road as her heels tapped out a steady pattern on the sidewalk. She was wearing a long, flowing dress with a split up the side that almost gave away too much. Everything about her was relaxed, even her long hair that blew in the breeze. Perhaps she was actually on vacation.

Maddy snorted, looking back at his feet. If his leaves of absence had been anything like that, then his problems would have been solved.

The people around him were the unbiased observers that he would normally trust during his investigations. Maybe they were right, and he was just another lazy man taking advantage of the system.

Either way, Maddy didn't have the right to waste Derreck's time. He had to get back to his desk and get to work, no matter how much the thought made his stomach churn. It wasn't the work— no, he enjoyed that—it was everything and everybody else.

"Maddy?"

Maddy blinked, his gaze glued to an ant that was trekking its way across the sidewalk. It struggled as it dragged a dead grasshopper that was at least four times its size, barely making headway as it climbed a crack. It would probably bake on the sidewalk, just like him.

"Maddy."

A touch on his shoulder seared straight to his skin and he jerked back, smacking his head against the brick as he stumbled. His eyes flew wide, his heart jackhammering as he tried to see who was standing in front of him, their arm still outstretched. The familiar palms and thick cord of muscle of the person's biceps jogged his memory.

It was Derreck. *Oh God.*

"I'm sorry. I shouldn't have touched you without permission," said Derreck, dropping his hand to his side. His eyes were squinted against the bright sun, a tiny piece of sleep clinging to one eyelash. The tight curls on his head were dusty, with a small leaf clinging just above his eye.

Had his skin always been the color of a caramel macchiato? Maddy couldn't remember. Or perhaps he had noticed, but it hadn't mattered. It still didn't.

But he remembered those hands and arms—the same ones that had given him strength.

"Derreck." His voice was barely a breath, but at least he'd managed to say something. Derreck tilted his head, just like he had done when Maddy had asked for more during their scene. Settling back on his heels, Derreck clasped his hands behind his back.

The sun baked down on Derreck as he stood in front of him, the rays soaking into his white T-shirt that had a streak of something smeared across the middle. His pants were dirty too, with hand-shaped prints along his hips, and his shoes had actual chunks of dried mud that had left a trail along the sidewalk.

A man passed them, eyeing both Maddy and Derreck with narrowed eyes before giving them a wide berth.

"Tell me what you need," said Derreck, his voice so deep that it made something in Maddy ache.

"I need..." He trailed off, looking down the sidewalk as he tried to shake off the twinge. He couldn't express how relieved he was that Derreck had come rushing to him. But conversations about himself had always been limited to the moments spent within the bleak walls of his therapist's office. How was he supposed to know what he needed when he wasn't even sure where to start?

Maybe the best defense was a good offense? Maddy raised his gaze to Derreck's heaving chest, the outline of his body stark under his tight shirt. Maddy hadn't met many other men who managed to look like Derreck, but physical strength was often misleading. It only took one kick to the balls to take down a bear. "I need to know that you're okay."

His boss's words had tipped him over the edge, but it was his uncertainty about Derreck that had hooked into him and dragged him all the way to the bottom. Forget a spiral, he'd just sunk.

"Walk with me if you're up to it. There is a park down the street where we can talk in private," said Derreck. He turned as Maddy took a step toward him, leading the way a half-pace ahead.

Maddy paused mid-step. Derreck's car—a luminous Mustang that looked like it didn't get more than one mile per gallon—had jumped the curb, the parking meter blinking with an expired red light. Derreck glanced back, waving dismissively at his car before he continued his trek.

Maddy's lips twitched into a small smile as he followed, each step sizzling against the overheated sidewalk. His shoes grew heavier with each footfall as sweat slicked his skin and his clothing started to cling. His breath came in harsh pants as he struggled to keep up with Derreck's longer stride.

He let out a sigh of relief as the dark canopy of trees in the park came into view. The limbs on even the largest trees had started to droop, their leaves curled and tinting brown around the edges. The park only offered a small clump of maples, with wilted grass stretching for the rest of the three-acre plot that was nearly deserted. Even the bravest Labradors had retreated indoors.

It was a good thing that Maddy had a desk drawer stocked with toiletries, including extra deodorant.

Derreck paused by a bench beneath the pocket of trees, the sparse shade trickling over Maddy and finally giving him a hint of relief. He shuddered as a tiny breeze fluttered through his soaked hair, the scent of the wind sinking into his skin.

"You can sit if you're comfortable...or stand," said Derreck, taking a seat at the edge of the bench. He left the majority of the bench open, giving Maddy the option to put space between them or take the nearest spot.

Maddy let a breath out as he took the closest space, lowering himself next to Derreck so they were only inches apart. He didn't want to try to stand when his head was already filled with fluff. He'd already made that mistake once.

He could smell Derreck's sweat, mingled with the deep scent of earth as his ass touched the wooden slatted seat. A tiny whimper pushed its way through his lips as his weight settled on the bench, an ache radiating from every stripe and blister. His skin prickled beneath his clothes, his mouth going dry.

"I brought cream if you needed it," said Derreck, seemingly unaffected by Maddy's whimper as he pulled a small tube out of his pocket. The tube was slightly squashed, probably from being in a stiff denim pocket, and the cap looked close to popping from the pressure.

It was probably one of the single most thoughtful things that anyone had ever done for him — not the cream itself, but the option. When people offered help, they usually didn't take no for an answer.

"Thank you," said Maddy, dropping his gaze to the dirt path as Derreck looked his way. Derreck's eyes looked lighter in the sun and almost soft. He'd imagined that they would always have been hard, no matter what the situation.

There were a few dusty wildflowers weaved through the cracked path that led through the park, and even the resilient dandelions had started to turn brown. Maddy stared at the misunderstood flower, gripping his hands in his lap.

"The pain doesn't bother me. Something happened at work, and…I crashed. You see, I'm an addict, and sometimes with certain triggers, I get…cravings." Maddy swallowed. Cravings didn't begin to describe the desperate need that consumed the entirety of his being.

He took a deep breath. Telling someone about his addiction was harder than admitting it to himself. He'd practiced it in the mirror so many times, staring at his grim expression and wide blue eyes, but it didn't come close to reality. He'd told his family, and one friend who had been too brief in his life to even recall his name when he saw him on the street.

He waited for Derreck to laugh, judge him or at least start up twenty questions. People always pried deeper if they were given an inch. His mother had been in circle of rage, tears and denial for years as she tried to pin his *problems* on some sort of trauma. *And she wonders why I don't take her phone calls.*

"Work can be tough," said Derreck, taking Maddy completely off guard. Derreck scratched at a streak of dirt on his jeans, the sound of his nail against denim like a steady beat of radiating calm.

Maddy held his breath as he waited for the other shoe to drop. Derreck threw his arm over the back of the bench, his hand resting on the wooden slats across the top. Shifting on the bench, Maddy slid closer until Derreck's fingertips tickled the back of his neck.

Air burst through his lips as Derreck slowly threaded his fingers through Maddy's hair, sinking straight to the sweaty roots and tugging gently.

The touch was unlike anything Maddy had ever experienced. His hair stood on end as tingles raced from his scalp, pooling in his gut until the warmth spread out through his limbs. He leaned into it, craving more even as terror and uncertainty curled in his chest. *What is happening to me?*

He moved closer until he was plastered to Derreck's side in a way so similar to how Derreck had held him on the couch after their scene. He took a deep breath, letting Derreck's scent coat his lungs and languish inside him. His core warmed a few degrees, Derreck's presence chipping away at the ice better than global warming.

Derreck slid his hand down from Maddy's hair, slipping between the bench to trail over his neck and back before moving lower until he brushed the top of his ass. There were a few stripes of bruised flesh that high, and his fingers found one unerringly. Could Derreck feel the heat of them through his clothing?

A single soft press of Derreck's fingertip against his naked skin had heat rushing straight to Maddy's core. He turned his face into Derreck's chest, smothering his groan against the solid muscle there. Clutching at Derreck's shirt, Maddy relaxed into the touch. How was it that Derreck knew exactly what he needed when Maddy didn't?

A lady walking by with her dachshund did nothing to deter Derreck as he slowly mapped out the top edge of Maddy's ass. Derreck dipped his nail into a particularly sensitive spot, dragging over it until Maddy let out a whine.

Every touch sent Maddy higher. The fuzziness cleared as his chest loosened, the gnawing need receding to the back of his mind where it belonged.

Placing his hand over Derreck's dark bicep, Maddy squeezed until he went still. Sweat glistened over Derreck's skin and beneath his palm, every line etched in caramel ebony. His arms were thicker than Maddy had realized, his hand barely able to wrap around a third of the girth. He was tall, too, so much so that Maddy's head was comfortably tucked under his chin with room to spare. Derreck's chest was rigid, and the muscles under his cheek rippled with each breath, the steady sound of a beating heart drawing the last of the ice from his limbs.

It was something that he usually wouldn't notice. Maddy was lucky if he noted if someone was a woman or man, not to mention that he barely remembered skin color. He was a cop's nightmare witness — the details of the people in his most vivid memories slipping through the cracks in his mind.

But something about Derreck was *different*. He stuck around when even Maddy's family had faded.

"Thank you...for not asking," said Maddy, letting out a breath when Derreck's arms settled around him. He should have been boiling with another layer of body heat enveloping him, but he'd never been more comfortable.

"You'll tell me when you're ready and not before. I'll never ask you for more than you can give," said Derreck.

There was a pressure against the top of Maddy's head, and for a moment, he wondered if Derreck had placed a kiss there, but that was impossible. Derreck had insisted on sex as a limit, thank goodness.

That was something Maddy hoped he'd never have to explain.

"Walk me back to my office?" asked Maddy as he pulled himself away. The moment Derreck dropped his embrace, he had to fight the urge to lean back against him. He wanted to be held — maybe even more. Maddy shook his head.

A man walked by as Maddy stood, his green eyes carving toward them. The stranger's gaze didn't matter — not with Derreck there.

"Anything you need."

Chapter Five

Derreck

Getting ready for a *date* was nearly impossible when he had no dress clothes to speak of. He had work clothes, which consisted of jeans and whatever T-shirts caught his eye, and club clothes, which were a bit too tight or leathery for a restaurant. Then there were his grocery shopping clothes, which were the same as his work clothes, minus the holes and stains.

He paced in front of his dresser, all his drawers pulled wide and the usually neat contents scrambled about like an egg. Grabbing a black T-shirt, he held it up to his chest in the mirror before grimacing at the words scrawled on the front. It had seemed hilarious when he'd found it online, and he'd worn it to the club a few times, but it wouldn't work for daylight hours in the middle of the city. *'It's a kink thing'* would probably get him kicked out of a restaurant.

But what the fuck was he supposed to wear? And why the fuck had he agreed to it, anyway? He hadn't gone on a date in three years, when he'd invited an online friend out for drinks. No-strings-attached sex to blow off steam every few months was easy enough to find without donning a suit and bow tie.

He cursed as he glanced at the clock. He was down to the wire. He had to leave in five minutes to make it on time. There was still time to cancel, but...

Derreck swallowed, turning away from the mess at his feet. The truth was, he really wanted to see Maddy again. Their scene had been epic and enough to put him back where he belonged emotionally. The aftercare had been a touch stiff, but nothing unexpected for two virtual strangers.

It was the moments since that had him thirsting for more.

The half-hour in the park played over in his mind. Maddy's skin had been so soft under his fingertips when he had dipped below his waistband to press against a bruise. His delicate gasp and the way Maddy had turned his face into Derreck's chest had left him stunned and struggling to breathe. And the smell of Maddy's simple cologne mixed with fresh sweat had made his mouth water.

Derreck sighed and lay back on his bed, the scratchy comforter crinkling under his naked skin. He hadn't had a reaction like that in a long time. Nav aside, he rarely desired a repeat scene, let alone anything more. He would rather stand back and watch someone than feel their touch.

He hadn't been able to resist pressing a kiss to the top of Maddy's head, breathing in the scent of his hair and tasting the strands that stuck to his lips. His own hard limits were coming back to haunt him, his cock hard as he lay in bed and thought about Maddy's soft moans and delicate bruises.

Limits were there to protect both of them, and he took them more seriously than handcuffs. Not that limits couldn't change.

He had been dreaming of Maddy and reliving their scene in his sleep when his phone had woken him. He'd barely been conscious when Maddy had invited him to lunch. His eyes had snapped wide, all sleep instantly gone as the words had sunk through the last layer of his dreams.

He wasn't able to say no, even if he probably should have. He had to see Maddy again—touch him—even if it meant cutting his sleep almost in half to get ready. His head had throbbed in protest as he'd pulled himself from the bed and into the shower.

He grabbed a different black T-shirt from his drawer. The brand name was small and tucked away on the cuff, so it would have to do. Skin-tight black jeans completed the ensemble.

He ran a hand through his short curls, nodding to himself. His hair grew slower than a glacier, so that always gave him one less thing to worry about.

Three minutes left.

He rushed down to his car, the Mustang's engine roaring to life as he pumped the gas a few times. The pristine body of the Ford looked out of place next to its ratty neighbors, but he'd never looked down on them. He'd been in the same spot ten years before when he'd been fresh out of college with no aspirations. He'd driven a Volvo then, which had been held together by bits of duct tape and hope.

Slowly reversing out of his spot, he sent off a small wave to his next-door neighbor Carla, who was balancing three children and two golden retrievers. One of the little girls ran up to his window, tapping on the glass with a grin on her face. Cranking the e-brake, Derreck rolled down the window, leaning through and sending a false glare at the little girl.

"What do you think you're doing, Jeanine?" He leaned his chin on his arm, sending a wink at her mother.

Jeanine giggled and squealed, darting back to her mother and wrapping her arms around the older retriever with graying hairs around his muzzle. The dog stumbled from the sudden weight before turning to lick the little girl's face.

"Sorry, hon!" Carla shouted as she readjusted the baby on her hip and detangled her ankle from a stray leash.

Derreck waved her off, easing his brake down once they were safely inside the building. Squealing his tires as he hit the street, he gunned it for the restaurant. Maddy would have to forgive him for being late. He cranked the radio, the white lines flashing by as he doubled the speed limit.

Jumping the curb on the street, he glanced at himself in the mirror, wiping a stray streak of dirt from his cheek. No matter how many times he showered, his job always managed to follow him around. But as long as he didn't end up six feet under, he was fine with a bit of dirt.

He glanced up at the plain white sign above the door, checking to make sure he had the right place. He'd heard of McGuinty's before, but he hadn't been there himself. He didn't often find himself in a bar that wasn't kink-oriented or a restaurant that wasn't for his mother's birthday party.

There was a picture of two clinking pints on the clouded window and a blazing red open sign that couldn't have been tackier.

He hadn't pictured Maddy eating at a dive. He seemed a little too reserved for that. Derreck glanced at his own clothing. He would fit right in.

He stepped through the door, frigid air and loud music assaulting him in an instant. *A bar?* He paused inside the door, glancing around the small space that had the taint of freshly spilled beer, despite the early hour. Two men at the bar looked like they had just rolled out of bed, and a third looked like he had probably spent the night on the floor, using a sticky pool of alcohol as his pillow.

No date in the world should have ever taken place in a bar that seedy. So maybe it wasn't a date after all, and Maddy had simply wanted a drink between acquaintances before he went on his merry way. Derreck was used to rough and tumble, but he would have picked a different bar.

A woman at the far end of the room caught his gaze before she slowly strolled over to him, a folded menu clutched in her hands.

"Are you here to drink or eat?" she asked loud enough that he could hear her over the music. He smothered a chuckle as he glanced at her name tag. *Candylane, nice to meet you.* Parents these days. They would name their kid anything.

"I'm meeting someone," he replied at a normal volume. Her brows scrunched together as she gave him a quick up and down before her eyes widened dramatically.

"You here for Cuz?" she asked with a smile. "He's waiting for you upstairs." She turned away to lead him past the bar to a staircase along the back wall that he hadn't noticed.

The rowdy music dissipated and the air warmed as he followed her up the steps. The worn wood groaned under his weight, and he gripped the banister, just in case.

His jaw nearly dropped when he hit the upper landing and a tastefully decorated restaurant was revealed. The rich blue curtains, candle-lit tables and cattle-hide seats were a stark contrast to the main floor. He breathed deep, the scent of rich steak and seafood coating his lungs.

He glanced down the stairs, raising one brow in question when Candylane looked his way.

"Different owners, hon." She patted Derreck on the shoulder, and he struggled not to cringe from the touch. "Cuz helped me keep my place up here, and Bruno's place downstairs. That makes him family. He's never brought a friend here, though." She patted him once more before she dropped her hand.

He spied Maddy as he stumbled from his seat. Striding toward the booth, Derreck grinned as he got his first look at his sub in days. His imagination hadn't done him justice.

Maddy had a soft flush over his cheeks that brightened as Derreck stopped in front of him, looking down and breathing deep. He was wearing cologne, and it smelled expensive. His dress shirt and slacks looked expensive, too, and fit his thin body perfectly. *Maybe I am underdressed after all.*

"You found it okay?" asked Maddy, dropping his gaze to the yellow laces on his shoes. The waitress turned away with the menu still clutched in her hands.

Derreck nodded. Maddy looked like a completely different person from the one he had seen in the park two days before. His face had color beneath his blush, and his eyes were bright. The way he moved was looser, as if something had snipped the invisible strings that had been binding his limbs together. He looked free.

Derreck lowered himself into his seat, watching Maddy shudder as followed suit. Maddy slid his eyes shut, tilting his head back the barest hint as he opened his mouth, his tongue tracing over his bottom lip. It was utter bliss.

Derreck adjusted himself before Maddy opened his eyes. He had met subs who said they loved pain, only to have them tap out after a few hits. He could have sworn that Maddy was one of them, but the man had proven him wrong. Pain had obviously helped Maddy leap from his shell. He had wrapped himself in it like a blanket, filling all the little holes that his life had left behind.

Derreck had to clench his hand into a fist to keep from pulling Maddy over his lap and slamming his hand down on his ass. Would he cry out and pull away or beg for more? *Maybe not in a crowded room.*

"Thank you for coming, Derreck. You really helped me out of a tough spot the other day, and I couldn't go another day without thanking you properly," said Maddy, jumping into the next moment as if his ass wasn't on fire. Derreck knew how much the welts would have hurt. He had never hit a sub with anything that he hadn't tried himself first.

Derreck couldn't stop his frown. "You don't have to do this." He motioned around to the packed restaurant as his stomach sank. Why did it feel like he was being paid like a prostitute? He rapped his knuckles on the table.

Maddy's face fell, and he looked off to the side as he pulled his lip between his teeth. "If you're uncomfortable, you could have said no or canceled."

"That's not it," said Derreck, leaning back in his seat. There was a glass of water waiting for him already, condensation dripping onto the coaster below it and sinking through the thick paper. Maddy's glass was almost empty. He must've been waiting for quite some time.

"I enjoyed our scene together and the aftercare. I enjoyed taking you to the park as well. It gave me peace to know that I could help bring you back up when you were down." He dragged his fingers down his glass, spreading the moisture over his palm. "I don't want to be paid for something like that."

Maddy's eyes flew wide. "I didn't mean... Oh God, I'm so sorry. Please don't think that. I'm just...so sorry." A flush bloomed over his cheeks, the tiny mole below his right eye standing out.

"Don't apologize for wanting to see me again," said Derreck, letting his frown fade. He'd been told on more than one occasion that his frown was a touch too fierce. Perhaps he was laying it on a bit thick. "How have you been feeling? Anything you want to talk about?"

It wasn't a date. Derreck was just being a good Dom who was taking care of his sub. Maddy deserved it—and so much more.

Denial. You aren't here just to make sure he's okay.

He ran a hand through his hair to banish his thoughts. Maddy wasn't even his sub yet, but maybe he could change that. Their limits seemed to line up, and Derreck couldn't wait to get his hands on that pale skin again.

"Work is crappy, but what else is new," said Maddy, letting out a huff.

When Derreck had driven to Maddy's work, he'd eyed the government building with acrid distaste in his mouth. "What do you do?" He pegged Maddy for something lower in the ranks, consistent with the submissive attitude that he had shown to Derreck so far.

"What are your thoughts on auditors?" Maddy asked. Derreck had given him a blank look.

"You know. The guys that walk through your workplace and ask questions that give you an aneurism while your boss scowls at you." Maddy swirled his water around in his glass, the ice tinkling against the sides. Despite the people around them, their table was secluded, wrapping them in an artificial bubble of privacy.

"They're assholes," said Derreck. He'd never had to deal with them in his current job—they didn't really delve into dirt too much— but Clint had complained to him about them on more than one occasion.

Maddy chuckled. "Then you'll love me. I'm the one who audits the auditors. I sniff out anything fishy, like bribery. I'm like internal affairs—only they hate me, too."

"That sounds…terrible," said Derreck. He glanced around for the waitress, but she hadn't returned after depositing him in his seat. Even though he usually didn't eat until after six in the evening, his body must've been confused, because he was ready to start eating napkins.

"I actually kind of like it, believe it or not. I get to know a lot about the businesses in the city and the people running them. I learn about the people I work with without ever having to actually talk to them. If it weren't for the few bad ones, my job would be easy-peasy." Maddy fiddled with the sleeve of his dress shirt, the delicate material at his wrist stretched and worn at that spot.

"Oh. And I hope you don't have any allergies. I told them you didn't," said Maddy, looking up.

"We haven't ordered yet," said Derreck, looking back for the waitress again. *This is a date.* He gripped the edge of the table until his knuckles started to ache. How was he supposed to stop himself from touching Maddy if it was a date? He wasn't even sure if sex was on the floor, let alone the table.

"It's not a place where you actually order," said Maddy, speaking with rapid excitement. "The owner is an 'outside the box' kind of gal, and she has a set menu that changes every week. You pay a fee, and they bring you six courses. You don't have any allergies, right? I hope it's okay. It's really good food, but I've never brought anyone here before."

A flush stained Maddy's face as he finally seemed to realize that he was rambling. Derreck chuckled. "No, I don't have any allergies."

This was a date. There was no way that it wasn't. He'd never had a sub order his food for him, but it had been something that he'd secretly craved for a long time.

He glanced to the side at a couple who were leaning across their table, their mouths inches away from each other. Nobody ate cheesecake like that during a business meeting.

His stomach grumbled as Maddy started to ramble again, his topics switching rapidly between work, food and different areas in the city. Every time he shifted in his seat, he would let out a soft sigh, pulling Derreck's focus in until he was locked on, mesmerized by Maddy's lips.

He had the cutest bottom lip that was slightly swollen from the way he bit it every time he paused. Derreck doubted that Maddy even realized that he was doing it. And when Maddy dug into their first course, which was some sort of fancy salad with more decorations than lettuce, he let out a moan that had Derreck instantly on edge.

He brought his fork to his own lips. Either he was starving to death, or it was the best salad that he'd ever had.

"Is it okay?" Maddy asked, pausing with his fork almost to his mouth.

"It's delicious."

Derreck watched Maddy's every twitch and flutter as they moved through the courses, going from squash soup and oysters to lamb, then a sizzling meat on skewers that was supposed to be buffalo. It was, hands down, the best meal he had ever had at a restaurant, but as his hunger eased, his interest in the food diminished to nothing.

"Did you enjoy our scene?" asked Derreck, breaking the brief silence as Maddy took a breath. "You're still wearing my marks. I can see it every time you move."

Emotions flitted over Maddy's face faster than Derreck could follow, so he plowed on. Usually he would let the sub come to him, waiting patiently for their barriers to break down, but he was getting nowhere with Maddy, and dessert was due any moment.

"Tell me what you liked most about it. We didn't discuss it during our aftercare," said Derreck. They hadn't discussed it, because they had both been drunk on adrenaline and endorphins. Derreck was surprised that he'd even been able to speak at all as he'd held Maddy on the couch.

"I liked…" Maddy lowered his voice, glancing at the tables around them. "I liked when you gave me more when I asked for it. You didn't try to deny me, take it away or tell me it was too much and I couldn't handle it. It felt so good. It still does." He leaned back in his seat, his lashes fluttering against his cheeks. "Every time I move, I feel your cane against my ass."

Taking a deep breath, he tried to calm his racing heart.

"What do you think about most?" asked Derreck, licking his lips as Maddy sank deeper before his eyes.

"I think about when you touched me in the park. Your hands were on my skin, your fingers pressing into the bruises that you'd made. Everything my boss said just disappeared, and my colleagues didn't matter anymore. I just wanted you to touch me and never stop." Maddy let out a soft sigh, blinking as two slices of cheesecake slid on the table before them.

Derreck gave Candylane a nod, and she excused herself without a word. He shifted in his seat, uncomfortably hard from Maddy's words. Kink didn't usually fill his cock with blood or make his balls ache with the need to come. But knowing that every moment had been as perfect for Maddy as it had been for him went straight into his gut.

"What do you want?" asked Derreck. He had to push Maddy just a tad more. He had to know for sure.

"I want you to put your hands all over me and make me hurt. I want you to beat me, whip me and cut me. I want you to make it so I never need to hurt myself again."

Derreck was out of his seat before Maddy had finished speaking. He knew that kink was no replacement for therapy, but he had to wonder if Maddy had ever been as alive as he looked at that moment. Presumably, worries, bills and the world wouldn't matter to him if Derreck simply looked after him.

Maddy's eyelids barely fluttered as Derreck slid next to him. The sweater suddenly made perfect sense. Maddy was more than just shy. He was hiding every part of himself from those around him.

"May I touch you?" asked Derreck, moving close, but keeping his hands to himself. He waited for Maddy's nod before he ran his hand through Maddy's hair, tugging the strands until he heard the tell-tale gasp.

"Let me feed you dessert, then let me take you to the club after work today. I'll make you hurt until you beg," said Derreck, slicing off a small piece of cake and bringing it to Maddy's lips.

Maddy scrunched his face and fluttered his eyes open, his gaze dropping to the fork. His eyes were blue, with flecks of yellow that made them look like clear skies just before a tornado set in. Derreck had never met anyone who had eyes quite like them. Maddy opened his mouth, snatching the cake off the fork, sliding his lips over the metal twines before he licked them clean.

"I won't beg you to stop," said Maddy, slowly shaking his head as he licked his lips clean. "I'll take everything I can get from you."

"We'll see," said Derreck, a rare smile on his lips. *Fuck, I love a challenge.*

Chapter Six

Maddy

"I'm going to restrain you today," said Derreck, his voice slithering against the back of Maddy's neck. He shuddered, his mind and body on instant alert. He usually waited until he was at his lowest before he caved in to his addiction, but he was still floating from their lunch together, and now he was going to go that much higher.

How high could he go before he was truly addicted to Derreck's touch? Or perhaps he already was, and he was just in denial. He'd told Derreck things that he had never told anyone, and Derreck had *listened*. He hadn't tried to offer solutions or fix Maddy's problems. He had just listened.

He needed to come clean with Derreck, but not yet. He could enjoy one more time together before he risked their...whatever their arrangement was.

They'd already gone over their limits, which had been slightly unexpected. Maddy had thought that once he'd said them, they were set in stone, but apparently that wasn't the case. He could change his mind at any time, and he still had his safewords if he was uncertain.

Derreck gripped one of Maddy's wrists, dragging him over to the wall. He stumbled, falling against Derreck and getting a whiff of his clothing. There was sunshine, earth and clean laundry, an image of a grassy field with rich flowers popping into his mind. Saliva pooled in his mouth, and his face went hot.

That...had never happened before. He swallowed, peering up at Derreck's dark eyes. Indoors, it was difficult to tell his pupil from his iris, and they appeared as dark pools of nothingness that Maddy struggled to look at. He *wanted* to look at Derreck, as Derreck flickered his gaze over him, but something about the darkness terrified him. He had to look away.

He didn't have time to think before his other wrists was encased by a lined cuff that was imbedded deep into the wall. He clenched his hands into fists and pulled against the restraints, groaning at the way the metal edge cut into his skin, the padded softness of the middle warmer than he'd expected. It didn't even hurt, but Maddy was already losing focus. He was so ready to fly.

His sleeves dropped as he tugged at the cuffs, leaving the pale skin of his wrists exposed. His skin prickled as the cool air of the room touched it. He had never felt so naked in front of Derreck before. He tugged again, his sleeves settling farther down.

Derreck grabbed at Maddy's pants without lowering the zipper, dragging them over the abused flesh of his ass. The cane marks had still been purplish in the mirror, but the welts from the flog had faded from yellow and green. They still hurt, though, which was the only thing that mattered.

Kicking his legs wider, Derreck secured Maddy's ankles to the wall next, throwing him completely off balance with a few clicks. Maddy wouldn't be able to lean into any hits without putting pressure on his wrists, which were already starting to bruise with fresh purple lines.

"Looks good," said Derreck, bringing his hand down on Maddy's ass with a resounding slap.

Maddy let out a startled cry before clamping his mouth shut. He went tight as a fresh sting mixed with the aching bruises of his body. *I can take it.* Maddy gritted his teeth. It was unlike anything he'd ever felt, but if Derreck thought that it was going to make him beg, he had another thing coming.

"Do you look at my marks in the mirror every day?" Derreck asked, squeezing his ass hard enough to make Maddy's toes curl. Maddy clenched his jaw as he fell against his restraints, struggling to pull himself back up.

Maddy nodded, trying to find a grip on the sheer wall as he waited for the next strike. He hissed as Derreck grabbed him by the hair, pulling his head back until he had to arch. It put him so far off balance that he hoped that the cuffs would hold him, otherwise he would fall right on his aching ass if Derreck let go.

"Answer when I ask you a question. I deserve that much, at least," said Derreck, his voice dark.

You deserve so much more. Much more than Maddy could ever hope to give him. "Yes, I look at them all the time. Sometimes I lock the door in the bathroom at work and just stare at them in the mirror. I touch them, too, but I can never make them hurt as good as you can."

A second slap rang out, his skin tingling from the blow.

"Good. You should know that I'm the only one who can give you what you need."

Maddy couldn't stop the shudder. His body agreed, his adrenaline surging as something fluttered in his belly. He closed his eyes, pulling himself upright as he shook his head. *I can take care of myself, thank you very much.*

There was a small pause and a rustle before the hits started to rain down on Maddy's flesh. The bruises soaked up each strike, amplifying them in a way that he never could have imagined. Just when he thought he had Derreck's pattern down, the man would pause, hitting a new spot that would breathe fire into his veins.

Fuck, it hurts. Energy swelled under his skin, sending him to a place that only pain ever did. It was the only place that he was at peace—where nothing mattered except for feeling and living.

His chest heaved, his eyes blurred, even as he blinked rapidly. He slowly pulled himself against the wall, his wrists aching as the latest blow sent him rocking back. He didn't know what Derreck was using on him, but it was much more powerful than the first pathetic flogger he'd tried. It didn't have the focus and sting of the cane, though.

"Did you like my warm-up?" asked Derreck as he leaned against Maddy's back, the rough scrape of his jeans against Maddy's ass almost too much to bear.

Warm-up? Shit. That wasn't right. Maddy could take so much more. He scrunched his eyes shut, biting into his lip.

A flick against his forehead had his eyes flying open and his mouth dropping in surprise. Derreck had moved to lean against the wall beside him, a scowl on his lips. He pulled Maddy's lip out from between his teeth, pinching the spot that was almost perpetually bruised.

"Two things, Maddy," Derreck growled, holding onto Maddy's lip like a fishing hook. "If I ask you a question, you answer." He tugged Maddy's lip. "And the only one who gets to give you pain is me. In this room, your body is mine and your pain is mine. The only way you can stop me is your safeword."

How could that be? Goosebumps prickled over his skin as Derreck's words sank in. The haze in his mind pushed him higher, until Derreck's face unfocused into a blurry cloud of want. A second flick to his forehead brought Maddy back. He blinked the moisture from his eyelashes.

"I liked your warm-up. More, please," said Maddy, his voice low and raspy. Derreck's smile sent a rush of something through him.

Derreck couldn't really mean that—not when Maddy was still hiding from him. He wanted Derreck to possess him like no one had ever cared to before. He wanted to belong to someone, but it was impossible.

A sliver of ice trickled down his spine, but he pushed it away. It was not the time for his issues—not when Derreck was looking at him like that.

"And here I thought you'd had enough," said Derreck, huffing and turning away. There was more rustling behind Maddy, but he couldn't see what Derreck was doing when he craned his neck back. He settled his face against the cool wall as sweat soaked into his shirt.

The next hit almost broke him. It was as unexpected as it was swift, pushing the air from his lungs and any last thoughts from his body. The initial thud hit all the way to the bone, but the secondary sting was what pushed him over the edge, a yell exploding through his lips.

He clamped his mouth shut, stifling his cry. He wanted to bite his lip and draw blood, but he couldn't. He had to be good for Derreck.

"Too much?" Derreck asked, smoothing over the hit with his warm palm. Derreck should have been trembling and sweaty from exertion, but he sounded calm, like he really was just getting started.

Maddy shook his head, keeping his lips sealed as he glanced to the door. There had only been a few couples in the bar area when they'd walked in, but who knew how many were out there now. Would anyone come running if they heard him scream? He couldn't bear their eyes on him – not when he was stripped bare.

Another hit pushed air through his nose as he smacked his head against the wall, trying to keep the sound inside. What the hell was Derreck even using? He tried to look back and see, but his vision was blurry.

Three more hits and he couldn't hold back his deep grunt. Every strike felt like it was hitting the same spot, cutting deeper and deeper until his soul was bared, along with his bones. He clutched the wall as his knees trembled, his legs starting to give out beneath him.

Drifting in and out, his breathing slowed as his eyes crept shut. His cheeks were wet, and the wall steamed from his breath, but it didn't matter. The drop of drool slipping over his lower lip didn't matter, either.

"Will you scream for me, Maddy?" Derreck asked as he paused his blows. His hand creeped over Maddy's flesh that had gone numb as Maddy floated far away. It was a question, and Maddy knew he had to answer. He struggled to open his mouth and push the words out.

"I don't want them to hear," he said, his words slurred as if he were drunk. He didn't feel drunk. He was so fucking high that his skin buzzed with energy that couldn't be contained for much longer. Something was building inside of him, and it was ready to burst.

"The doors and walls are soundproofed. Your sounds belong to me, just like your pain does." Derreck's breath skimmed over Maddy's cheek as he loomed close.

Something shifted in Maddy's chest. He clenched his fists, struggling to hold it back. He shivered, terrified and free.

"I need your permission for what I want to do next. I want to whip your hole and your balls. I've tried to hold back, but I can't resist. It will hurt, though," Derreck warned him.

Maddy wanted to snort and roll his eyes, but he was barely able to move. He'd hardly ever paid any attention to anything down there, and the few times he'd tried to make something happen, it had all been for nothing. His ass and cock meant nothing more to him than the skin of his palms.

"Do it," said Maddy, turning his face back to the wall and letting himself sink down onto the restraints. His wrists ached. They would probably be bruised for weeks. *No mirror required this time.*

The fibrous and scratchy strands of some kind of flogger fluttered against his skin. His legs were already splayed and trapped in the cuffs, but he shifted his stance as wide as he could, exposing his hole and a bit of his sac to Derreck.

Maddy's cock hung down between his legs, flaccid and soft as it always was. He could count on one hand how many times it had gotten hard for him, and each time had left him baffled more than aroused.

There was a light snap of wind before the flogger struck between his cheeks, the fibers dragging over his hole. Maddy went tight automatically, pulling at the cuffs as the blow sank in. Whatever Derreck was using, it wasn't leather or any other kind of cloth Maddy was familiar with. The blow stung and itched, leaving a strange tingle that was nothing like the thud of the other implements.

"Did you like that?" asked Derreck, running his finger down Maddy's crack and soothing the sting.

Maddy nodded, his tension unwinding. The touch wasn't unwelcome, even with the slight sexual edge that it had. Sex was off the table, and there was no pressure. He could let himself go.

A second hit his stung across his sac, warmth spreading through his balls as a new kind of fire ignited. It didn't hurt—not like it should have. It was too good to hurt.

Squirming, Maddy tried to close his legs, sagging against the cuffs as his balance tipped.

Derreck went to work. The scratchy flog scraped over every inch of Maddy's skin, the sting lasting longer than it had any right to. His numbed flesh burst to life with a raging fire that burned from his core. And when the flogger hit low, glancing between his legs and over his sac, his belly flared.

A moan mingled with a gasp pushed through his lips, and he opened his eyes wide as something new started to build within him. His gut clenched as his groin throbbed and the dampness on his cheeks dried. The sudden urge to rut against the wall and bury himself within something was overwhelming.

Everything he'd ever been certain of in his life was gone. He was hard. *Impossible.*

He bit back a cry as his sac was struck, the sting zipping straight to his cock.

It didn't make sense. It had been years since he'd taken himself in hand for a few minutes of confusing pleasure. His cock had always been a dormant piece of flesh that he held only when he had to piss or when he was cleaning himself. It had nothing to do with his pain or with Derreck.

"Wait," Maddy cried out as the pressure between his legs pulled his control from him. His chest went tight as the warmth grew, fresh tears building in his eyes. "Derreck, stop."

The blows ceased instantly as the flogger fell to the ground with a thump. Through his panting breaths, Maddy couldn't hear Derreck anymore, and the pause in his hits was like a shattered metronome. Derreck's gaze burned into him, stripping the last of his defenses away. His breath caught, his heart thudding.

"Are you using your safeword to slow down or stop?" asked Derreck, his voice deathly calm. He was directly behind Maddy, so close that Maddy would have been able to touch him if he hadn't been cuffed.

How could he be so calm when Maddy was breaking at the seams? Maddy was so high that he was fucking shaking, but his cock throbbed, too, the ache bordering on real pain. He'd never been more confused in his life. It was too much, but he craved more like he desired the cane on his skin.

"I want to stop," he said, tugging at his wrists. The metal edge had to have been close to breaking his skin, each movement a vivid ache.

"May I touch you so I can release your restraints?" Derreck's voice was closer—nearly touching him now, and still calm. So fucking calm. How could he do it? *Can't he see that I'm breaking?*

"Yes. Get them off, please," he said, his strength fading as he struggled to stay on his feet. Three seconds flat and all four of his limbs were released. Snapping his legs shut, Maddy leaned into the wall, breathing against the cold surface. He couldn't turn and let Derreck see him like this. His cock throbbed as it glanced against the wall, pre-cum spreading over the paint like fresh primer.

"Leave me alone please," he begged, his shoulders shaking as his chest went tight. Another crack in his armor formed, the dam so close to breaking that he was holding on by a thread.

"I can't do that, Maddy. I need to know that you are okay. Turn around so I can see your face. Don't hide from me now, not when you are more beautiful than ever. You took every hit so well, but I need to know what happened."

The dam broke and a sob heaved its way out of Maddy's chest. Derreck must've thought it was his fault, but it wasn't. Maddy was so fucked up, and now he'd dragged Derreck into his muddy life.

"I'm hard," he said quietly, pressing his forehead into the wall. His hole clenched as his cock throbbed, a residual sting shooting up his spine. "I'm so sorry, Derreck. I don't know what happened, but it started when you whipped me down there, and I don't know how to make it go away." *Sex is off the table, but I fucked that up, too. Why do I fuck everything up?*

"Look at me," said Derreck, his voice low and commanding. "I'm not upset. You need to know that."

"But you said no sex," said Maddy, choking off another sob. "And I don't think I want sex, either… I've never wanted it. I just want you to hurt me, but I fucked up and now you'll never want to see me again." He slid his hands down the wall, his sweaty palms slipping easily over the surface.

"Maddy, look at me *now.*" His voice left no room for argument, and Maddy had to obey. With a deep breath, Maddy turned.

Derreck was staring at him, his dark eyes watching and stripping Maddy further. His thin T-shirt stuck to his frame, his chest rising and falling faster than Maddy would have thought from his voice. Maddy's gaze dropped to Derreck's obvious bulge trapped in his jeans. *Fuck,* Derreck was hard, too.

"Can I touch you?" asked Derreck, his gaze never leaving Maddy's face. He didn't look down, not even with Maddy's erection poking out into the room like a help wanted ad. But Maddy couldn't keep his eyes off Derreck's concealed package.

Maddy had seen hard dicks before. He'd tried porn, without success, and he'd seen one up close when he'd thrown caution to the wind and had set up an account on a hookup app. The latter had been a huge mistake — but also an eye opener.

He'd realized that maybe he was one of the rare few who didn't desire sex. Nothing got him hard — not tits, or dicks, or tits *and* dicks, or any other body part in between. But why did his mouth flood and his cock throb when he looked at Derreck's bulge?

"I think so," said Maddy, finally filling the silence as it stretched. "Don't touch me there, but anywhere else is okay." He looked down at his cock and the purpling head that was oozing a few drops of pearly fluid. He did not want to find out what would happen if Derreck touched his cock.

Theoretically, he knew what would happen, but he had no desire to experience an orgasm at that moment. He was already a jumbled mess without adding one of those to the shit pile.

Derreck touched his shoulder before he smoothed his hand down Maddy's arm, threading their fingers together and squeezing. The simple act was more intimate than anything they'd done together, and it sent a burst of calm to Maddy's core. Derreck wasn't leaving.

"Come sit on the couch with me," said Derreck, tugging Maddy along. Each step was a monumental effort that he could not have done without Derreck holding and catching his weight with every step.

The last time they'd snuggled, Maddy had rested his head against Derreck's chest. Maddy almost balked as Derreck pulled him until he straddled his hips, the fire on the back of his legs and ass igniting as he brushed against Derreck's jeans.

"If you are comfortable, I would like you to tell me what happened," said Derreck, bracing a hand against Maddy's back to hold him close. The outline of his cock was rigid against Maddy's ass. "Sometimes our triggers are unexpected, but I don't want to risk triggering you a second time. I need you to tell me, Maddy, so I don't upset you again."

Maddy pressed his face to Derreck's chest, taking a deep breath of earth and sweat. He couldn't believe that Derreck was still holding him when he had disrespected Derreck's limit. But how long would that last? *Time to come clean.*

"I don't get hard," said Maddy, his voice muffled in Derreck's T-shirt. "I've tried sex and other things, but I hardly ever get hard. Sometimes I have dreams, but by the time I wake up, the feeling is just…gone. I'm sorry I didn't tell you, but I didn't think you would care. You said sex was a hard limit."

The silence stretched. Maddy cringed and pulled his lip between his teeth. He shook with the effort of not biting down.

"Don't apologize for something you have no control over. I can understand why you're uncomfortable and why you're scared. Do you know what was different this time compared to the last? You didn't respond like that from just the pain."

Maddy shuddered as Derreck ran his hand down his back. He couldn't squash the urge to thrust a hand between his legs to clutch his aching sac. His skin was hot to the touch, the nerves so sensitive that they made him whimper. His cock drooled, moisture dribbling on his belly as well as Derreck's.

"Here," said Maddy, releasing his sac and squashing his face into Derreck's warm chest. "It didn't feel like that on my ass or between my cheeks, but there…" He shuddered.

"Fuck," said Derreck, flexing his hands. They dug into Maddy's ass, the relieving fog flooding Maddy's mind for a moment. "I'm sorry. I shouldn't have pushed you." His cock pulsed against Maddy's ass.

"I know why I don't want sex, but why don't you?" asked Maddy. He lifted his hips so he could see the bulge in Derreck's jeans. It looked monstrous behind the thick cloth. Reaching out, Maddy pressed his palm to the tent, testing the rigid flesh beneath him. It was rock hard and so hot.

He'd always found a person's pleasure somewhat fascinating. He knew sex was supposed to feel good, but he'd never had the chance to really explore except for on his own unresponsive body. His singular experience with another person hadn't left him with any clues, either. He'd just stayed limp on the bed while they'd pushed his face into his pillow and rutted into him. Underwhelming and bizarre had summed up those three minutes of his life.

But he was inches from Derreck's face, his eyes nearly black and his hard cock only a layer away. Maddy could feel the pulse of blood pass through Derreck's shaft when he pressed down, and when he squeezed, the whole thing twitched like a caged feral animal.

"Fuck, Maddy, don't," said Derreck, his head falling back against the couch as he let out a gasp. He gripped his hands harder on Maddy's hips. "I won't be able to control myself if you keep touching me like that."

Fear seeped into the fog and Maddy jerked his hand away. "You'd force me?"

He'd had his brush with that, too, and he never wanted to go down that road again.

"What? No, of course not," said Derreck, leveling Maddy with a stare. His eyes were pinched, a lighter fleck in his iris standing out like the sun against the shade. "I won't be able to stop from coming if you keep touching me like that. I don't want to push your limits more than I already have today."

"Oh." Maddy looked down, a flush rising on his cheeks. Of course, Derreck wouldn't force him. As crazy at it may have been, he trusted Derreck.

"I don't usually mix kink with sex," said Derreck, removing his hands from Maddy's ass and threading their fingers together again. Maddy relaxed at the touch, his uncertainty draining away. "Sex can be fulfilling for me, but not in the same way that kink is. The few times I've tried to incorporate the two, it didn't end well."

"I'm sorry," said Maddy, his hand burning at the memory of Derreck's cock. His own cock started to waver, each breath shrinking it back to its convenient carry-on size. Taking a deep breath, he tried to keep from reaching out and touching. The tented fabric called to him, still so big. How long would it stay that way?

"It's okay, Maddy," said Derreck, following Maddy's gaze. "You couldn't have known. You can still touch me, but you *will* make me come. I won't be able to stop that — not even for you."

Maddy wasn't exactly sure what that meant, but it was meaningless compared to the bulge in front of him — the thing that he had permission to touch.

He ran his finger down the zipper, his skin peaking into goosebumps as Derreck's breath hitched. Tracing the outline, he circled it, committing every subtle bump and ridge to memory. He didn't know if he would ever be able to touch it again, and he wanted to remember every part of it. It hardened beneath him, straining against the black jeans.

"Can I see it?" asked Maddy, licking his lips. Derreck nodded, letting out another curse as Maddy reached for his zipper, struggling to get the metal teeth open. When he adjusted himself in Derreck's lap, his sac scratched against Derreck's leg, sending a tingle of pleasure to his groin. He shook the feeling off, singularly focused on his prize.

Violently, it sprung from its confines, bursting into the air the moment he tugged at the unzipped edges of Derreck's jeans. It was huge and curved with a thick vein along the underside and smaller veins around the rest of it. The shaft was darker than the rest of Derreck's caramel skin, but the hooded head was a vibrant pink and moist with a drop of pre-cum.

Maddy's mouth watered as he stared at the pre-cum that dripped from the head and down the shaft. He licked his lips as uncertainty filled him. Would Derreck mind?

He swiped his finger over the tip, marveling at the way it twitched beneath him. It was more expressive than Derreck's face, which had been unreadable, even when Maddy had opened his pants. Gathering the moisture on one finger, he brought it to his lips before sucking it deep into his mouth. The flavor wasn't wholly pleasant, but not enough to make him gag, either.

I wonder. He glanced at his own cock, which had hardened again as his sensitive sac scraped against Derreck's leg. Maddy was definitely smaller than Derreck, but that wasn't a surprise. He was smaller than any man he'd seen online, too.

After dragging his finger through the dollop of pre-cum on his own cock, he brought it to his lips, scrunching his nose at the taste. He was a lot stronger than Derreck.

"Fuck," said Derreck, groaning again as Maddy shifted so their cocks lined up. Derreck practically eclipsed him in both length and width, and the color difference was even more startling and alluring.

"Can I touch it?" asked Maddy without even looking up. More pre-cum escaped from Derreck's cock, dripping down the crown and along the shaft. Maddy nudged his hips forward, the undersides of their cocks touching for the first time.

Derreck's skin blazed next to his own until his groin felt like it had been dipped in molten chocolate. His sac throbbed, heavy and full. Maddy's eyes rolled back in his head as he gave in to the urge to thrust a few times. The sensation was captivating.

"Fuck, yes," said Derreck, fisting the slick material of the couch.

Maddy's hand was too small to wrap around both of them at once, and his own pleasure was inconsequential. He reached for Derreck's cock, wrapping his fingers around the shaft and squeezing. It pulsed, going even harder.

"Shit." Derreck bucked beneath him, the head of his cock getting slicker. "I'm trying to hold back for you, but I won't last long." His breathing was ragged, his pupils dilated so his eyes were almost completely black.

Maddy forced his eyes to stay open so he could capture every moment. Sweat had gathered beneath Derreck's curls, and his mouth was open, his pink tongue moving as he let out tiny sounds. Maddy wasn't sure if *attractive* was the right word for Derreck, but he was enthralled, regardless. He'd never desired anyone the way he did Derreck. He'd never longed to just touch. Derreck was the first man that Maddy wouldn't hesitate to call *beautiful*.

He blinked as Derreck's throat bobbed with each swallow, the column of his thick neck flexing. The sight made Maddy's cock throb, and he tightened his thighs around Derreck's legs, his brutalized skin prickling with life. Derreck's lips pursed, his pink tongue peeking out as he panted and groaned low as Maddy twisted his hand.

Maddy shuddered, his eyes falling shut as something inside him broke.

Pleasure that he'd only felt a few times in his life rushed through his body, battering his cock and balls like an explosive baseball bat. There was a moment of fear before he surged higher, the ache of his ass and sac encompassing him as he let go.

Was that what it was supposed to be like? He wanted to scream and cry and run a mile, all at once. That part had never happened before, not even when he'd taken himself in hand, not stopping until he had painted his belly with cum. That had been a prickle of nerves in comparison.

It was over just as suddenly as it had begun. The pleasure receded to nothing, and the pain sunk its claws deeper than it ever had. It was the most complete he had ever felt.

Derreck stared at him, his eyes wide and his mouth open in something akin to shock. Maddy's hand was still on Derreck's cock, gripping his shaft in a way that was probably too hard. Slowly, he pulled back, an apology on his lips.

"Come home with me tonight," said Derreck.

Cold fear plunged over him. *No. No. No.* Sex would ruin everything that they had built together.

"Maddy, wait. Not for sex. I would never ask you for that unless I knew you were completely ready," said Derreck, slipping their fingers together. "I can't let you walk away right now. Please. We don't even have to touch. I just need you with me."

Maddy sank his teeth into his lip as he wiped his filthy hands on his dress shirt. The liquid soaked straight through the fabric, leaving a film on his skin. He needed a shower or a change of clothes at the very least, especially since he had rushed straight to the club after work without stopping to get changed. Derreck's clothes wouldn't fit him, but he was bound to have something appropriate.

Perhaps Derreck's still-hard cock didn't matter as much as Maddy had feared. And what did he have at home except for a bunch of empty rooms and a television that always told dirty jokes that he didn't quite understand? Being alone didn't sound like a great idea.

He understood Derreck — now more than ever.

"Okay."

Chapter Seven

Derreck

Fuck, that smarts. Derreck pressed his lips together, breathing deep through his nose as he tried, and mostly failed, to shove his cock back into his pants. Every touch sent a whisper of pleasure through his body as he battled his self-control.

It was like trying to put a tent back into its original packaging — futile and probably the cause of thirty percent of all divorces. He wasn't meant to fit into his jeans hard — especially his club jeans. It hadn't mattered before, because he didn't get hard from sceneing with a typical sub.

"You ready to go?" asked Derreck, cringing as he pulled the zipper all the way to the top. He would probably end up with a permanent bend in his cock, but it would have to be okay. Once he got hard, he stayed that way for a long-ass time.

"Yeah," said Maddy. He had wiped his shirt with a damp cloth and had guzzled almost a full water bottle as Derreck struggled with his zipper. Maddy's eyes were downcast, tracing the nonexistent pattern on the flooring. His lip was between his teeth again, but he hadn't bitten down.

"Hey," said Derreck, gripping Maddy's chin and tilting his face up. Maddy blinked, his bloodshot eyes still wet. "You don't have to come if you don't want to."

"It's fine, I just..." He tugged his chin away.

If Derreck hadn't known any better, he would have guessed that Maddy was dropping, but something told him that wasn't the case. There was something else hiding behind those beautiful blue eyes.

"Let's go," said Derreck, pulling the door wide. His erection would be obvious to any who cared to look, but that was another reason he loved Unkinked. There were enough hard cocks floating around that one more was hardly big news.

The air was cooler outside the door, and it sucked the heat away from his skin, his pants somehow pulling tighter. He cursed, casting his gaze to the rugged ceiling. He was determined to get through the next few hours and keep his promise.

He slid his hand along Maddy's shoulder, hoping to steady his sub. Maddy had slumped his shoulders as they exited the room, and he had shrunk in on himself in a way that he always seemed to do when there was anyone watching. His sub was the furthest thing from an exhibitionist.

Derreck didn't need a crowd to fuck someone up, though.

Maddy shrugged Derreck's hand off without a word, his face beaming red in the low light. *Shy, too.*

"Did you want me to take you home?" Derreck asked. It would kill him to do it, but he wouldn't keep

Maddy without his consent. His skin thrummed with the need to hold Maddy close, but he held himself back. He had already pushed both of their limits — perhaps too far to repair.

"I — Phil?" Maddy jerked to a halt as he stared at someone in the nearest booth. A middle-aged gentleman's head jerked up, his sparkling eyes going fierce and his smile pressing into a thin line.

Derreck tried to connect the name and the face, but Maddy's blanch tore his focus away. Maddy's eyes had gone wide, his mouth open in utter surprise as every muscle went taut. Taking a step back, Maddy collided with Derreck's shoulder, flinching at the touch.

"Madison," said Phil, looking over Maddy's shoulder as Derreck took a step forward, putting himself between his sub and Phil.

Derreck narrowed his eyes in recognition. Phil was a Dom so far off Derreck's radar that he didn't even register as a blip. The young woman at his feet with dried tears on her face and a far-off look in her eyes was of more interest to him than Phil, and Derreck didn't even like to get involved with women all that often.

Women could hide secrets beneath the thinnest veneers. He had no chance of breaking their shields and building them back up again. They were just too strong. Men were simpler...usually. *Except Maddy.*

"It's Maddy," Maddy responded, his voice harder than Derreck had ever heard it. He turned back, stunned at the force of the rage that was etched in Maddy's every movement.

"What are you doing here, Phil?" Maddy's voice dropped into a low hiss. The dungeon master was nowhere in sight, but Derreck spied Clint as he glanced their way from behind the bar. To anyone who didn't know Clint, he appeared relaxed as he polished a glass and refilled another. Derreck knew him better than that.

"I certainly have more right to be here than you do," said Phil, leaning back in his seat as he spread his legs wide. Threading his hand into his sub's hair, Phil tugged once before patting the top of her head. Her expression crinkled. "At least I have a membership. I'm surprised they even let you in here with your background and all."

Maddy stiffened, curling his hands into fists until his knuckles bled white. "*My* background?"

A smirk slithered its way over Phil's features as he nodded. His silver hair glinted in the low light, the stubble on his chin the perfect mix of scruff and definition. *Is it bad that I want to shave his face and slit his throat?* Derreck shook his head. He wasn't there to bury anyone.

"Or maybe they don't know." Phil leaned forward, his eyes twinkling. "It would be interesting to see what would happen if anyone in here found out about you. And think about your coworkers... If they knew you were in a place like this, with your problem, it might not go well for you." He shook his head, clicking his tongue.

Rage had never felt quite so palpable before. It burned its way along Derreck's hands, whirling higher until his chest ached and his gut boiled. Phil hadn't been a blip before because he was a good-looking douche with a capital '*d*'. But blackmail in a place like Unkinked? That made him a big fucking problem.

Derreck had Phil by the throat before he could utter another word. His hand clamped down against his will, choking Phil's yell off with a few pounds of perfectly placed pressure. The fear that crept over Phil's face and obliterated his smirk had Derreck's gut throbbing with glee.

"Tell me that I didn't just hear you try to blackmail my sub," said Derreck, not letting up the pressure until Phil's face morphed from red to purple. The vein at Phil's temple throbbed as the pressure increased, his eyes popping wide.

Phil's sub scrambled away on her hands and knees, letting out a garbled shout as her long hair tangled in his fingers, tugging a few strands free.

"Derreck, what are you doing?" Maddy shouted, tugging at Derreck's shoulder.

Derreck turned to him, glancing from the horrified flush on Maddy's face to the way he gripped Derreck's shoulder hard enough to bruise. *Nah, I'm not done yet.* "Check on his sub. She looks like she might be high." Then he turned his attention back to Phil. "You didn't answer me," he said to Phil, who was still struggling, only able to get the tiniest breath of air when Derreck allowed it. "Your membership is suspended either way, but if she's high, you're fucking done."

Clint rushed in, at Derreck's back before he even had to call out to him. Clint knelt next to Phil's sub, taking her hand to lead her away from the commotion while he spoke to her in hushed tones.

"Maddy's a freak," Phil whispered, his words barely audible. "Your sub lied to you."

Derreck tilted his head, watching the way Phil's temple thudded in time with the pulse under his hand. With just a little bit more pressure Derreck could end him and bury him in the dirt where he belonged. Not with this many witnesses, though, and with Maddy at his side looking more frightened of him with each passing throb.

"It doesn't matter. Get the fuck out or I'll take you the fuck out." Derreck released him, stepping back as Phil fell to his knees. Phil hacked as he clutched his throat, his chest heaving as he tried to suck in a breath. His perfect suit had been crumpled in the struggle, the button torn from the hole that was now beyond repair. *Who the fuck wears a suit to a kink club? Seriously?*

Derreck took a step back, checking in with Clint, who was back by the bar with Phil's sub. The bruises around Phil's pale neck would brand him with a collar. Men like Phil wanted power for power's sake, and the collar would be as much of a threat as it was a warning. Derreck had the feeling that Phil wasn't a true Dom anyway, only a manipulator of the system so he could feel better about his own dick size.

"You won't get away with this," Phil hissed at Maddy as he struggled to his feet. Grabbing the table, he hefted himself off the ground, taking a step toward Maddy with his fist raised. Maddy blanched, his already pale face going snow white.

Is this guy for real? The second the choking stopped, did he really think he was God again?

Derreck moved in close, reveling in the way Phil flinched. Grabbing Phil's shoulder, he dug his fingers into the meat, pinching every nerve within his grasp. His lips hovered by Phil's ear, the smell of cologne and aftershave overpowering.

"Excuse me?" asked Derreck, letting his voice drop into a growl. "I don't recall giving you permission to speak. A *boy* who can't listen and speaks out of turn isn't worth anything at all."

Phil struggled to pull away, flinching as Derreck gripped harder. He was like a fly battering at Derreck, his useless wings breaking off with every movement.

"You can crawl out of here. Bad boys don't deserve to walk." Derreck leaned back, soaking up the fury as he spoke loud enough for the onlookers to hear. "Push me and see what happens."

It was *technically* on the edge of the rules. The audience that was silently looking on had not agreed to be part of their little *scene*...but neither had Maddy. Phil's sub looked like she wasn't in a state to consent to anything from the way her eyes darted around, her gaze lost and unfocused.

Phil dropped back to his knees, grumbling as he glared up at them. Maintaining eye contact, Phil coughed as he went down on his hands, his face blazing as he touched the slightly sticky floor. No matter how many times the place was cleaned, a bar was still a bar.

Derreck could imagine the humiliation that was enveloping Phil, but he couldn't bring himself to feel the least bit sorry. *Fuck with me, and you'll get the bull's horns, but fuck with my sub? You might wish you were dead.*

Derreck let out a breath as Phil dropped his gaze. Humiliation really wasn't his thing, although he'd been with a few subs who had liked it, so he knew his way around the kink. Watching Phil struggle across the ground, his knees probably burning under his weight as he shuffled over the hardwood, did absolutely nothing for him.

If it had been Maddy doing the crawling? Derreck shook his head. His sub was as shy as he was polite. Asking Maddy to humiliate himself would be the end of their agreement. He silently added it to Maddy's hard limits.

"Oh, Phil, just one more thing." Derreck waited until Phil was nearly at the curtain before he called out. "You can leave your key card at the door. It won't work again after today."

Phil slapped the floor, his back going straight as he glared at Derreck. His face was bright red, steam almost visible from his ears. The curtain slipped wide as the bouncer rounded on Phil, his hand outstretched. Phil reached for it, presumably to pull himself back up, but the bouncer slapped Phil's hand away.

"Your card."

I hope this bouncer sticks around. He seems like a good guy. Derreck could always appreciate a man who had his back.

Derreck didn't even wait until the outside door slammed shut before he turned to Maddy. Most of the couples around them had gone back to their conversations, a bubble of noise wrapping around them as the tension dissipated. The sound of sobs reached him as Phil's sub broke down.

Some of the onlookers had probably seen a similar show before, because Derreck didn't have a reputation for no reason. If there was one rule that he followed in his life, it was consent, and allowing the scum of the earth to violate that was just as bad as doing it himself.

"What did you just do?" asked Maddy, taking a step back when Derreck reached for him. His eyes were wide and terrified, and Derreck's heart thudded uncomfortably as he lost his internal balance.

"What needed to be done. You remember the rules?" asked Derreck. Consent was the rule that reigned above all in the community. "There are no second chances here, Maddy."

Derreck longed to touch him and slide his thumb over Maddy's cheek until his terror fizzled away, but he knew when to stop pushing. Maddy was shutting down, a shield snapping over him before Derreck's eyes. Maddy fiddled with the sleeve on his shirt, tugging it down until it slipped over his knuckles, hiding them from view.

Clint had moved Phil's sub to one of the bar stools, a glass of water before her and a blanket over her shoulders. She wobbled visibly, a hand to her lips as she listened to whatever Clint was saying, her head bobbing every few seconds.

"I didn't take anything," she said as Derreck moved closer. "Phil only gave me an aspirin when I told him I had a headache. I wasn't really up for anything today, but he was going away on a business trip."

Derreck grimaced, catching Clint's gaze and nodding once. The poor girl had definitely been lied to. Aspirin didn't make you slur or throw you off balance so you could barely sit on a stool. He would leave it up to Clint to convince the girl to go to the hospital and get treatment.

"We're good," said Clint as Derreck hovered at the edge of their bubble. "You can take off."

Derreck grunted, turning back to Maddy...who wasn't even there. The middle of the bar was clear, the so-called dancefloor where he had almost choked Phil out, deserted.

Shit. Things were going from bad to worse.

He pushed his way through the curtain at the front door, bowling by the bouncer who was clutching Phil's white key card and looking like he was barely keeping his questions behind tight lips. He grabbed the door handle and threw it open.

The heat and humidity of summer struck him like a physical force, tearing the breath from his lungs and compressing his chest. After two steps, sweat brimmed on his skin, dripping down from his hair to the collar of his T-shirt.

His heart raced as he looked up and down the street. Derreck had picked Maddy up at work because he had been worried that Maddy would somehow slip away before he made it to the club. His blue Mustang was parked just down the sunbaked street, the paint glinting in the sun. There was no one around him except for the two black crows that pecked at the remains of a dead frog a few feet away. They looked up, their beady eyes glaring at him before they took off into the still air.

Panting, he jogged to his Mustang, pushing himself faster with each step. There was no way that Maddy could have gotten far so quickly. His sub was strong and fast, but no one would be able to run for long with the sun glaring so fiercely that each breath was a struggle.

His last hope died when he saw the passenger seat of his car empty. Maddy was gone.

Chapter Eight

Maddy

He hit the street before Derreck could notice that he'd slipped away, the familiar heat sinking beneath his shirt and stifling his thoughts. He looked both ways before he let the door fall shut, making sure that Phil had already moved on. Phil had about forty pounds and four inches on him, and he did not want to get caught alone with the guy.

What the fuck just happened? He bit his lip, not holding back until the tang of blood spilled into his mouth. He had promised himself that his search into the kink world would be a secret, just for him. He hadn't told anyone about it except for a few anonymous friends online. His therapist didn't even know, for Christ's sake.

But Phil? He was the last person in the world who Maddy would have willingly told. The guy developed a beef with him since the day Maddy had started snooping into his files to stack up evidence against him.

Accepting bribes, condoning unsafe work practices and, of course, the extra little tidbit Maddy had stumbled upon when he'd dug deeper. Phil was the type of person who gave auditors the wrong reputation, and he was a goddamn sex offender, too.

But he still hadn't deserved to be put on his knees or strangled by Derreck, who had turned into some kind of attack dog the moment Phil had started to speak. The look in Derreck's eyes when he'd wrapped his hand around Phil's throat told Maddy that he hadn't wanted to let go. Maddy had seen hatred and rage, but there had been more than that. There had been murder in Derreck's eyes, too.

It was as if a veil had been lifted from over Maddy's eyes. How had he never noticed that Derreck was so tall and so strong? He could've killed Phil with his pinky finger alone without breaking a sweat. His dark eyes had shone bright, his lips twisting with brutal glee.

Maddy shuddered, despite the heat. He was in too deep, and there was no paddle in sight. He couldn't believe that he'd had his hands on Derreck's cock, his own cock harder than it had ever been as he'd come all over himself. *What is wrong with me?*

None of the journey was supposed to have been about sex. It hadn't been until the flog had slapped over his balls, leaving them itchy and bruised. Pain had never done anything like that to him, though.

His chest ached, and he ran his knuckles over his sternum. It was all falling apart because of the stupid piece of dangly skin that had pushed its agenda before his mental health.

He booked it down the street, running despite the brutal ache of his ass. Every welt scraped against his clothing with each movement, the pain almost unbearable without Derreck there to soothe it. His cum that had crusted to his shirt pulled at his skin, stiff and awkward as he started to sweat. It didn't matter if he was close to boiling on the sunny street. He had to run.

Derreck was going to find out what he was desperately trying to hide. He would lose his only outlet, then his job and maybe his freedom last of all — all because he had been in the wrong place at the wrong time. He should have known that he might run into someone who would recognize him. All the planning and waiting and he'd been foiled by the simplest mistake.

The same thoughts echoed over in his head as his chest tightened, his breath barely satisfying his need for air. He rounded the corner, speeding to the closest bus stop as his mouth went dry. His vision wavered from the full-bodied ache and the heat. He blinked at the foggy outline of the sign and a few people, his heart pounding as he slowed to a stop.

He'd mapped out every inch of the city roads, planning every escape route before he'd even attempted to track down Derreck. He hadn't known what kind of shape he would leave the club in or if he would have been safe to drive. As much as he longed for the privacy of his own vehicle, he was probably better off standing.

Plunging his hand into his back pocket, he grabbed for his wallet, the welts on his ass screaming in outrage. They were so fucking raw, as if every bit of his flesh had been brutalized. A few people glanced his way as he grabbed for the sign, wobbling as he struggled to stay upright. Their gazes cut straight through his clothing. He burned.

Waiting for the bus and riding among its patrons was like swimming through a heavy fog. He was sure that someone had tried to start up a conversation at some point, but their voice had been muffled beneath the blood rushing through his ears. The bus driver gave him a strange look as he departed, calling out to him as Maddy nearly plunged down the steps.

With the last of his strength, he tripped through the door of his house, slamming it shut behind him and taking a deep breath of isolated air. His back touched the door, the coolness seeping into his skin as he slid to the floor. His ass touched the ceramic tiles, the cold leeching the ache from his skin. Shivering, he dropped his head into his hands, tugging his hair in the same way Derreck had.

It didn't help. If anything, it made him tremble harder. It was a reminder that Derreck wasn't there and that Maddy probably wouldn't see him again.

How could he have ever thought that things would work out? Derreck was sure to talk to Phil, and once he did, it would be over. Maddy would probably have to steer clear of work as well. Gossip traveled faster than bullets and could be just as deadly.

"Stop it," he said into the silent room, tugging harder as his thoughts continued against his will.

His boss hadn't understood his need for a leave of absence, and he sure as hell wouldn't understand Maddy's addiction. It didn't matter how useful he was to the company. It didn't matter that they had gone through four employees while he was on leave for one month. Every time they hired someone new to fill his position, the newbie called it quits. Nobody wanted to be everyone's enemy.

They wouldn't outright fire him. They couldn't. No, they would make his life a living hell until he had no choice but to leave. Their looks were hard enough, even on the best of days, and their whispered accusations always struck home.

His chest pulled tighter as he started to pant, his head spinning out of his control. The walls loomed closer, his clothes clinging to his skin so tightly that he couldn't take it. He played with the hem of his sweat-soaked shirt, unable to pull it from his body.

A knock above his head startled the breath from his lips and he tumbled forward in his rush to get away from the sound. They couldn't know already, could they? Was that his boss telling him not to show up? His head swam as he started to hyperventilate.

"Maddy, you in there?" Derreck's muffled voice called through the door as the heavy knock sounded again.

Maddy didn't have time to think about how Derreck knew where he lived before rage curled in his gut. This was *his* home, his paradise and his solace. It was his only safe place in the world where no one came but him. He'd never had to defend it before, and his will to fight was all but gone.

But he couldn't let Derreck see it, any more than he could invite Phil or his boss inside. His heart was laid bare in each of the rooms, his soul exposed and his defenses gone. He couldn't muster the strength to build his walls up in his house like he did everywhere else.

"Maddy, can you hear me?" Derreck's voice came again, stronger than the first time. The neighbors would start wondering soon. Mrs. Davidson was probably peeking through her lacy curtains, already planning her tale for the next cribbage night. "You don't have to open the door. I just need to make sure you're okay. You are crashing hard, and I need you to know that we are okay and I'm here for you. I would never judge you for anything, Maddy. You're safe with me, I promise."

The tightness eased in Maddy's chest, and he took his first full breath since he'd touched Derreck on the couch. *I'm okay. He says I'm okay, so I must be. I have to be.* Derreck had never lied to him.

His hands slipped over the tile as he tried to stand, his knees wobbling so hard that he almost hit the floor a second time. Grabbing the knob, he steadied himself, pulling himself all the way to his feet. He looked down at his dress shoes, the yellow laces untied and one missing the plastic end. They were scuffed with dirt from his run, one of the soles worn down so he would probably slip in the slightest bit of rain.

Cracking the door, Maddy peered outside. Derreck was sitting on the top step with his back to him, his shoulders slumped as he let out a deep sigh. It was just another line in the long list of Maddy's offenses. Derreck was upset because of him.

He withdrew behind the door, shutting it so quietly that he hoped Derreck hadn't heard. His eyes burned, his throat closing as a sob tried to push its way free. He was breaking. After so many years of holding it together, all it had taken were a few well-aimed words when his guard had been down, and he'd folded like a card table.

"Derreck." The sob escaped as he fumbled with the knob. He couldn't keep himself away from Derreck. As much as it terrified him, he just wanted to slip back into Derreck's arms and feel those hands on him again.

Derreck was the only thing that had ever made him feel whole.

When he cracked the door a second time, Derreck was still sitting on the porch, his head turned toward Maddy as he took a step through the threshold. He looked so tired, and as worn as Maddy felt.

"Are you okay?" asked Derreck, tapping his knuckles against his knee.

Maddy shook his head. He hadn't been okay for a long time. The shaking and trembling were nothing new, but he'd always been able to hold back his tears.

"You look worse than I feel," said Maddy, swallowing the lump in his throat. His breath hiccupped as tears poured down his cheeks. Derreck's lips thinned and he shifted on the concrete porch. Sweat was soaked into the back of his T-shirt and glistened on his shoulders as the sun carved through the sky toward them.

Derreck's keys jingled as he leaned back against the banister next to the steps. Derreck's metallic blue Mustang was parked askew in his driveway, the front wheel on the grass and the rear almost in the neighbor's yard. That would give the neighbors something to talk about. The Mustang was the only thing out of place along the identical row of houses.

"You can go if you want," said Maddy, gripping the edge of his door. He blinked the tears from his eyes, wiping his cheeks with the back of his hand.

Derreck shook his head, turning to look back out onto the street. A rickety Honda tumbled down the road, clearly in the wrong part of the city.

"What can I do?" asked Maddy as he stepped out from behind the door, leaving his last bit of protection behind. His own problems, he could deal with, but he didn't know how to help Derreck.

"Don't run out on me again…ever." Derreck's voice was soft, but there was steel hidden in his words. "You won't deny me aftercare, even if it means we just sit in the same room without touching. But you don't run."

Oh shit. Maddy had been looking at everything all wrong. He'd thought he'd been sparing Derreck from his problems, but he had done something so much worse. He slid down next to Derreck on the front step, leaving an inch of space between them. His welts didn't even hurt as he settled on the unforgiving concrete.

It was the inch between them that burned, drawing and pushing him at the same time. Would Derreck's hands feel different now that Maddy had touched his cock? Or would Derreck go for his throat in the same way he had done to Phil? His skin tingled, his cock twitching in his pants as he imagined Derreck's hand wrapped around his neck.

"Something is wrong with me," said Maddy, finally closing the distance between them to lean against Derreck's shoulder. "And you won't even ask what it is."

Derreck grunted. "You'll tell me when you're ready." His skin was nearly vibrating under Maddy's touch. Derreck clenched his hands into fists, his muscles going taut. He was so strong, but maybe he was just as fragile as Maddy was.

"Why won't you just ask me?" asked Maddy. He wanted to run back into the house before slamming and locking the door behind him, but Derreck looked like he was barely hanging on by a thread. Maddy refused to leave him because he couldn't conquer his own fear.

"Because I respect you," said Derreck, his voice dropping into a growl. "You are a grown-ass man, Maddy, and we all have secrets. You barely know me, so why would I expect you to divulge everything about yourself?"

"What?" asked Maddy, an ache sparking in his chest. Was that how Derreck really felt? He had seen Derreck's soul, and Derreck had seen his. "I know you, Derreck. You aren't a stranger to me."

Derreck let out a humorless chuckle. "What do I do for a living? Where do I live? Who are my parents? When's my fucking birthday? You don't know anything about me, Maddy, because I haven't told you anything. You've already told me so much, but you don't even realize it. I know where you work, where you live and what kind of person you are. I know that your favorite food is bacon and your favorite color is yellow. I know that you're the most sensitive and sweet man I've ever met, but you are terrified of yourself and your sexuality. You're an addict, but not of any standard drug or quick high. I already know, Maddy, but you're still terrified to tell me."

"How?" Maddy's heart pounded. He hadn't told Derreck any of those things that he could recall, even though they were all true.

"I've seen you in three different pairs of dress shoes, but the laces were always yellow. That's how I know it's your favorite color. Your phone case is yellow, too, and the business cards in your wallet. The waitress gave you a side of bacon with your food and winked at you in the restaurant, even though no one else was served bacon. You already told me that you were an addict, and the rest was easy to put together." Derreck shook his head.

Ice trickled over Maddy's skin, even as the sun blazed down and struck them on the uncovered porch. "Does everyone know?" He wondered more to himself than to Derreck. Was he hiding himself for nothing?

Derreck snorted, shaking his head. "With most of the people I've met, you could tell them a dozen times that your favorite color is yellow but they still wouldn't remember it. They wouldn't know."

Relief was so strange after the heap of uncertainty that had piled into his afternoon that it stopped his tears in their tracks. He leaned closer, resting his head on Derreck's shoulder. The man relaxed under his touch, his tight muscles starting to go lax.

"I want to tell you, but I don't know how," said Maddy. He reached for Derreck's hand before threading their fingers together. Each callus scraped against his palm, the blisters soft in comparison.

"It's okay." Derreck encircled him with his free hand, pulling him in close and enveloping Maddy with earth and salt. The lacy curtains across the road shifted and Maddy let out a low laugh.

One plus of living in the part of town where everyone was retired was that the houses always looked nice. Bert was out every morning at eleven o'clock trimming, sweeping and watering his grass. His wife would follow a few minutes later, painting some part of the exterior while she gossiped with her next-door neighbor. The downside was that no one could make a move without everyone knowing about it.

"Come inside before my neighbor has a heart attack. I wouldn't want to give her too much excitement so late in the week," said Maddy, standing and trying to tug Derreck to his feet. Derreck followed stiffly, his limbs seemingly resisting Maddy's urging.

"You don't have to invite me in if you aren't comfortable," said Derreck as he ducked through the entrance.

Maddy tightened his grip. "I've never been more sure of anything in my life. Stay with me tonight." He cut off the rest of his sentence. He was going to add 'not for sex', but he wasn't so sure anymore. His single orgasm had polluted his body somehow, making him attuned to Derreck's every movement.

He'd never considered someone attractive before, but Derreck was filling that role more and more every time Maddy saw him. It had to be something. Looking at a man like Phil made him want to withdraw and hide, but with Derreck it was the opposite. And those hands… He wanted to suck each finger into his mouth to see what they tasted like.

"I have to work, but I'll stay as long as I can," said Derreck, shutting the door behind them.

Maddy led Derreck through the house, grabbing a quick glass of water for each of them in the kitchen before he headed upstairs. Derreck followed a few steps behind, his gaze shifting back and forth as he glanced at everything within the walls.

"You have a nice place," said Derreck as they moved past Maddy's collection of horse figurines. They would have been better suited for an old lady's house, but Maddy loved them. He'd never even ridden a horse and had petted two in his entire lifetime, but something about them just captivated him. The little sculptures were all he could bring into his world.

"Come with me," said Maddy, touching Derreck's hand again. He wondered if he would ever be able to let Derreck go for longer than a few breaths without the need to reach for him. "I need to show you something."

Chapter Nine

Derreck

Derreck looked from one room to the next, swallowing his surprise with every bit that was revealed. Somehow, he'd missed the fact that Maddy was loaded. It was nearly impossible to afford a house in the city, especially one that had more rooms than Derreck could keep track of. It wasn't that the house was a mansion, but it dwarfed his apartment and everything in it.

Maybe it was the affordable red Toyota Maddy drove, or the fact that he'd never sent a single judgmental look Derreck's way for his crappy clothes that had more than one hole. After seeing Maddy's workplace, he'd figured he was lower middle class, but the house was unreal.

Granted, it was nearly identical to all the other houses on the street with their neatly trimmed lawns that had just started to brown from the summer's sun when everything else in the city had bleached weeks ago. But in Maddy's part of town, people made six figures and up. Derreck could never dream of affording a single square foot of the place, let alone twenty-five-hundred.

Beyond the stained antique wooden door, which was something that had been unique to Maddy's house, Derreck's surprise thickened. The walls were covered in what he assumed were family photographs and a few paintings that looked like they belonged in a museum. The knickknacks were a cute touch, though.

It was the family photographs that surprised him. Maddy had never mentioned his family, except for his pseudo-adoptive cousin at the restaurant. But there they were, Maddy's mother a slightly taller and blonde version of Maddy, with the same eyes and nose.

Maddy didn't seem to notice what was around him, even when Derreck complimented the place. Derreck was sure that his eyebrows were somewhere in his hairline, and he wasn't sure if they were coming down any time soon.

Derreck had poured his pride and money into his car—something that he could touch, tinker with and polish to his heart's content. Sinking his money into a home was unfathomable.

He let out a soft sigh as the ache in his core was momentarily soothed when Maddy threaded their hands together. He longed to pull Maddy close and kiss the top of his head, but he had no idea where they stood with each other.

The last time a sub had run from him, he'd taken weeks to pull himself out of his spiral. It was that same wound that Maddy had reopened.

Derreck's soul had poured out onto the street, sizzling as it hit the pavement when he'd found his car empty and Maddy lost to the wind. Going after Maddy hadn't even been a question. Finding his address had been as easy as slipping into Clint's office while he was still busy with the stoned sub.

The waivers and consent forms were supposed to be private and confidential, but Derreck had been around long enough to know the codes to all the locked doors in the club. Hell, Clint had called him before when he'd spontaneously forgotten his passwords after a rough day.

Privacy was secondary to Maddy's wellbeing. Maddy had looked so fucking shattered when Derreck had wrapped his hand around Phil's throat, and Derreck wasn't letting up until he'd pieced his sub back together. Fear had never felt so ugly.

"Come upstairs with me," said Maddy as he tugged Derreck up the stairwell, his full glass of water still clutched in his hand. There were six doorways on the landing, each with stained wooden doors and rich trim. A dark blue accent wall with a reading nook heaped with pillows guarded the top of the landing, the sun streaming in the skylight like a sign from above.

Maddy slipped left, pulling Derreck to the last door. *An office?* Maddy squeezed his hand as he pushed the door wide, revealing a bedroom.

Derreck froze, his mouth going dry. The bed had to have been a king, with a duvet of blue flowers and pink pillows with the same design. There was one small nightstand with a floral lamp, it's antique brass shimmering as Maddy flicked on the overhead light.

Sex had been the last thing on his mind, even if his cock was still a bit chubbed up. Sex wasn't aftercare — well, not usually.

"I don't expect anything, Maddy. I didn't come here for sex," said Derreck, even as his cock went harder as he spied the bed posts. They were solid and looked sturdy — perfect for tying up a wayward sub.

But there was a reason he usually kept his *activities* to the club. Kink and sex had always been two separate things in his mind. The line had thinned with Nav, but Maddy had obliterated it.

The image of fucking Maddy on the bed, his hands and legs cuffed to the posts and his ass aching from the flogging had him rock hard. Every time Derreck would sink into Maddy, he would feel the heat of the welts on Maddy's ass against his groin. Maddy would cry out beneath him, begging for more while he struggled through his confusion about the sex itself.

He'd never imagined sex in his perfect scene, but it was there, and he couldn't get it out of his head.

"I...I need to show you something," said Maddy, dropping his hand and stepping to the bed. Derreck couldn't see Maddy's ass through his slacks, but he knew how perfect it was. It would be even better with his marks on display.

Is it your cock? Derreck shook his head. He couldn't get the image of Maddy's perfect cock out of his head. He shuddered as he remembered how it had felt against his own.

Shifting, he thrust his hands in his pockets to try to subtly adjust himself. It was a tight fit, but he managed to flip his cock up under his waistband, the tight band trapping it like a collared rogue animal. The pressure was almost too much, a bit of pre-cum soaking into the bottom of his shirt.

Sex and kink were one thing, but Derreck couldn't remember the last time he'd been so turned on. It was almost embarrassing how distracted he was.

Maddy tugged at the hem of his shirt, taking a deep breath before he started to pull it over his head. Derreck struggled to keep the surprise off his face as Maddy tossed it to the ground, leaving himself naked from the waist up.

Maddy's gaze dropped to the floor, his face pale as he gnawed at his lip. Clenching his hands at his sides, Maddy slid his eyes shut, a visible tremble running through his body.

Derreck was next to him in an instant, cupping Maddy's chin and tilting it up to him. Maddy's eyelashes fluttered, his blue eyes pinpoints as he finally opened his eyes wide. Tears still clung to his clumped lashes, his sclera pink from his sobs. His lips were so full, the bottom one swollen and bruised from his incessant nibbling.

"Thank you for showing me," said Derreck, moving his hand through Maddy's hair before cupping the back of his skull. Maddy's breath tickled his lips and he struggled not to lean down. A few centimeters and their lips would touch, but what they had was too new. Maddy's sexuality probably felt like a raw nerve and Derreck didn't want to push him any further.

"They're terrible—ugly." Maddy shuddered as Derreck massaged his scalp, easing the tension from his body with a simple touch.

"No," said Derreck quietly. "Your fear is the only ugly thing in this room. Don't be afraid of me, Maddy."

Maddy's face crumpled a moment before his sobs began. Derreck could hit him a hundred times, going deep until he drew blood, but it had never broken Maddy the way his exposure had. The designs themselves were just that and nothing else. They were as unimportant as skin color. Derreck's adoptive parents had been on two different sides of that spectrum, and Derreck had been the third.

"May I touch you?" asked Derreck, moving them to the bed as Maddy nodded. He pulled Maddy to his chest as he lowered them down, breathing in the deep scent of laundry detergent and his sub. His chest hummed as their skin touched.

Carefully, he slid his hand down the back of Maddy's neck, then lower. Maddy's back was nearly smooth, with only a few ridges and bumps interrupting his exploration. Slipping down Maddy's sides, he felt along every ridge between and over Maddy's ribs, like intricate spiderwebs of banded tissue.

Maddy shivered under his touch before he tucked his head under Derreck's chin. Goosebumps burst over Maddy's skin, his prickled hair tickling Derreck's fingertips.

"I'm sorry," said Maddy, another sob pushing through his throat as he clung to him. Derreck winced at the grip but didn't complain. If he had his way, Maddy would be even closer to him, gripping him so hard that they would never be separated again.

"Why are you sorry?" asked Derreck. He reached around to unexplored spots where the worst of the marks were. There wasn't an inch of Maddy's stomach and chest that hadn't been drawn on by some sort of sharp object, and his arms matched the continuous design.

Maddy shook his head, pressing his face into Derreck's chest. Maybe Maddy didn't know why he was apologizing, either.

"I should have told you when I first met you. I'm not exactly stable. I don't belong in a place like Unkinked, and I never should have even tried." Maddy's voice leveled out as he spoke, and Derreck stilled his hands on Maddy's hips.

"Are you sorry that you found me?" asked Derreck. Maybe that was it. But Maddy had been looking for him from the very beginning, and like some sort of fucked up fairytale, they had found each other. "I'm not sorry you found me. You've given me so much, Maddy. I could never repay you."

"But I'm an addict, Derreck. Don't you get it? Pain isn't something I could ever give up. It's my heroin and my reason to get up every day. I've tried so hard to quit. I even took a leave of absence from work and checked into a center to try to stop it. It didn't help as much as I'd hoped, and some days it's the only thing I think about."

That hurt more than it probably should have. Derreck swallowed against the ache, stilling his hands. "Your marks are old, Maddy — more than six months, if I had to guess."

Some of them were even older than that. There were faded strips that looked like they had been inscribed over and over again with years lapsed between them.

"I've been using you," said Maddy, letting out a long breath. "Why would I do it myself when I can get you to do it for me? It feels better when you do it, anyway, and the high lasts longer. You get those places that I've never been able to reach, and I don't feel guilty afterward. I don't feel like I've failed again."

Derreck traced down to Maddy's ass, still warm and ridged with the welts from his touch. He cupped one cheek, squeezing hard until Maddy let out a whimper. The sound was laced with pain and something akin to relief. It was the same sound that an addict would have made when they'd finally got their fix after too long. Derreck had heard it before in the darkest places.

"Is that all this is?" asked Derreck, his heart aching but steady. He could close himself off and shut down. He'd done it before, and he could do it again. It shouldn't have been that hard, anyway. He always was a cold-hearted bastard.

"What else could it be?" asked Maddy, lifting his head. His blue eyes were clearer despite Derreck's grip, his mouth parted in a sigh.

It could be so much more. We could wake up together in your bed or mine and I could hold you. Maybe someday you would let me kiss you. I just need to be close to you, to hold you, beat you and piece you back together until you forget all about being broken.

Derreck gazed into Maddy's soft blue eyes. It was all so clear. Maddy saw him as a Dom and only a Dom. Derreck was there to break him and comfort him, but that was it. Maddy had no desire for them to spend a moment more than necessary together. *How did I miss this?*

"The restaurant," said Derreck, his mouth dry. "Why did you take me to that restaurant?" It had been a date. He had been certain. They had snuggled in the booth after they ate, and Maddy had ordered and paid for him.

"To thank you. I told you that." Maddy leaned away before pulling himself onto his knees, his separation like a wall. The bed creaked as he shifted, the polished wood groaning with age.

What would Derreck get for rushing to Maddy's house to make sure he wasn't dropping? A Hallmark card? Or maybe just a silent wave before Maddy saw him to the door?

Derreck shook his head in disbelief. The warmth that had started to soothe his limbs was dragged away. He'd experienced top drop before, and he knew the signs. He knew he was just a few minutes away from soul-crushing guilt and uncertainty. His remedy the last time had been to hide himself in his work, digging himself into the ground until he felt lower than the ones around him who were actually six feet under.

"I thought there might have been more," said Derreck. He owed it to them both to get that out in the open, even if it amounted to nothing.

"You said no sex," said Maddy, his lips pressing into a firm line as he crossed his arms. "Or did you lie about that?"

"Sex isn't intimacy, Maddy. You can see inside of someone's soul and lay them bare before you without ever laying a finger on them. I've stripped you of your defenses, and I know who you are—the real you who you try to hide from everyone. I want more from you, and I don't mean that I just want to fuck you."

Maddy snorted humorlessly and stood from the bed, wrapping his arms around his middle. "*Just.* You make sex sound like it's nothing and like it wouldn't even matter either way."

"It doesn't."

"Yes, it does," said Maddy, his voice ringing off the walls. "It matters to everyone, Derreck. You can't deny that you got hard, because so did I. The difference is that you wanted more, and I was just terrified of what was going to happen."

"I won't hurt you—"

"Yes, you will." Maddy threw up his hands, reaching for his discarded shirt before pulling it on again. He tugged the sleeves down, covering every inch. "That's the only thing I'm sure about. I want you to hurt me, but I certainly don't want you to fuck me."

Derreck ground his teeth together, his jaw aching from the strain. Things were not turning out the way he'd thought they would when he had stolen Maddy's address and parked himself on the stoop. He had been gung-ho for a snuggle session to try to lift their mutually broken spirits, but instead, he was getting his emotional ass handed to him.

"Do you want me to leave?" asked Derreck, slowly picking himself off the bed. His limbs were slow and sluggish, the drop starting to set in like a fierce ache. He had failed Maddy and himself. *Useless Dom.*

"I think you should," said Maddy. His mask was back, the tears dried from his cheeks as if they'd never been there. He was a completely different person to the one that Derreck knew — the one he thought he knew, anyway.

When he walked from the bedroom, his heart plummeted, his throat closing up in the beginnings of a panic attack. It was so much worse than what he'd experienced with Nav, and he knew it had only just begun. At least he'd known that Nav would reach out to Trick, but Maddy had no one — just an empty house with too many empty rooms.

Descending the stairs alone, he turned back, the doorknob creaking beneath his hand. "You know where to find me when you need your next fix, Maddy," he shouted loud enough so his voice would carry through the house. It was the first time he'd raised his voice in years.

He would take anything he could get. His skin was already prickling with the visceral need to hold his sub, his chest aching with every heartbeat. His vision blurred and he pushed out of the door, slamming it behind him with his full strength.

The sun had dipped behind the roof of the nearest house, the air cooling as it slowly descended. A few crickets chirped by the white picket fence, pausing their song as he marched to his car.

There was only one place for him to go. Digging someone an ill-timed grave had never sounded better.

Chapter Ten

Maddy

Maddy slid into his office chair, feeling lower than the bug that he'd squashed on the way from his car. Unrecognizable emotions oozed from every part of him, just like the bug's green...jelly. Perhaps someone would come stomp on him and put him out of his confused misery.

Fear... He understood that emotion hiding just beneath his skin. It was the culprit for his sweaty palms and pale face, but the ache in his chest was new. He had tried Pepto Bismol and Gaviscon, but they had done nothing to relieve the discomfort.

Whether it was a side effect of the useless medications, Maddy wasn't sure, but for the first time in as long as he could remember, there was something at the forefront of his thoughts that wasn't his next rush of endorphins.

Three weeks. It had been three strenuous and terrifying weeks without Derreck. The first few days had been a numb blur, the only clarity the welts on his ass. He had stood before the mirror, cupping and squeezing them until tears sprang to his eyes. But they had faded, along with the numbness, leaving him lower than the Grand Canyon.

His days had blurred, and even Phil's smirking face and his boss's concerned one did little to rouse him from his purgatory. He knew what he needed, but there was no way that he was going to get it any time soon.

A week before, he'd dialed Derreck's phone number, but it had gone straight to voicemail. He had let the computerized recording beep, then he'd taken two deep breaths before he'd chickened out and hung up. He'd tried every day since, but his calls had stopped going through. Either Derreck had changed his number, or he was ignoring Maddy's calls.

He'd thought briefly of going to look for Derreck, but his Dom had been right. He knew nothing about him. He didn't know where to find him at work, or where he laid his head at night. He had no idea what his favorite foods were or his favorite color. He didn't even know his last name to look him up online.

But why did it even matter? *Because it's Derreck.* He'd been kidding himself by thinking there was nothing between them but scenes and pain. His addiction had never made him feel that way.

He had tried and failed to jerk off, rubbing his ass against the bed when it had still been marked and sore. He'd stayed pathetically soft no matter how hard he'd tried to make himself hurt—another thing that seemed to be tethered to Derreck.

A knock at his door startled him from his thoughts. He looked up to see Phil's slightly distorted face looking at him through his glass door. Even through the mirage, Phil still looked like he hadn't showered in a week, dandruff clinging to the grease in his hair. He had the nasty habit of covering everything up with cologne and aftershave instead of spending his time showering. Maddy shuddered, waving Phil into his office.

Phil took two steps inside, a smirk on his face as he went to close the door.

"Leave it open," said Maddy, his voice loud enough so that more than one person in the office would overhear him. He thumbed the file on his desk — the one with Phil's name on it. His boss had been waiting for progress, but Maddy had held back.

Phil hadn't said anything to Maddy about the afternoon at the club, but he'd also never made excuses to visit Maddy in his office before. Maddy could count on one hand how many times Phil had willingly spent time in his office before their altercation, but after Phil had returned from his week-long business trip, he'd been in Maddy's office every day.

"Is it starting to rain out yet?" asked Maddy, despite the windows at his back. Watching the smirk drop from Phil's face was worth every bit of feigned stupidity. He could talk about nothing all day, and with his door open, Phil wouldn't try anything.

He would never want to be alone with a man who had drugged his sub into submission. But from the file on his desk, he wouldn't have to worry about him much longer. Phil had more problems than pending charges.

"I came to ask what you thought about my proposal," said Phil, clasping his hands behind his back as he moved closer to Maddy's desk. Thick perfume choked Maddy as Phil's broad shoulders blocked the view of the door—and Maddy's only real escape. The windows were option two, but that would leave him with one more broken leg than he wanted.

"I don't know what you're talking about, Phil," said Maddy, slipping the file into his desk and locking the drawer. Standing from his seat, he moved past Phil, making sure to keep a wide berth. He fiddled with his sleeve, tugging the fabric down over and over.

"About you being my sub," said Phil, lowering his voice just enough so that he wouldn't be heard in the neighboring office. "Or did you want me to ask you where everyone can see?"

Maddy skirted to the side as Phil reached for him, his skin crawling at the very idea. *That* proposal was so ridiculous that he had laughed it off the first time Phil brought it up. The man was nothing if not persistent.

"I already told you no, and I'm not going to say it again," said Maddy, staring out through the glass walls. Denise glanced his way, and he gave her a wave, despite the frown on her face.

Oh yeah, she's next up on the docket. There were a few accounts that didn't look quite right that she had investigated. Just another colleague relationship down the drain.

"Well, the way I see it, you owe me," said Phil. "I could have pressed charges against your Dom. Hell, I could have had your ass fired weeks ago, but I didn't. I've tried to be patient and wait for you to come around, but your time is up. You sub for me or the whole world finds out how much of a freak you are."

The concept didn't seem nearly as frightening as it had a few weeks ago. He slid his phone from his pocket, checking for the hundredth time if there was any reply from Derreck. Nothing but an email notification that he dismissed with a sigh.

"Are you even listening to me?" asked Phil, his voice dropping into a low whisper.

"No," said Maddy, leaning against his door frame and looking at the gathering near the water cooler. "Getting fired isn't worth kneeling for you. I'd rather leave than let you touch me." He let out a long sigh as Phil marched past him, his hands clenched and his lips pressed tight.

"You better start packing your shit then." Phil snarled over his shoulder before he cut directly over to the next office where Maddy's boss was hard at work.

The numbness was back, sealing over his emotions until only one peeked through. Could he live without a job? Yes, he could, but he didn't want to. The office had been a mess of corruption and under-the-table deals when he'd started, and after years of hard work, he was finally starting to see the light at the end of the tunnel.

He pulled out his phone, typing Derreck's number in by memory. There was a long stretch of silence before he heard a woman's voice. *The number you have dialed is not in service...* He ended the call, slipping it back into his pocket.

Low mumbles reached his ears from one office over and something entirely unexpected happened. When his boss turned his head, looking straight at Maddy with a frown on his lips, the numbness retreated like a sudden tide, and panic blossomed in Maddy's chest, tightening like a corset. Phil shot him a triumphant smirk, and Maddy's heart dropped.

Eyes from every corner of the office burned into him, piercing through his clothing to the monster underneath. It shouldn't have mattered what they thought of him, but it did, and it hurt so goddamn much. It would finally give them all a tangible reason to hate him.

Oh, there's Maddy, our resident psycho. We had to take everything sharp away from him, so no paperclips or staples on any of his reports. When you hear the timer go off, that's for his meds. Just steer clear and don't worry about a thing. No one trusts the word of a freak.

Everything that he'd worked for was starting to unravel, and his skin ached under his shirt, suddenly too tight for him to even breathe. He recognized the panic attack for what it was, but he had no way of stopping it.

His therapist wouldn't have helped him. A new dosage of mediation and a few days of taking it easy wouldn't solve a thing. The letter opener on his desk wouldn't help him either, the very idea of it making bile surge up his throat.

He needed Derreck.

Grabbing his keys, he pushed his way through the office, elbowing the elevator door when it tried to close on him. He didn't care that he could hardly breathe or that sweat dripped down his back as he tried to stay on his feet. He got a few strange looks on the way to his car, but they were just another pin in his crumbling armor.

Dodging through the rain and into his car, he sped out of the parking lot, his tires hydroplaning over the worn pavement. The yellow lines had long since faded to speckled streaks, dust coating the surface along with a few slicks of floating oil.

He panted as he pulled in front of the club, the rain pounding on the window and blinding him even with the wipers working overtime. Despite the downpour, he flung himself out of the car, running the few steps up to the club entrance. His hand trembled as he brought it down on the door as hard as he could.

Of course, he didn't have his own key because he had only been a guest—one without a Dom and without a single friend to his name.

He knocked louder, his knuckles aching under the strain. Rain pounded on the street, his shirt clinging to his body and pulling ever tighter around his skin with each drop.

He lifted his hand to knock again, ignoring the way his knuckles split, blood mixing with the rain. The door flung open, his hand hanging in the air mid-knock. Clint stood there, a scowl on his lips as he glared down at Maddy. Water ricocheted off Maddy's chest, speckling Clint's clothing.

"Can I help you?" asked Clint, his voice calmer than Maddy had expected. Maddy took a step into the rain so the drops wouldn't strike Clint with each wind gust.

"I'm looking for Derreck," said Maddy, shouting as the wind pulled at his clothing. He stumbled, catching himself against the brick and scraping his palm. He hissed at the unwelcome sting.

"You'd best try to call him, kid, 'cause he isn't here." Clint leaned back, letting the door go. It started to swing shut, the thick material like an impenetrable blockade.

"No, wait!" Maddy grabbed the door before it could slam shut, forcing it open and soaking Clint's feet as water splashed inside the threshold. "I tried calling him, but he won't pick up. I just need to make sure he's okay."

"He's a big boy, kid. He can look after himself," said Clint, crossing his arms. His biceps bulged in a way that was probably supposed to be threatening. "I haven't seen him in a few weeks, anyway." A frown slipped over Clint's lips.

"Shit. *Shit*." Maddy stumbled back into the rain. Derreck had told him not to run — but Maddy had run like the fucking gingerbread man when he'd ordered Derreck out of his house.

He knew about sub drop for his research online, and he knew it could happen to Doms, too. His chest pulled tighter as he imagined Derreck going through the same thing he had been for the last three weeks. The numbness, the fear, the guilt and the crushing sense of worthlessness — all of it Maddy's fault.

He fell to his knees as a pothole grabbed his foot, a warm puddle seeping into his pants as they soaked up the rain. Grit slipped against his skin, grinding into his flesh and scraping him raw.

The arms around him startled him enough that he struck out — something that he'd never done in his life. Perhaps it was the way his skin was still crawling from Phil's demands or the vile wriggling of a worm next to his knee, but the touch burned.

Clint stumbled back, grabbing at his chin where Maddy had accidentally nailed him. He grimaced, his clothes soaking through almost instantly.

"I'm so sorry," said Maddy, trying to stand even as his knees wobbled. "Oh my God, are you okay? I've never ever hit anybody before, and I just don't know what's gotten into me. Please forgive me."

Before Clint could reply, Maddy turned away, racing to his car. Distantly, he heard Clint call out for him over the rain.

He was running again. *What a fucking coward.*

* * * *

Derreck

The thing about a hard rain after a long drought was that it really fucking sucked. People always had this image of grass reviving and fucking butterflies fluttering around fresh flowers, but that was all bullshit. When the dirt was so hard that it cracked, the rain just ran off and fell into the closest pit in a muddy swirl.

Derreck scowled as he nearly slipped in the squelching mud beneath his feet. Three fucking graves that he'd busted his ass over to get perfect and all of them were filled with water and slopping mud. A few twigs swirled in the mess as more mud crumbled in from the side.

He was coated in filth—absolutely fucking coated. He was pretty sure that it was in every orifice, including under his eyeballs, because they scratched every time he blinked. He was going to plug his shower drain at home from the sheer amount of sand in places where sand was not supposed to be.

And it was still fucking raining.

He tossed the shovel to the side, swiping his arm over his face. Grit ground into it, but what else was new. His boss was going to have his ass, but at that point, he didn't fucking care. He'd already added thirty hours to his usual forty, and he was done.

"Hey, Derreck!"

If he hadn't already dropped his shovel, he probably would have when the shout nearly startled him out of his skin. He usually tried to listen to the sound of people coming so he could slip away before anyone saw him, or, worst case scenario, tried to talk to him.

"Clint," he said, looking back at the club owner as he pressed a hand to his chest, covering his movement with a scratch that dug rocks into his pec. Clint was dressed for the weather, wearing blue rubber boots that matched his blue polka-dot umbrella perfectly. It was the only cheerful thing in a place full of bodies.

"Did you fall in?" asked Clint, taking a step off the path and onto grass that looked more like a weedy pond. He grimaced as his boot sank into the muck, taking a step back until he was back on the gravel path. *Fucking pansy.*

Derreck shook his head. Clint was a good guy, and he didn't deserve to take on any of Derreck's shit. The man had gone through hell and back more times than Derreck could count, and he still came out on the other side with blue fucking polka dots.

"Well, I can see that you're in a sparkling mood, too. And here I thought that it was just your sub with an attitude problem." Clint lowered his hood, tilting his umbrella into the wind as the treetops tossed.

Derreck clenched his hands into fists to keep from reacting. "Don't talk about him like that." His voice dropped into a growl. He wouldn't let anyone disrespect Maddy — not Phil, not Clint and certainly not himself.

Clint held up his free hand in surrender, his boot squelching as he took a step back. "I didn't come here to give you shit, but when someone shows up at my place looking like they are barely able to stand because they are dropping so hard, and they can't get ahold of their partner, you don't give me much choice. Why aren't you answering your phone?"

"Fuck." Derreck reached into his pocket and fished out his phone. The screen was blank, water dripping from the corner as he held it up. He hadn't charged it in...he couldn't even remember. It had probably been dead for at least a week or two, and he couldn't remember when he'd last had the ring tone on.

"Well, that makes sense, then," said Clint as he eyed the steady stream of water coming from the phone.

Derreck tossed the phone to the side. The corner bounced on a rock at the edge of the grave, sending it spiraling down to his feet with a loud splash.

Breaking shit usually filled him with satisfaction, but watching a few bubbles emerge from where his phone had disappeared made him sick. He'd had Maddy's number stored in the phone, but he hadn't thought to put it anywhere else.

Maddy, who had gone to the club in search of him... How many times had he called Derreck before he'd dragged himself to the club, exposing himself in the way he hated most?

"Fuck," he said as he scrubbed his hand over his face. He wanted to puke, but he couldn't remember the last time he'd eaten. His stomach growled at the thought. *Fuck, what time is it?*

He squinted up at the rising sun that was attempting, and failing, to break through the clouds. It was overhead and peeking through the branches of one of the poplar trees that had more roots than leaves.

He'd been digging since midnight, but before that...he couldn't remember. The days had started to blur together, the dirt on his hands never coming clean, no matter how hard he scrubbed.

"You okay, Derreck? You look like shit. You could be dropping, too. It happens to the best of us."

Derreck stared off into the rain, blinking every time a fresh drop splashed into his eye. *Dropping? No.* He had dropped three weeks ago when Maddy had asked him to leave. Since then, he hadn't got much higher than floor scrapings. He couldn't drop if he was already at the bottom.

Scrambling in the mud, he pulled himself from the grave, water pouring from his shoes as he hauled himself free. He slipped as he tried to push past Clint, catching himself on his hands as he slammed to his knees. Water seeped between his fingers, sucking him deeper into the over-saturated ground. His reflexes were shot, his hands trembling from exhaustion. Fresh blistered covered his palms, stinging as dirt sank into them.

"Shit, Derreck, what can I do to help? I've never seen you like this before." Clint took a step in his direction, but Derreck waved him off, summoning the last of his pride as he pushed himself to his feet.

He stumbled to the path that led mourners to the last resting places of their loved ones. The path was gravel and looked more like a creek than anything else, but it had more grip than the sodden earth. He forced his burning legs into a fast walk, his arms burning as they pumped with each step.

"Where you going, man?" Clint called, his umbrella threatening to turn inside out in the wind. A tree branch overhead gave way, crashing to the ground where Derreck had been digging moments before.

"Maddy," said Derreck, turning back and focusing every thread of his being on getting to his car. The Mustang had never looked so far away, its paint still clean, despite his recent neglect. He would have to take a day off just to buff it and get the shine back.

"You can't go like that," said Clint, rushing to keep up and seemingly having no trouble at all on the slippery path. "At least change first. You look like you just escaped from being buried alive."

"I'm not waiting," said Derreck, sending a glare over his shoulder. He should have felt bad for glaring at Clint, but he couldn't bring himself to care.

"Okay, man. Just put a jacket on or something, and tell Maddy I said hi." Clint waved him off, twirling his umbrella around as he looked toward a grove of trees where a few scattered gravestones stood. "I have a few people I want to say hello to while I'm here."

I'm such a jackass. Derreck cursed himself as he looked back at Clint. Clint was going out on a limb for him, and Derreck was being nothing more than a dick. A short distance away, Clint's husband lay under the soaked ground. Derreck had dug the spot himself beneath the twisted roots of a maple where no machinery could have reached.

"Say hi to Ross for me," he called back, raising his hand. "I owe you, Clint."

Clint nodded once, his lips turning up in a small smile that didn't reach his eyes. It had been years, but grief like that never went away. "Everyone gets one for free."

Rushing toward his car, Derreck pressed the remote start, the engine grumbling to life in the quiet field. His leather seats would have to forgive the state of his clothing. At least they weren't cloth.

Wiping the rain from his eyes, he powered out of the cemetery, headed straight for Maddy's house. He was almost certain that Maddy would have been at work two o'clock on a Wednesday, but Maddy's house was closest. He grimaced, gripping the steering wheel and cranking up the wipers as he passed by a scrolling sign at the gas station. It was Friday – not Wednesday.

The house was empty, and the driveway was too, except for a brimming puddle in the middle of the concrete pad.

Putting his gas pedal to the floor, he gunned it to Maddy's work, squealing into the employee-only parking lot before double parking behind someone's Buick. He scanned the lot, spotting Maddy's car along the far edge. It was squished between a suburban and a Jeep, small and unassuming next to its neighbors.

Passing through the first roadblock was surprisingly easy. The front entrance opened under his hand to a well-lit interior that was just on the right side of overdone. His shoes squished on the scuffed black mat below his feet, muddy water sloshing over the sides with every step.

His jeans, which had been faded blue when he had left the house, were now closer to tan, with grit clinging to every surface. They wouldn't have looked that bad if it hadn't been for the huge streaks of mud at his knees from when he had fallen. At least his shirt was relatively clean, if not dripping.

"Oh my," said the receptionist, looking slightly less bored than when he'd spotted her from outside the doors. She had a shitty poker face to match the elevator music she was playing at her desk. Derreck pushed the *See next attendant* sign to the side before leaning on the edge of the counter.

"Can I help you, sir?" she asked, her eyes going wider as she looked him up and down.

"Looking for Maddy," he said, glancing down at the spots where his hands stained the desk. His touch left a brown muddy streak filled with sand over the surface.

How much was in his hair? He squashed the need to check.

"I'm sorry, sir, but I can't let you up to the fourth floor without an appointment." She shook her head, glancing down at her screen. One hand crept to her phone, probably ready to dial security.

"Sounds good. I'll make my appointment once I get there." He slapped the desk, leaving a handprint of mud on the surface as he pushed through the door to her left that was clearly marked *Stairwell*. Hopefully security was as slow in government buildings as it was at the mall.

Reaching the fourth floor, he shoved his way through the door, stumbling out into an area that probably looked identical to the floors above and below. All offices were made up of depressing little squares containing bored humans jammed into tight spaces with the smell of ink and paper in their hair. He usually wouldn't be caught dead in one, but desperate times and all that.

He recalled Maddy telling him that he had an actual office, which was one tiny step up from the padded cubicles. Looking around, he spotted one row of offices in view of the stairwell. *As good a place to start as any.* He wasn't leaving until he fucking found his sub.

Chapter Eleven

Maddy

"I need to know what your goals are in this company, Maddy." Mr. Jameson crossed his arms, his steady gaze pinning Maddy to his chair.

Why they were doing this in *Maddy's* office, with the door wide open, was beyond him. His office was a comfort zone, even if it had been getting steadily less so in the last few weeks. No one bitched him out in his comfort zone, and no one threatened him.

"I've had a few concerned colleagues approach me with some very interesting things. I have already been on the fence about your...behavior. Someone in your position requires stability to get the job done, and, from what I understand, you aren't stable."

His boss's voice was loud — too loud for a small office with more ears than telephones.

Un-fucking-stable. Phil. Maddy ground his teeth, looking down at his desk before he could say anything he would regret. The papers before his eyes blurred, their secrets locked away as his temple throbbed.

"What the fuck did you just call him?"

A voice that Maddy hadn't thought he would ever hear again carved through the office and straight to his heart. He looked up, a gasp pushing through his lips. Derreck stood in the open doorway, glaring at Maddy's boss like he was two seconds away from strangling him.

Their three weeks apart seemed to have treated Derreck about the same as they had Maddy. He was absolutely filthy, as if he'd just rolled around underneath a street sweeper before dousing himself in a river. His face was gaunt, his eyes bloodshot and weary.

None of that mattered. He was the most wonderful thing that Maddy had ever seen. Relief surged through him, so powerful that he would have gone to his knees if he'd been standing.

"Excuse me? Who are you?" Mr. Jameson curled his lip, taking a step back as Derreck moved into the office. Derreck's shoes squeaked with each step, letting out a rasping sound as he lifted his feet, as if they were gasping for breath.

"I'm the one who digs your fucking grave," Derreck growled, sending a thrill up Maddy's spine that he didn't fully understand.

It wasn't the only thing that he didn't understand. His skin was on fire, longing for Derreck's touch, and his cock was tingling in a way that only seemed to happen around Derreck. He had to touch him — had to go to him. He didn't care if he got filthy or if it cost him his job.

His boss spluttered, taking another step back until his back hit the glass wall. Derreck's eyes were wild, his lips curled into a snarl.

"Tell me why you would say that," said Derreck, only stopping when he was centimeters from Mr. Jameson, his nostrils flaring wide. "Tell me why you would corner one of your best workers — the one who has been fighting to turn this office around from the very beginning — and call him unstable."

"His leave of absence —"

"You'll be taking one yourself if you don't shut the fuck up. And it won't be voluntary." Derreck snarled like a deranged beast. He clenched his fists, his arms bulging beneath the filth. Maddy was mesmerized. Had anyone ever stood up for him? He couldn't recall.

"Call security." His boss looked over at Maddy in absolute terror.

"Derreck," said Maddy, his voice so soft that it was barely there. "Derreck." It was stronger the second time, and the third. Finally, Derreck turned to him, his gaze softening.

"Why are you here?" asked Maddy. "Not that I'm not grateful. I'm so glad you're here but you weren't returning my calls. I was worried." Maddy bit his lip, cutting himself off as he looked back at his boss. "Why are you still in my office?" He glared at his boss as he asked.

Rage from weeks of holding back suddenly surfaced. Phil, Mr. Jameson and the beady eyes of his coworkers had kept him on edge for so long, but he was done.

"You think I'm unstable? When the 'concerned person' who told you that is a sex offender and a rapist? Phil has been accepting money under the table for years and giving passes to places that should have been shut down. But you can absolutely believe him if you choose to, because I don't care anymore. You can't hold this place together without me. You literally can't."

"Madison—" his boss started.

"It's Maddy," said Derreck, turning on Mr. Jameson with a snarl that made the man pale a few shades. Derreck looked back to Maddy, a hint of a smile on his lips. "You wanna get out of here?"

Maddy couldn't stop his answering smile. "I thought you'd never ask."

* * * *

Maddy

Maddy let himself relax as he slid into the passenger seat of Derreck's Mustang. Derreck had apparently double parked behind Phil, who was pacing and talking on his phone, probably trying to track down the owner of the car blocking him so he could get out for his late lunch break. When Phil spotted Derreck, his phone slipped from his hand, tumbling to the ground and shattering into two pieces.

"Shit, that felt good," said Maddy, leaning back in the seat and stretching his arms over his head. "Not as good as it is to see you, though. Sorry for freaking out back there." A warm fuzziness had settled over his limbs the moment that he'd seen Derreck's deranged face. Or maybe it had been when Derreck had stood up for him, ripping Mr. Jameson a new asshole.

Derreck grunted, shifting his car into gear before backing out. Something crunched under his tire and Maddy could hear Phil's cursing, even through the glass, and saw the man himself shaking his fist at them.

"I should be the one to apologize," said Derreck. "I forgot to charge my phone, and now it's really dead. I had no idea you were trying to get ahold of me until Clint tracked me down. I honestly thought that you didn't want to see me again after last time, so I didn't check in with you."

Maddy shuddered at the memory. He still couldn't understand why he'd chucked Derreck out of his house when the man had only been trying to look after him. "I'm such an asshole. I was just...scared...I think."

Maddy looked away, watching a bolt of lightning streak across the sky. He squinted at the unfamiliar street sign as Derreck turned. The first few buildings were worn and ragged, giving way to slightly nicer ones with more cars in their driveways than should have been legal.

"Thank you for coming back and defending me, even though I was so horrible to you," he said quietly. "Have you been doing okay? You don't look okay." That was a terrible thing to say, even if it were true. Up close, Derreck looked exhausted, with puffy bags under his eyes and blisters covering his hands and seeping through the drying layer of muck.

"I fell in a grave," said Derreck as he looked down at himself. "And I haven't slept in...a few days, I guess."

Any reply Maddy had was swept away when Derreck pulled into the lot for a shabby apartment building. His car was the only one in the lot that looked less than twenty years old, and the only one that didn't have at least one piece of duct tape on it.

Maddy wasn't usually one to judge, but they were on the side of town where people keyed your car and pissed in your gas tank if you didn't buy drugs from them.

"Is this your place?" asked Maddy, his voice quivering just a bit as he looked outside. It was still pouring, and it made the crumbling apartment building look almost haunted. One balcony was covered in potted plants that were definitely marijuana. It was legal, but Maddy hadn't exactly seen it kicking around everywhere.

A group of teenagers hung by the covered front door, making a blockade of flashy clothing and sinister looks.

Derreck gave him a strange look before he nodded, pulling himself out of the car and leaving a smear of gravel and mud in his wake. Maddy glanced at the seat and cringed. Maybe there was a special polish that would buff it out, but he doubted it.

Scrambling out of the car, he followed Derreck as close as possible without entangling their feet. "Aren't you worried someone will trash your car?" *Or steal it.* Derreck hadn't locked it and it stuck out like a diamond ring in a pile of trash.

"No," said Derreck, his confusion evident. The sea of teenager parted around Derreck as they approached the door and Derreck nodded to one of them. Maddy struggled not to shrivel away to nothing as they turned their curious gazes at him.

He was taller than most of them, but they all had teenage brawn, so they were definitely a hell of a lot stronger than him. One of them looked like an actual football player in both height and width, and his steady stare was incredibly unnerving.

"Who's the ice-cream cone?" the largest teen asked, his lip curling back over his perfectly straight teeth.

That's totally not fair. Yeah, he was pale—okay, maybe more than a bit pale. It was his dark sweater that made him look even worse—like fresh snow on Christmas morning. And he *was* soaking wet. It dripped down his neck and into his collar, making his shirt droop from the extra weight.

Shit. I am a fucking ice-cream cone.

Derreck paused with his hand on the door before turning to the teen slowly. He eyed him up and down, towering over him and looking so out of the teenager's league that it wasn't even funny. "Is there a problem, Blake?" His voice was soft, but Blake took a small step back, his eyes going wide.

"No, sir," said Blake, shoving his hands into his pockets. "Just haven't seen you with someone in a long time. Didn't know if you were still into that stuff." He looked away, and Maddy could imagine a blush on his cheeks.

"He's my sub, if that's what you're asking," said Derreck. It was Maddy's turn to flush, his mouth dropping open. That was not something that Derreck should have been telling random people. "And we're gonna get cleaned up. Who knew that sceneing in a graveyard could be so fucking messy?"

Holy shit. My Dom is a fucking bad ass. No wonder he wasn't worried about his car.

The teenagers gave them a quick goodbye as Derreck held the door open for Maddy, letting him slip inside the humid building. The air was hot with a side of spicy food that was strong enough to make his eyes burn. He glanced at Derreck, who didn't seem to notice.

After following Derreck through the doorway, he strode a short way down the hallway before Derreck stopped at the first door. *Apartment one on the first floor.*

Easy to remember. Maddy committed it to memory. It had nearly killed him when he'd realized that he hadn't known anything about Derreck, and he wasn't going to make that mistake twice.

"You live here?" Maddy looked down the hall when he heard the muffled sound of a scream. His skin prickled, until he saw the little girl running from her brother at the end.

"Let me get cleaned up, then we'll talk," said Derreck, opening his door without a key before waving Maddy into his apartment.

There was a small sound, like a strangled wail that had the hair on Maddy's body standing on end as he stumbled inside. The door slammed shut, darkness enveloping them as the wail came again.

Something touched Maddy, scraping along his lower leg that was still damp from the rain. He barely held back his scream as he tripped backward and rammed into Derreck's chest.

"It's just Demon," said Derreck, chuckling as he grabbed Maddy and flicked the hall light on.

The 'demon' in question was a cat who was wrapped around Maddy's ankles. The cute — no, adorable — orange tabby, who apparently had the voice of Satan, flexed his claws into the carpet, snapping the strands as a whining purr split the air. Demon rubbed against Maddy's leg again before turning to Derreck and scrunching up his tiny nose as it spied the mud.

"So cute!" Maddy dropped to his knees and scooped the cat into his arms as Derreck shuffled by. He wasn't a cat person per se, but Demon was too adorable to pass by without petting. The cat let out another meow, the sound making Maddy shudder, despite the silky-soft fur beneath his fingers.

"You are so cute. Give me kisses." Maddy smooched the cat until its pupils started to constrict—a sure sign that he was about to get swatted. He'd thought about getting one of his own a few times, but he hadn't been sure he would have been able to bear the moment that it passed away.

When he looked up, Derreck had already disappeared into the apartment. The distant sound of a shower started as Maddy stood, giving Demon one final pat. Muddy footprints trailed all the way into the apartment, even with Derreck's sodden shoes resting at the door on the small tray.

Slipping off his own shoes, Maddy headed deeper into the room, tripping over Demon twice before he shooed him away. The interior was surprisingly tasteful, made up of mostly grays and whites with a few colorful accents on the walls. The kitchen, although tiny, had high-end appliances that gleamed in the dim light. It was a stark contrast to the yellowed ceiling and the cracks in the walls that looked years old.

He followed the sound of running water, turning a corner into Derreck's bedroom, which was surprisingly spacious. The blankets were a deep blue on a bed that was probably a queen. The headboard and footboard were dark wood with a natural grain that made it look expensive. It was all surprisingly tasteful.

His eyes were drawn to the bathroom door, which was...open. Steam poured out, the room beyond looking bright with white tile lining the floor. There was the scratching sound of metal against metal like shower rings against a bar before the sound of water dimmed slightly.

Swallowing, he moved closer, looking down at his own sodden and sweaty clothing. He hadn't dried well sitting in his office chair while drowning in his own sorrows, but he hadn't been able to bring himself to just head home. He had perfected his mask at work over the years for a reason.

He leaned against the door, peering around it and inside the room. It was tiny but bright and tasteful, with the only things out of place being a heap of clothes on the ground and a towel down on the tile. Behind the thin white curtain, a shadow moved.

The curtain was the only thing that separated them, and the sight of it drew Maddy into the room until he was close enough to touch. He'd never felt that way about anyone before, but maybe it was about time that he tried to figure it out.

He tugged at his sweater, lifting it over his head after a moment of hesitation. Derreck had already seen him and touched the marks that decorated his body. Taking a deep breath, he fumbled with his pants and boxers, letting them slide down into a heap on the floor.

A shiver traveled through his body as the cool air of the apartment sank into his skin, a stark contrast to the warmth that wafted from behind the curtain that obscured the man he wanted. He didn't quite know *how* he wanted Derreck, but he wanted him, all the same.

He pushed the curtain aside softly so the shower curtain rings didn't drag against the rusted bar and give him away. Stepping over the edge of the tub, he pulled the curtain back in its place before the warmth could escape.

There was just enough room for two people to stand in the space without touching, but Maddy pressed his back against the wall to give himself another inch, smothering his gasp at the coolness of it.

Derreck was facing away, his body on display like the statue of David. Maddy's dreams and imagination hadn't come close to reality. A gay man and a straight woman would have probably swooned, and Maddy certainly found Derreck's body pleasing, but it was nothing to the *man* himself.

He was big, though, in every sense. Derreck had never seemed quite as tall as he did in the small space, or as broad as he ducked his head under the water to scrub at his short hair. His cock peeked between his spread legs, his sac heavy and swinging slightly as he moved.

Maddy's mouth watered. *What does it taste like?* He could still imagine Derreck's pre-cum on his tongue and how salty and thick it had been. His hand had smelled like Derreck's arousal after he'd touched him, and Maddy had brought it to his nose over and over, breathing deep each time.

He slid down the wall, sitting on the small ledge as Derreck scrubbed at himself. He moved like he didn't know he was being watched, which ignited something deep inside of Maddy that he hadn't known existed. He wasn't sure if it was the image before him that made his cock start to stiffen unexpectedly or the thought of Derreck not knowing Maddy was watching his every move.

Derreck slid his hand back between his cheeks, spreading soap in such a perfunctory way that Maddy's mouth started to water. Derreck smoothed the soap down his legs next, which were hairier than his arms and rock solid. As he bent over, Maddy got the first look of Derreck's hole between his cheeks. It was darker than his skin tone and furled tight.

His gasp at the sight was completely involuntary.

Derreck froze with the soap poised above his shin. He turned his head slowly, his eyes going wide when he saw Maddy sitting on the ledge. Maddy flushed, looking off to the curtain as shame swept away his confused arousal. He slid a hand over his groin, shielding himself from Derreck's eyes.

"You can watch. I don't mind," said Derreck, his voice gentler than Maddy had ever heard it. With that, Derreck turned, revealing his front to Maddy as he continued to scrub himself as if there had been no interruption.

His pecs were smooth and defined, with dusky dark nipples that hardened under Maddy's gaze. He had hardly any chest hair at all, but his groin was covered in thick, dark hair that was in need of a trim. His cock still looked huge surrounded by the hair, so much thicker and longer than Maddy's. It twitched under his gaze, and he bit his lip to hold back the groan.

"Can I help?" asked Maddy, slowly standing from the ledge. Derreck handed him the soap without a word, and Maddy grasped it in his palm, squeezing hard so it couldn't escape. It shot out of his hand like a torpedo, smacking against the wall and sliding to the bottom of the tub. "Shit, sorry."

Leaning down, he had a sudden thought of the teasing phrase 'don't drop the soap', but when he looked over his shoulder Derreck had tilted his head back into the water, his eyes closed like a gentleman.

Grasping the soap again, he brought his hands to Derreck's body. It was strange touching skin that didn't belong to him, his hands standing out in stark contrast as he spread bubbles up and down. Derreck was so hard under his fingers, with muscling that Maddy could never dream of possessing.

Derreck flinched when Maddy circled over his nipples. He looked up, biting his lip when Derreck nodded for him to continue.

"I'm going to get hard." Maddy glanced down at Derreck's plumping cock. It twitched every time he passed over Derreck's nipples, like his hands were suddenly electrified.

He lathered each ridge of Derreck's abs, then lower to the scratchy hair on his groin and to his heavy sac. Holding it in his hand, he felt the weight, trying to keep his surprise off his face. *How much cum does Derreck have in there?*

With each touch, Derreck filled out, his cock getting longer and thicker until it stood up at a ninety-degree angle from his body. Maddy reached for it, looking up at Derreck as he finally touched the soft skin.

Pulling back the foreskin to expose the head, Maddy lathered the tip, rinsing the suds away a moment later. A white pearl gathered at as he moved it away from the water, the salty sweetness calling to Maddy.

"Fuck." Derreck let out a shuddering breath as Maddy drew his slippery hand up and down Derreck's cock, the suds slicking the way to make his movements so much easier. "Fuck, Maddy, that feels so good."

Maddy's cock throbbed to the tempo of his heart, getting harder with each noise that Derreck made. It was...interesting to find pleasure when he wasn't actually touching himself.

Slicking his hands with soap, he moved down to Derreck's sac, gripping it softly and gliding over the surface. Derreck shuddered under the touch, a low groan coming from his throat.

If that feels good, what about this? Maddy's mind checked out as he reached back farther, to the place that most gay men, and some straight ones, apparently loved to play with. He'd never had much success with it himself, but he had only tried a few times.

He circled Derreck's hole once, watching for any sign that Derreck had changed his mind. On the third swipe, he sank the tip of his finger inside. It was so hot and tight, clinging to his finger perfectly as he touched Derreck's silky walls for the first time. He wanted — no, needed — to go deeper, to where Derreck was warmest.

"Fuck." Derreck let out a startled shout as Maddy sank his finger all the way to the last knuckle.

Maddy's eyes went wide, his mouth dropping open as he allowed himself to soak up every sensation. Derreck's breath was loud in the small shower, his chest rising rapidly as he flung his hand out to slap the shower wall. He had parted his lips when he had shouted, closing his eyes as he tilted his head back under the stream of water.

So, that was what all those guys online had been talking about. It was as fascinating as it was enthralling.

"Does it feel good?" asked Maddy, twisting his finger a bit and gentling his movements when Derreck's expression tightened. Derreck nodded, letting out a long breath as he spread his legs wider.

"I've never... Can you do it to me? I want to feel what it's like." Maddy withdrew his finger, turning around and spreading his legs to present himself. "I've only had one guy finger me, and I didn't really like it with him, but you seem to really enjoy it. Maybe it will be different with you."

"Fuck, Maddy, I can't do this if you are going to leave again. I can't watch you walk away every time you get scared." Derreck leaned back, shutting the water off before pulling the curtain aside. Cold air rushed into the shower, stripping Maddy of his warmth.

"I'm done running, and I want to know what this is," said Maddy, gesturing between them. "I can't get you out of my mind, and I don't understand why. I can't promise that I'll be here forever, but I'm here now and I don't want to leave. You make me feel whole, Derreck."

Derreck looked at him for a long time, water dripping to the tile floor with each breath. It looked slick, despite the towel soaking up the majority of the puddle. Derreck's cock hadn't deflated in the least, but his breathing had slowed as a frown settled on his lips.

"Okay." Derreck threaded their hands together and led Maddy to the bedroom.

Maddy's skin prickled into goosebumps as he followed Derreck, his mind and cock thrumming together in anticipation. He was level and focused, even if he had no idea what was going on with his body. He wouldn't break his promise, no matter what happened in Derreck's bedroom.

"Can I still use my safewords? Or are they just for when we are at the club? I'm just worried that I might get nervous or something, and I might need to slow down—"

"Maddy," said Derreck, cupping his chin and moving in close, "you can always use your safewords. You have them for a reason—so you never have to feel uncomfortable or forced. Even if you ask me to stop, I'll always stop."

That was amazing. He couldn't remember the last time someone was so considerate to him or so understanding. He just knew he needed to take it slow.

"Can we lie on the bed?" asked Maddy as the soft mattress called to him. Derreck sat on the edge and Maddy followed a moment later, leaving a few inches between them. The mattress was firmer than he had expected, but the comforter was soft against his skin, despite the cheap perfume of what was likely powdered laundry detergent.

"Lie down, please. I want to play with you." Maddy flushed, his eyes wide as Derreck tossed the comforter and sheets back before he laid on the bed. His dark hair touched the pillow and Maddy followed, zeroing in on the cock that he couldn't seem to look away from.

He paused when Derreck's cock hovered inches from his lips, his own groin close enough to Derreck that he could feel his breath. Letting his eyes fall shut, he focused on the sensation, each breath making him tremble and crave more.

Another mystery solved itself as he let the minutes stretch. Men in comedy or online had always boasted about their endurance, but it finally made sense. Maddy wanted the moment of intimacy to last forever.

"You can tell me to stop, too," said Maddy, opening his eyes to stare at Derreck's length. He didn't know where to begin. *Touching him is probably a good start.*

"I know," said Derreck, his voice thick as Maddy traced the head of his damp cock with his fingertips. Derreck's smooth skin was almost familiar, but he took his time tracing the veins before he wrapped his hand around it, pumping once.

"How does it feel?" asked Maddy.

Derreck didn't answer. Instead, he wrapped his hand around Maddy's cock, mirroring Maddy's movements. Maddy let out a gasp, his toes curling at the sheer overload. It was so different than the times with his own hand when he had tried to get hard, demanding an orgasm from his body that had no plans to respond.

When he trailed his hand down Derreck cock to his heavy sac, Derreck did the same thing on him. He cradled Derreck's balls in his hand, squeezing until Derreck's hips twitched and his Dom swore.

Derreck spread his legs as Maddy traveled farther, back to the hole that had him absolutely fascinated. Something thudded against his arm. *Lube.* He grabbed it, smearing it over his fingers before trailing back to Derreck's furl. He heard the cap open again, and watched Derreck slick up his own fingers.

Okay, we are doing this. He took a breath.

Pushing inside and feeling Derreck wrap around his finger at the same time his hole parted for Derreck had a groan pushing through his lips. It was equal parts pressure, uncertainty and a feeling a fullness that he vaguely recalled but had never felt so good. He was instantly addicted.

"More," he said, even as he sank a second finger inside Derreck. He hissed at the echoed intrusion, a sweet ache flaring along his spine that made him grit his teeth. "I feel like this is a bit unfair because your fingers are way bigger than mine."

"It's not about size," said Derreck, letting out a low chuckle as he twisted his hand and *oh dear.*

Maddy inhaled, his hips jerking as Derreck touched his prostate. His cock jerked once before Maddy was coming unexpectedly with a shout, his toes curling as his body went taut and pleasure burst outward from his groin.

"Keep going," said Maddy, his voice a strangled scream as Derreck tried to withdraw. His orgasm faded except for the distant tingle in his cock and a smear of cum on his belly and the sheets.

Somehow, Derreck's fingers were so much bigger than they had been moments before. He braced down on them, wanting to feel every ridge and callus inside as his hole twitched with the aftershocks.

A third finger sank inside, and the ache flared like the sweetest ecstasy. "More, please, Derreck. It feels so good. It's never felt like this before."

His cock was already throbbing again. Maybe it was trying to make up for lost time or maybe Derreck had just pushed Maddy's *on* button. Derreck *was* hitting his spot, and Maddy's cock kept leaking as he collapsed against the bed. He inhaled the scent of earth and Derreck, wishing he could wrap himself in it forever.

"Would you fuck me if I asked?" asked Maddy, belatedly withdrawing from Derreck's body. He immediately ached to push back inside, maybe with something other than his fingers. But he would probably come before he was even able to get the condom on. Longevity was making more and more sense. *Shit. Condoms.*

"Are you asking?" Derreck looked at him, his pupils blown wide until the brown was a thin rim in a sea of black. "Having sex isn't the same as something like this, Maddy. Once I'm inside of you, there's no going back from that type of intimacy."

Maddy nodded, licking his lips as Derreck moved, his fingers slipping from Maddy's ass. Derreck paused when their lips were inches apart, his breath fluttering against Maddy's mouth.

"I need you to say it," said Derreck, his dark eyes gazing straight into Maddy's soul.

Maddy had to prove it somehow. He needed Derreck to know how much he wanted this—wanted them. A 'yes' wasn't good enough, but his mind had blanked. He took a breath, following the tug of his gut and bringing their lips together.

It was sweet but hard at the same time—and so completely unexpected that it made Maddy gasp. It was nothing like holding hands, or even Derreck's fingers inside him. It was…intimate.

Derreck tasted like toothpaste, but as his mouth opened and their tongues touched for the first time, Maddy was overwhelmed by the rush. He was absolutely terrified, but that didn't stop him from wanting to pull Derreck closer and take everything.

Bodily fluids were right up there with pocket mints that had hair and fuzz stuck to them. But there he was, sucking on Derreck's tongue and swallowing him down as their mixed saliva gathered in his mouth. His cock throbbed, hard and leaking, as Derreck pushed him down onto the bed, his larger body hovering over Maddy's while Derreck claimed his mouth.

There was no question as to who was Dominant. It may have been Maddy's exploration, but Derreck was still in control, and as unyielding as the blazing sun on a summer's day. Maddy wouldn't have had it any other way.

"I'm asking. Please fuck me." The words slipped out between kisses, and Derreck growled, nipping at his lips until he was sure they would be swollen for days. The hint of pain mixed with pleasure was nearly as perfect as the pain itself. Derreck's weight held him down, keeping him from bucking off the bed as his hips twitched, seeking out any form of pressure.

The crinkle of foil drew Maddy's attention, seconds before the cap of the lube bottle clicked open. Derreck leaned back, rolling a condom onto his cock before slathering himself with lube. Maddy's legs shook against his will as Derreck slid between them and moved back in, capturing his lips in another kiss.

"I'll go as slow as you need, but I think you want it to hurt," said Derreck, growling against his lips as he lined himself up against Maddy's hole, his blunt cock so much wider than three fingers.

Between two stuttering breaths, Derreck pushed inside. He was so thick and blunt that at first it didn't seem like he would ever be able to breech him. But when Maddy finally relaxed and parted, and his nerves sang to life, he understood what Derreck had meant.

The ache flared along the base of his spine, more exquisite than he had expected and better than any flog or cane. Their breaths mingled until he could scarcely tell where he ended and Derreck began. Derreck was everywhere—his hands, his mouth, his cock—everywhere.

Sceneing was allowing Derreck to take control and see his soul, but sex with his Dom was about giving himself up completely and throwing a part of himself away, hoping that Derreck would catch it and hold it tight and not let it break on jagged rocks.

"Ah, Derreck," said Maddy, clutching at Derreck's shoulders as his voice went high. It was so much, the sensation of fullness tipping until it was like nothing he'd felt before. There was agony but it was mixed with pleasure, sending him floating as Derreck settled himself all the way inside. He was going to break. There was no way his body was meant to take something so big, but he reached for Derreck's ass, sinking his nails in to the firm globes to tug him closer.

Derreck pushed Maddy's knees to his chest, hooking his legs over his shoulders until he was fully on display. Maddy should have been embarrassed about his exposure, but he let his legs fall wider, arching his back so Derreck could see where they were connected if he chose to look. He was exactly where he wanted and needed to be.

Leaning down to bring their lips together again, Derreck started to thrust, pushing Maddy's legs wider so their chests touched. Maddy's hole flared as his rim stretched over Derreck's cock, every vein pushing him that much wider. Moving slowly, it still burned, the ache intensifying as Derreck shifted so he went deeper.

Maddy cried out, his scream lost to Derreck's lips as his prostate was struck for the first time. The force of it nearly hurt the sensitive bundle, tears gathering in his eyes as he grabbed Derreck's sides and held on. Digging his nails into Derreck's skin, he urged him on—faster, deeper, harder. He didn't care, as long as it was *more*.

Derreck let loose, their skin slapping as he pulled Maddy onto his cock with each thrust. He leaned back, and Maddy let out a shout as Derreck went even deeper. *How am I not broken?* Everything ached, and he was almost there.

With a single touch to his cock, Maddy came, painting Derreck's chest with his cum. His body clamped down, but Derreck pushed through every defense, slamming himself deep each and every time, and leaning down to capture Maddy's lips in a brutal kiss.

He longed for air but didn't dare to pull away—not until Derreck came inside him and claimed him in every way that would ever matter. Carving his nails into Derreck's back, Maddy arched, trying to get him to go fast and deeper.

His Dom had no problem with giving him everything he wanted, slamming inside until it was nearly unbearable. He was broken and he would never be the same, but there was no turning back.

Derreck's pace stuttered and he bottomed out one last time, going taut as his breath rushed out of him. Derreck groaned, his eyes closing in bliss as his eyebrows drew together and his mouth dropped open.

Beautiful. Maddy finally saw it for the first time. It was intimacy and trust and pain and pleasure. If Maddy could have, he would have come again.

"Derreck." He threaded his hands through Derreck's tight curls, tugging at them gently as Derreck collapsed against his chest, still inside. His heart pounded, thudding against Maddy's chest in a rhythm that matched his own. "Mmmm, no, stay," he said as Derreck went to pull out.

"Can't." Derreck leaned back, letting Maddy's legs fall as he gripped the base of the condom and tugged his way out. He was already shrinking, some of his load creeping back up his shaft like it was trying to escape. Derreck tied it, tossing it to the side and hitting the garbage can beside the bed.

"Can I fuck you next time?" asked Maddy, reaching for his hole. He was slick and swollen and *ouch* really tender.

"Fuck, kid, let me catch my breath first." Derreck collapsed back onto the pillows with a smile on his lips. They both had to be thinking the same thing.

Next time.

Chapter Twelve

Derreck

Maddy was on his chest, his breathing even and deep now that their bellies were full and they'd had a second round. Derreck had offered up his ass, like a gentleman, but Maddy had pushed Derreck down to the bed, sliding a condom onto his cock before sinking down and riding him like a legitimate cowboy. The thought of bucking him off hadn't crossed Derreck's mind.

Fuck. He couldn't believe it, and he didn't dare fall asleep. If he closed his eyes, he would wake and discover it had all been a dream. That would have been torture worse than working another three days straight in the rain.

While they had been eating, Derreck had sent a text to his boss, a simple *"can't dig in the rain"* using Maddy's phone. As far as he was concerned, he would rather buy a new phone than try to dig his own out of that fucking grave. *May it rest in peace.*

"Did you really fall into a grave?" asked Maddy, pulling Derreck from his thoughts. Derreck ran his hand down Maddy's back, settling on his ass and squeezing one firm cheek. Maddy was so light on top of him that even his weight seemed almost imaginary.

"Thought you were asleep, but yeah, I did." Derreck yawned as he slipped his fingers between Maddy's cheeks, prodding the swollen hole that was probably bright red. It was soft and hot, still slick with a bit of lube that he had missed with the cloth. His cock started to thicken, ready for round three, even though he was exhausted.

Maddy let out a gasp that morphed into a giggle as he wiggled against Derreck's hand, rubbing his soft cock against Derreck's belly as he pinched one nipple between his pale fingertips. "Should I ask how? I feel like there's a great story behind that."

"That's what I do for a living. I dig graves," said Derreck, slipping in a second finger in and scissoring Maddy wide. He hadn't tightened up yet, but the swelling at his rim certainly made him feel tighter. *Fuck,* he was fully hard again.

Maddy leaned on his elbow, staring down at Derreck as his face flushed. He squirmed as Derreck pushed deeper, cranking his wrist to try to hit his sub's prostate. "I honestly didn't know that was a real job. I thought they used a machine for that kind of thing. No wonder you're so strong."

He tried not to preen, he really did, but he failed miserably, his chest swelling and his ego inflating against his will. He searched Maddy for any trace of judgment—like the look he'd given the apartment building—but there was none.

"Usually, yeah, but machines can't get into some spots, like under trees. Smaller cemeteries just can't afford them, and when the ground is really soft, they would just tear everything up, so that's where I come in. It's not glamourous and it doesn't pay all that well, but it keeps me out of an office." He slipped a third finger into Maddy, who winced, his face flushing brighter.

"Sore?" Derreck asked, not pausing for a moment. He knew what Maddy liked, and it certainly wasn't a soft fuck. He kept half an eye on Maddy's cock, though, which was still soft against his hip.

Maddy hummed, looking down to Derreck's length. "Every time I look at it, I still can't believe that it fit inside me. It's just huge. I'm half expecting it to start talking on its own."

Maddy snickered and rotated until his face pressed against Derreck's groin. His tongue peeked out of his mouth, so pink and delicate against Derreck's dark cock as he swiped at the head. Grimacing, Maddy pulled back. "Tastes like lube and plastic."

A real laugh burst from Derreck's chest, startling him as he shook from the force of it. It had been a long time since he'd laughed that hard — probably years. It had also been years since he'd brought anyone back to his place.

"The look on your face," said Derreck, still chuckling. Scooting up and leaning back against the headboard, he patted his chest, hoping that Maddy would accept the invitation. He did, sliding back into Derreck's arms and pressing a hesitant kiss against his lips.

"You were my first kiss," said Maddy quietly. "It's weird... I never thought that I'd ever want to kiss someone. It always looked a little gross, to be honest. But with you? Your lips are just perfect — so sweet."

He placed another peck as Derreck tried to cover his surprise. Maddy didn't look young, maybe mid-thirties, and it was astonishing that no one had ever tried to kiss him. "Was that your only first?" His heart thumped much too quickly as he thought back to how rough he had been.

"It was the first time I've enjoyed sex — or come during sex. I tried once before with another guy and he was rough, like I thought I wanted, but it wasn't good. It didn't get me off like you did, and he left right after, so it left me a little on edge. I thought that was how it always was. I mean, in porn, the bottoms sometimes aren't hard at all and they don't seem to come very often." Maddy shrugged, staring down at Derreck's cock. "I couldn't have stopped myself from coming if I tried with you. You blew my mind."

Is murder still a crime? Probably somewhere. Derreck held his tongue. He was not going to ask the guy's name, because if he found out, he was going to prison.

"I wonder how it would feel if you beat me then fucked me," said Maddy, his eyes glazing over as he licked his lips.

"Shit." Derreck's cock dribbled pre-cum as the image played through his mind. He had kept the two things separate for a reason, but maybe it was time to start letting the line blur. "If you promise not to run, I'll fucking destroy you, then fuck you so hard that you'll never come down."

Maddy shuddered, fluttering his eyes shut. His dark eyelashes stood out over his pale cheeks. He didn't have a freckle on his face, only his single mole and semi-permanent blush.

"I'd like that," said Maddy, his cock showing the first signs of interest. "But I need you tell me something first. You've never really looked at my marks or asked me about them. Why?" His eyes stayed closed as if he were afraid of what Derreck might say.

"Because they don't matter," said Derreck honestly, smoothing his hand down Maddy's ridged pec. There were more lines than he would ever be able to count, but it still didn't matter.

"How could you say that?" asked Maddy, biting his lip as he let out a shudder. "They matter. Of course they matter. Everybody who has ever seen them treats me like I need to be put away and medicated for the rest of my life. People don't just accept them."

"Tell me what you think of them," said Derreck, tracing down one line that was ragged and bumpy, as if it had become infected at one point. Marked or not, the skin was still warm and it still felt like Maddy. It still smelled like Maddy, and tasted like him, because it *was* him.

"I... They kept me sane." Maddy swallowed. "I've never told anyone this, not even my therapist. I think she would agree with the majority, too, because she wants me on meds, and she wanted me to take a longer leave of absence. I mean...some people bite their nails and some smoke or drink or do cocaine, but I just need pain. I can't live without it, and to be honest, I don't even want to try. I don't want to kill myself or hurt anyone else. *I* just want to hurt. It's an addiction, just like gambling, only cheaper."

Maddy let out a humorless laugh. "Sorry, I didn't mean to drag you into my shit storm of a life. Pain was the only thing I thought that I ever truly needed, but then I met you, and *shit...*" He ran his hand through his

M.C. Roth

hair. "You made it so much better, and you took my guilt away. I owe you so much for doing that for me."

"No, you don't," said Derreck after a long pause and a few deep breaths. "You don't owe me a thing." Maddy couldn't know how much he'd given Derreck in return. He'd been so fucking lost, but holding Maddy in his arms, with his cock hard and his sub happy, was fucking heaven. If it ended, he would never recover. It would be the last time he ever trusted someone.

But he couldn't tell Maddy that and weigh down his shoulders that were already carrying such a heavy burden.

"Show them off if you want...or don't," Derreck said instead. "Just know that you're the same to me either way."

A chime sounded from the bathroom, with a ring tone that definitely didn't belong to Derreck. Of course it didn't. His phone was still six feet under.

Sliding from the bed, Maddy disappeared into the bathroom, reappearing in the doorway with his phone. Maddy stood taller than he had before, his shoulders back and down as he marched back to the bed. He looked fucking proud.

"You okay if I put it on speaker? My hands are still sticky." He held his phone between the tips of two fingers, swiping with his pinky before tossing the phone down on the sheets.

"Maddy here," he said, sliding back onto the bed and onto Derreck's lap. Derreck wanted to growl with satisfaction, but he opted to kiss the back of Maddy's neck instead, hugging him tight until Maddy's hip brushed against his hard cock. A smile flitted over Maddy's lips as he gave him a half-hearted glare.

"Madison, it's Mr. Jameson."

177

That time Derreck did growl, nipping the back of Maddy's neck to keep from reaching for the phone and crushing it in his hand. Maddy shushed him softly, pulling himself out of Derreck's lap.

"It's Maddy, and how can I help you? I'm not scheduled to come in tomorrow, and you're lucky I had my ringer on." Maddy pulled at the sheet on the bed, covering his legs and fiddling with the edge.

The sweet, undeniable Maddy that Derreck knew wasn't the one that was on his bed, glaring at his phone. This was the man he'd only had a peek of when he'd rampaged through a government building like a swamp monster.

The snarky behavior that would probably get him kicked out of most offices was coupled with uncertainty. He watched as Maddy gazed around the room, pausing as he spotted a shirt hanging out of a dresser drawer. The snark had to have been a farce — a defense to keep himself more hidden than he already was.

Maddy had started to sag his shoulders again, his newfound confidence obviously smashed to nothing. It just made Derreck want to break the phone more.

"I think we should discuss whether or not you will be returning to work at all," the asshole continued, his voice pitched like he had a three-foot stick up his ass. "I've spoken with our human resource department as well as upper management about your *stability*, and we have decided that it would be in your best interest if we let you go. The job is clearly too much for you, and we can't have a situation on our conscience."

Derreck tangled his hands in the sheets, clenching his jaw tight to keep his anger at bay. *That's it.* Jameson was going to have an unfortunate accident before the week was through. He knew exactly where to bury the body, too.

"I don't understand," said Maddy, flashing a confused look at Derreck. "You think you can make a decision for my best interest without consulting me?" His voice rose steadily.

"Yes, that's exactly what we did. You are ill, Maddy, and you can't work here until you've taken care of your illness. Your termination is not up for negotiation, but you will be getting a generous severance package." Maddy's boss sniffed once before clearing his throat.

"You entitled prick," said Maddy, taking the words out of Derreck's mouth. "You're going to sweep me under the rug and shove your head in the sand? Well, here's a news flash for you. I don't fucking care. If you want to take the away checks and balances that keep employers and employees safe and hire ex-cons and rapists, then by all means. But here's a warning for you— Whatever your package is, you'd better double it unless you want thirty lawyers crawling up your ass."

"Six weeks' pay and benefits—and that's final." The jackass huffed and Maddy rolled his eyes.

For a guy with maybe one-hundred-and-seventy pounds on his frame, Maddy could be a terrifying motherfucker. Derreck was ready to jump ship and hang up the phone because he was getting intimidated. Murder could only get you so far, but lawyers? *No thank you.*

But Maddy gripped the sheets hard, glaring at the phone as if it would burst in to flames if he stared hard enough.

"I might consider that if you let me find and train my replacement," said Maddy, his voice strong, despite the tremble in his body. Derreck lifted himself to his knees. Maddy's chest was rising fast, his eyes going wider with each passing moment.

Derreck knew the first signs of a panic attack when he saw one. His sub had already been through so much. Reaching for Maddy's chin, he tilted Maddy to him, smoothing along his lip as he flinched and shuddered.

"Are you okay?" he whispered soft enough that the phone wouldn't have been able to pick up his voice. Maddy shook his head, tugging his chin from Derreck's grip. Derreck dragged a hand down Maddy's spine instead. "You don't have to pretend anymore, Maddy. Tell this fucker what you really want to say."

Maddy took a shuddering breath before he leaned into Derreck's touch, his body molding against his chest. Humming in approval, Derreck traced the designs with his fingertips.

"You know you can't replace me," said Maddy, his voice cracking for the first time.

"Everyone is replaceable," Mr. Jameson said roughly.

Derreck tensed, leaning down to Maddy's ear. "He's wrong. There's no one in the world like you, but he'd just too blind to see it. Let it go. He can't hurt you anymore."

"You're right," said Maddy, looking up at Derreck.

"I'm glad you understand—"

"Not you, dirtbag. Derreck. He's right, because you don't see the good that I've done, and you never will. You are so blind, but I doubt you'll miss when my lawyer pays you a visit." Maddy smirked, his eyes going alight.

"I don't think that's necessary. Our offer is more than generous—"

"Sorry! My give-a-shits have officially expired. Goodbye," said Maddy, reaching for the phone and disconnecting the call. Leaning back into Derreck's embrace, he let out a long sigh.

"I won't ask you if you're okay, because I know you aren't," said Derreck. "Just let me know what I can do." He slipped his hand over Maddy's trembling form, his erection faded to nothing.

"I can't believe they fired me," said Maddy, shaking his head with a huff. "Like I really can't believe it. With all the laws in place to protect workers and all the campaigns about mental health, they still tucked tail at the first sign of trouble."

Derreck stayed quiet as Maddy continued to ramble, his breathing slowing as he eventually wound down. It had been a long time since he'd held someone and listened to them while aching to do anything to help but knowing that he couldn't. He was about six feet above his comfort level.

"I guess I should get out of your hair," said Maddy, pulling away. "Sorry if I'm not really in the mood for a beating right now. I think I just need to go to bed and crash for a bit." He looked back at Derreck, holding his gaze. "I'm not running. I'm just tired of hiding."

Derreck nodded once, trying to ignore the pang in his chest as Maddy pulled away. It wasn't a drop or anything close to that. He just wanted Maddy in his arms, preferably forever. He clamped down on that feeling fast before it could spread. Maddy was still his sub first and foremost.

"Let me know if you change your mind. You'd be surprised how often a good beating can fix a few problems." The offer sounded dull, even to his own ears. "Or a hug. I'm good for those, too." Derreck kept his hands on the bed as Maddy moved away. His sub had to stand on his own, even if it hurt.

"I'm sure you are. I'm going to head out, but text me when you get a new phone. I'd like to call tomorrow and chat if we could." Maddy's smile looked more forced with each passing breath, tension wrapping around his body like a zip tie that slowly clicked tighter. "I'll leave my number for you in the kitchen."

Maddy grabbed his clothes, slowly pulling them over his frame and tucking his phone in his pocket. He looked back at Derreck before he slipped through the bedroom door. Demon dashed to intercept, letting out a warbling meow that only a mother could find endearing. "I'm not running."

Maddy reached down and patted Demon on the head, turning away from Derreck without looking back. Derreck leaned against the headboard as he caught the distant sound of his front door opening and closing. Dragging his hand through his hair, he glared at his crumpled and stained sheets that were still warm from Maddy's touch.

If Maddy isn't running, why does it hurt so much?

Chapter Thirteen

Maddy

It was the most awkward situation of his life. He was standing in a clean pair of slacks and a blue dress shirt that had little red diamonds on it, but his ex-colleagues were staring at him as if he were a street bum. The entire water cooler gang hovered in the corner like a fight club looking for their fix of violence.

Their eyes weren't actually as beady as he recalled and were more like the watery brown of an over-tired basset hound. They had similar expressions to the dog, too, as if they couldn't quite believe he had the audacity to step into their territory.

He had to laugh as he looked around the place that had once been his office. How could he not laugh? They were like hyenas circling a baby lion, just waiting for the right moment to grab a bite.

Luckily, Maddy had never felt further from a helpless baby lion. He was more like the lioness that stalked out on the plains, grabbed a buffalo by the throat and squeezed — the lioness with a dick and balls, that was. A functioning dick and balls too, which was something that he'd never thought he would have been able to claim.

Derreck's cock inside of him had pushed more than one button. Apparently, there was another button directly beside his prostate that had turned his horniness meter to the max. Since his first fuck, he'd climbed on Derreck's cock as often as he could.

"Madison, thank you for waiting." Mr. Jameson greeted him exactly how Maddy had expected. *Maybe he's hard of hearing?* There was a pinched look about his boss's eyes, as if he had just started to realize the shit storm he had created. But there was also that little concerned glare, as if he was watching Maddy for any signs of a meltdown.

"Now that I'm no longer one of your employees, you are welcome to call me by my actual name," said Maddy, reveling in the wash of joy the words that gave him. He'd always been…abrupt…in the office, but now he could say anything he wanted. Anything besides death threats, at least. His lawyer had made that abundantly clear.

"Your things have been packed away. I believe they are just inside the door of your old office space. Please follow me." His boss turned to lead the way, as if Maddy had somehow forgotten where he'd spent his days for the last ten years.

Ten wasted years. That sat in his gut harder than he'd thought it would. He had loved his job, despite the stress, and he already missed it after a week away. In his office, he had made a difference in the world, but now…now he was nobody again.

He cleared his throat, looking up to his old office. It was the same door and the same glass windows but somehow it looked different.

"Hired a replacement already? I wonder how long that will last," said Maddy as he spotted someone sitting in his old chair. The last record had been fourteen days before they had quit. Before Maddy, the position had sat vacant for nearly two years after a steady stream of hire, quit, fire and repeat.

"Yes. I believe the two of you are acquainted, and with his education and skills, he was an obvious choice."

Why the hell does he sound so smug? It was obvious that there was no love lost between them, but Maddy had done good things for the company, even earning a bit of public trust back.

He tried to keep his face blank when he stepped into *his* office and the person behind *his* desk looked up. The smirk that spread over Phil's face as he leaned back in Maddy's chair, could have starred in horror movies.

Maddy felt the blood drain from his face, and he clutched the doorknob to keep upright. *A man like Phil in a seat of power?*

"You hired Phil to replace me?" asked Maddy, unable to keep the disbelief from his voice. *Sex offender, Phil? Rapist, Phil? Ex-con, Phil?* His faults were like the tally card at a golf game, and he had just struck out.

Okay, so I don't exactly know anything about sports...

"He is perfect for the position. He obviously has attention to detail if he can see things about his fellow employees that I can't, and he's not afraid to report it," said Mr. Jameson. "He is more than qualified. I thought you would be happy for him, Madison."

"I am," said Maddy, clearing his throat when his voice came out weak and strangled. "Congratulations, Phil. I hope you make it longer than fourteen days."

There was no way he will make it that long. He doesn't have the balls for it.

"Did you take your meds today, Maddy? You are looking a bit pale. Maybe a trip back here wasn't good for your *illness*," said Phil, tapping his finger against his greasy chin. There was a smear of mustard at the corner of his mouth, and his cologne practically soaked the room. It would never come out of the carpet.

I am going to kill this motherfucker. Maddy glanced at the boxes of his things. His mug and a few pictures were there, but all his notes and journals were gone.

The journals that his therapist had suggested keeping at work with him so he could write down his frustrations throughout the day to keep them from building up. The journals that he'd rambled in and poured his negative thoughts onto the page so that they didn't cloud his life.

"Where are the rest of my things?" asked Maddy, his voice hollow as he looked at the empty bookshelf where he'd kept a few cards from loved ones. He had opened them on down days, to remind himself that it wasn't all bad.

"Everything is in that box," said Phil, his smirk going wider. "I cleaned out your desk myself."

Phil had seen his journals and his cards. He knew every detail. Every vulnerability. His breath came faster, clogging his throat as an invisible hand squeezed.

"My cards from my family? My books? My files?" Maddy stumbled over to the box of his things, falling to his knees as his heart started to pound.

"Your files belong to me now. And as for the rest? Well, how was I supposed to tell the junk from the keepers? Most of it looked like the ravings of a lunatic." Phil's eyes danced with glee, and Maddy's head started to swim.

"You're really enjoying this," said Maddy, rubbing at his sternum, which had started to ache.

"Of course he isn't," Mr. Jameson cut in. "It was very nice of Phil to go through the office and pack away your things for you."

Had Maddy's office always been so fucking lonely? He was surrounded by people, but no one really knew him or anything about him—except perhaps Phil. He had probably jerked off to the inner workings of Maddy's mind, or he was storing them away and waiting for the chance to break Maddy's life apart again.

He stared down at the mug in the box—a company present when he'd celebrated five years with the office. There was a chip at the rim that hadn't been there before, and there was a bit of dried sludge at the bottom of the cup, which didn't make sense, because Maddy only ever used it for water.

The pictures in the box were old and replaceable, with the better versions and duplicates at home. Two of the picture frames in the box had cracked and a third one was twisted out of shape.

"You can keep this too," said Maddy as he stumbled away from the box, leaning on the wall for support. "This stuff means nothing to me, and you've stolen the only things that did." Phil's condemning files were probably among his missing things, the proof of his nefarious past hidden away by his new position.

"Are you sure you are all right, Madison? Do I need to call someone for you?"

Maddy shook his head, stumbling out of his old office as he reached for his phone. The hyena in his chair cackled at his retreating form. He should never have come back.

Chapter Fourteen

Derreck

Derreck looked down at his phone, swiping his finger across the pristine screen. Despite just having washed his hands, he still left a dirty print behind. The phone was bigger than his last one, and he'd purchased a waterproof case that was bright orange so he'd hopefully never lose it. The old one was probably under a body, and definitely equally as dead.

Glancing back to the curtain at the front of the bar, he scanned the gap beneath it. As much privacy as it offered from any outsider's eyes looking in, there was still a crack of light along the bottom. The running shoes of the bouncer shifted as he moved from the sign-in table to a stool, but there were no other signs of life.

Maddy's text had roused him from sleep an hour before and had sent him straight to one-hundred-percent when he'd read the few simple words on the screen.

Meet me at the club.

His hands tingled as he imagined holding a flog or even a cane between his fingers with Maddy stretched out on the other end. Their vanilla sex had been amazing over the last few days, but Derreck knew it wasn't enough for either of them.

Something had been holding Maddy back—something Derreck hadn't been able to figure out, even when he'd been balls-deep with Maddy's cum on his chest—which was one of his new favorite positions that he had locked in his memory forever.

The door clicked and Derreck looked back to his phone automatically. Maddy was supposed to text him when he got to the club so Derreck could let him in. He wasn't technically a member yet, which was something that Derreck hoped to rectify soon. He didn't have room in his one-bedroom apartment for play, so the club was the only place where he could really be himself.

He didn't keep any implements around his place in case the neighbor kids visited or came to pet Demon. A few of their mothers had tried to get lucky by bringing him food, even when he'd gently declined. If anything, his refusal had spurred them on until it was commonplace to find casseroles inside his door with Demon licking the lid where a bit of cheese had escaped.

Some people might call his side of town sketchy, but to him, it was home. It was a place where nobody gave two fucks if the lawns were trimmed perfectly or if there were a few dandelions, because everyone was family. Everyone watched out for each other.

The curtain parted, and Derreck let out a sigh when he spotted another Dom. Henley — like the shirt — was a slim five-eight but could take any man twice his size to the ground in seconds. He'd also been cruising the club for a new sub, but his tastes were far different than Derreck's.

"You don't look happy to see me. I won't take it personally," said Henley as Derreck looked over his shoulder to the curtain that was falling shut again. Derreck grunted.

Henley had appeared out of thin air a few years before with no clue about anything in the kink world and one hell of a chip on his shoulder. Clint had taken him in, and Derreck had given him a few demos before Henley had been able to cruise on his own. As far as Derreck knew, Henley had scened and slept with over two-dozen subs and had never gone back for seconds.

"I heard you found yourself a new sub, so congrats," said Henley, sliding into the chair next to him. He smiled at Derreck's nod.

"Does he have a brother or a friend? It's been pretty slim pickings around lately. All the good ones have been snatched up."

Derreck stared at his sometimes-friend-but-never-play partner. There was a tightness around Henley's eyes, even with the smile on his face that looked genuine. Although Derreck didn't find Henley overly attractive, most other men and women did. He had soft, boyish looks with the mouth of the devil, and arms that could bench press Derreck with ease.

Derreck scanned the room, noting the few couples there. It was nearly two, so the bar was fairly quiet, but that didn't stop people from ordering soft drinks and socializing. Most were in pairs with a few triads, but there were only a select few singles floating around.

It didn't seem to matter what time Derreck came to the club. He was hardly ever alone. Even on a slow day, Clint was there to chat his ear off and treat him to stories of his nursing days. One of his favorite things seemed to be telling Derreck the strange things he'd found jammed up people's assholes.

"No feral pups out there right now," said Henley, following Derreck's gaze, "or domesticated ones, for that matter. None that would be my type, anyway." He swiveled in his stool, ordering a 7 Up before turning back to Derreck. "Not many subs wanna play my games. They all want to get flogged or spit on nowadays. No offense on the flogging."

"None taken," said Derreck, glancing back at the still curtain. The general motto of the club was 'To each their own, together', and as long as that lined up with consent, then Derreck didn't have a single beef with it. He didn't exactly understand the appeal of a collar, but all kink boiled down to the same two things for him.

Consent and power exchange.

Without those, it was an excuse or abuse.

"I don't think I've ever seen you this antsy," said Clint as he slid a drink Derreck's way. He glanced down at the bubbling dark liquid before knocking it back. A little caffeine would do him good when he was running on four hours sleep. "You look better than you did. I mean, better than when it looked like you were digging your own grave, but I've still never seen you so...impatient."

Henley gave Derreck a once-over, his emerald eyes probably picking up every detail. There was a reason that the guy worked for some kind of secret government agency, and it wasn't for his looks. Derreck was pretty sure that he wasn't even supposed to know that little detail, but after one altercation where Henley had fought with a drunken Dom, he'd cornered Henley for answers.

No one Henley's size could break a man's arm like it was nothing, but Henley had...with ease. The guy would have been intimidating if he weren't so packaged-sized. Derreck still tried to be cautious, though.

"Maddy should have been here by now," said Derreck, glancing down at his screen again. He bounced his leg on the lower rung of the stool, tapping his fingers over the bar top. It wasn't like him. Derreck was like a sniper that could wait for days for the perfect target, but something about the way Maddy had closed himself off lately rubbed him the wrong way.

Maddy wasn't taking his unemployment well, that was for sure.

"He's picking up his things from his work today. They fired him," said Derreck, not really sure why he was telling the others. He worried his lip, tapping his fingers faster and faster.

"Shit, man, that sucks. Why did they fire him?" asked Clint, leaning down on the bar. His elbow slipped in a bit of condensation from Henley's glass, nearly sending his face into the bar top.

"They accused him of being mentally ill," said Derreck. It sounded ridiculous, even to him. Maddy may not have fit into society's norms, but he was slowly discovering himself with Derreck's help.

He really did hope that Maddy had hired a lawyer and it hadn't been a bluff. No one should have to go through something like that again.

"Fuck, really?" asked Clint, wiping at the bar top with his towel. Henley let out a low whistle.

"That's low, really low. I mean, as long as he didn't lose it and start handing out death threats instead of valentines," said Henley with a chuckle. Derreck shot him a glare. *It's not funny.*

"He took a leave of absence, and his boss thought that made Maddy unstable," said Derreck. He wouldn't say more without Maddy's okay. He didn't know all the details of Maddy's leave, anyway.

His phone buzzed in his hand — a text from Maddy announcing his arrival. He stumbled out of his chair, uncharacteristically off balance as he marched to the curtain and flung it aside. The bouncer startled on his stool at Derreck's approach, quickly standing.

Grabbing the knob and flinging the door wide, Derreck let out a sigh when he spotted Maddy there. They'd only been apart for a day, but it felt much longer. An hour was too long, as far as Derreck was concerned, not that he would say anything.

Derreck didn't fall hard and fast. He just didn't. His heart had been locked away for the entirety of his life. Maybe the reason it was different was because he had blurred the lines between being boyfriends and play partners.

Boyfriends? Is that what we are? They hadn't discussed it, and Derreck had no intention of bringing it up himself. As soon as he put a name to it, it was bound to disappear.

Pausing, he took a second look at Maddy before he let him into the bar. Threading their hands together, he tugged him off the street, pushing aside the curtain and waiting for the privacy of the club to settle over them.

Maddy's face was pale, despite the sweat at his temples, and he tugged his sleeve down to where Derreck's held him. It could have been a trick of the light, but Maddy's eyes looked swollen and bloodshot.

"We can go somewhere else," said Derreck, pausing just inside the curtain. Despite the busy interior, hardly anyone looked their way, and the air was threaded with peace. He wondered if it felt the same to Maddy, though, as he continued to fidget.

Maddy shook his head, his nails biting into Derreck's palm. "I need this."

Maddy pulled him past the bar, bypassing the booths and stools before heading straight for their room. The alarm bells in Derreck's head were getting louder with each step, but Derreck let himself be tugged along. If Maddy needed him, he was more than willing to give whatever it took.

"We don't have this one today," said Derreck, glancing at the door labeled *Impact* when Maddy paused before it. Someone else had beat him to it with the short notice. Maddy deflated before his eyes, his jaw clenching until his molars squeaked together. His grip went tight—tighter than Derreck had thought Maddy was capable of.

Most of the rooms had been claimed by the time Derreck had gotten to the bar, leaving two available to choose from. Sometimes a little imagination went a long way. He didn't need a wall of implements to break Maddy.

Derreck headed for the last door, tugging Maddy along before tapping his card to the door lock.

"*Wet?*" asked Maddy, glancing up to the name. "Please tell me it's not what I'm thinking, because that is a hard limit for me." His blue eyes narrowed, a bit of the real Maddy starting to peek through his haggard shield.

"It's exactly what you're thinking, but I won't be pushing those limits any time soon," said Derreck, opening the door wide and flicking the light on. Piss play wasn't his thing.

It was dryer than Derreck had expected, but in his defense, he had only been inside the room once and could barely remember the details. He had been too focused on the scene that he had been invited to – the one that had shown him in absolute detail that he wasn't into piss play.

The room hummed as a fan started along with the light, sucking the humidity from the air. The entirety of the room was tiled, but the floors were covered with waterproof mats that offered some grip. The floors slanted away from the door, dipping along the far end where there were three drains.

There were two shower heads that dropped out of the ceiling above the drains, with several sets of manacles bolted into the ceiling and the walls. There was a restraint bench, but it was coated with a special plastic over the cushions and the wooden legs had been switched out for stainless steel.

"Oh," said Maddy, looking around the room. "Not what I expected." There was a couch tucked next to the door, which had the same covering as the bench, and there were about twice as many towels than any other room.

"Which was?" Derreck tugged Maddy to the couch.

"I thought there would be like five toilets in here," said Maddy. "It's for people into watersports, right? Hey, don't laugh at me."

Covering his snicker with his hand, Derreck muffled his laugh, preening under Maddy's smile. Sliding his hand down Maddy's belly, he stopped at his abdomen, right where his bladder would sit. He pushed into the soft skin until Maddy winced from the pressure.

"Hey," said Maddy, tugging at his hand. Derreck instantly released him, lowering his mouth to Maddy's ear.

"It's not all about watching someone piss into a potty," he said, keeping his voice low. "It's about control. The Dom could ask the sub to hold it in, even if they were desperate to go. They could fuck them hard, until they had no choice but to let go." He pointed to the manacles by the showers and hummed as Maddy's eyes went wide and a flush rose to his cheeks.

"Are...are you into that sort of thing?" He flushed brighter, dropping his gaze to the tiled floor.

"Nah," said Derreck, sitting on the couch. "But I'm always willing to explore if you want to." As much as it wasn't his thing, he would make the necessary sacrifices to keep Maddy happy.

Maddy shook his head, clasping his hands together as his gaze flickered between the walls. "There's nothing here. No flogs, no cane and no whip. I-I need them, Derreck, please. Today wasn't good."

Derreck let out a humorless chuckle as he grasped Maddy's wrist and dragged him onto the couch. He clamped down, grinding the bones in Maddy's wrist until he let out a pained gasp. "You think I need a whip or a flog to hurt you? Maddy, I can take you apart piece by piece until you can't even remember your name, and no one would ever see a mark."

Maddy trembled, closing his eyes as his breathing came faster. He was already starting to zone out and slip into his space, even though Derreck hadn't begun.

"I want you to mark me," said Maddy, his words barely above a whisper.

"I thought so. Tell me your safewords as you strip," said Derreck, nodding as Maddy quickly blurted them out and stumbled to his feet. To Derreck's surprise, he went for his shirt first, slipping it over his head and tossing it onto the arm of the couch. His pants went next, then his boxers and socks.

Maddy squirmed as Derreck raked his eyes up and down his form. He was still slim, but had thickened a bit since Derreck had first met him. Derreck nodded his approval. Maddy's ribs no longer poked out like secondary elbows, and he held himself straight, his body on display for Derreck's perusal.

Fuck, he was already getting hard. Derreck shifted to ease the pressure on his smothered dick. He was going to have to get new outfits if he planned to keep getting hard at the club. His current club gear was way too freaking tight to handle him.

Maddy was still soft, his cute cock nestled on a bed of trimmed dark hair with his sac hanging loose between his open legs. His legs were spotless and without a single scratch mark, despite the designs on his torso and legs.

"Where did you want me to mark you?" asked Derreck, leaning back on the couch even as Maddy squirmed again. *Adorable.*

"Can you please—I mean—would it be okay...my back?"

So freaking cute. How anyone could throw someone like Maddy to the curb was beyond Derreck. Maddy was ripe for cherishing, and so polite in his submission.

"Did you want me to leave something permanent or something that will heal?" asked Derreck. As much as he wanted to brand himself into Maddy's flesh, he didn't want to stray too far from Maddy's designs. They were methodical as well as exact.

"Can you please?" asked Maddy, his voice rising. "Leave something permanent, I mean. I've never been able to reach my back for anything, but I always wondered what it would feel like."

Shit. He should have grabbed a flog from one of the other rooms or a cane at the very least. Maddy's back was an untouched canvas that he could paint over and over until he begged.

"Stand beneath the shower to the right and put your arms above your head." The time for discussion had officially expired and his cock was starting to bend from his position on the couch. Nodding to himself, he waited for Maddy to scramble into position before he grabbed the manacles and snapped them around Maddy's wrists. He shortened the chain as soon as Maddy was secure, until he had to stand on his tip toes to keep himself from hanging.

Fear and anticipation. The air was ripe with it. Derreck licked a stripe up the back of Maddy's neck, reveling in the taste before he took a step back to admire his handiwork.

It was one of Derreck's favorite predicaments. Maddy could stand on his toes until his calves burned and turned to molten lava from the strain, but if he let his heels drop to try to ease the ache, the manacles would bite into his wrists and pull his shoulders taut, creating a new type of fire.

It could have been dangerous for an inexperienced Dom, but Derreck had put his subs through worse. "You'll be feeling this for days." He traced a single finger from Maddy's biceps and over his straining shoulders, then all the way down to the back of his knee. "You probably won't even be able to walk straight tomorrow."

He pressed his finger between Maddy's cheeks, to the tiny entrance that lay at the heart of him. He rubbed in dry circles, massaging the little bud that submitted so well for him. Peering around Maddy's hip, he waited until his cock was showing the first signs of life before he dipped his tongue between Maddy's cheeks, pushing his legs wide.

Maddy's weight hit his wrists as he scrambled for his footing. Derreck only swiped once, until he had Maddy's taste on his tongue, before he pulled away and let him regain his footing. Maddy panted as the chains jingled above him. They could take over four-hundred pounds of weight before they would start to fail, and there was no way that Maddy could escape.

Reaching for the lube in his pocket, Derreck smeared it over his pointer finger, pressing himself inside of Maddy to spread it around.

"Thought we would start out differently this time," said Derreck, pulling out a condom and lubing up his cock before he lined up with Maddy's hole. "I always like to eat my dessert first."

He ground his hips against Maddy, letting his cock slip and slide up his crack and between the perfect pressure of his cheeks. There was something about the threat of sinking in at any moment that would hopefully keep Maddy on edge and settle him deeper into his state of bliss. He never knew when Derreck would catch at his rim and sink inside.

"Nice and tight," said Derreck, squeezing Maddy's cheeks together and picking up the pace of his thrusts. He wasn't usually one to talk much during a scene or sex, but Maddy was soaking it up with little whimpers and groans, and he was more than happy to oblige.

His cock caught, then he was sinking inside, forcing Maddy to take him with next to no preparation. Derreck let out a cruel laugh as Maddy choked on a sob, the sound echoing off the tiles. "Oops, I guess I should have warned you."

They had fucked enough that Derreck knew it wouldn't harm him, especially with how much lube was between them, but it would still hurt like a motherfucker.

Maddy let out a whining gasp as Derreck bottomed out, the chains clinking as he jerked and writhed. Derreck peered around to see Maddy's cock hard and leaking against his belly. He was obviously loving every minute of both pain and penetration, and he had his safewords if that changed.

He didn't pause to let Maddy adjust before he pulled back and forced himself deep again, with Maddy fluttering around him as he let out high-pitched whimpers. If there was any doubt as to Maddy's enjoyment, it was abolished a few seconds later when Maddy pushed his ass back, forcing Derreck even deeper.

Sometimes prep was overrated. Derreck slammed in hard and fast, jerking Maddy in his chains until his wrists had to be aching. Derreck's own legs were burning from the position, but it only spurred him on faster.

Embarrassingly quickly, he emptied himself inside the condom. He tugged free, tying off the condom and tossing it toward the couch where it landed with an enthusiastic *splat*. Maddy's cock leaked and dripped, but he hadn't come yet, even with the abuse that Derreck had made sure to dish out to his prostate.

Well, that takes a bit of the edge off.

He spread Maddy's cheeks wide, tracing over his red and puffy rim while letting the moans and whimpers sink in. "One day I'm going to fill you up with my cum and watch it leak out as I whip you."

Maddy trembled, his cock dripping onto the mat below as his calves shook. His wrists and legs must've been close to agony, but he hadn't opened his mouth to complain yet. Probably because he was so fucking amazing.

"Perfect," said Derreck, echoing his thoughts as he circled Maddy once, stalking him like a leopard would have stalked its prey. Maddy's face was flushed, and his wrists were starting to get a touch red from the manacles. His gaze was still steady, though, despite the distance in his eyes. "I'm going to blindfold you. You know your safewords, and I expect you to use them if you need them."

He waited for Maddy to nod before he pulled the fur-lined blindfold from his pocket and tied it over his head. He was asking a lot of both trust and patience when his sub was close to breaking again, but the payoff would be so much better in the end.

"I'm good with a shovel, but there's one thing I really excel at," said Derreck, double-checking to make sure Maddy's wrists were secure. There was a bit of slack, which he immediately tightened, holding Maddy higher on his weakening toes.

"You're being awfully chatty, Derreck," Maddy snarked right back at him, clenching his jaw tight. A bit of his attitude was slipping through the cracks, and Derreck recognized it for exactly what it was—a defense mechanism. He just had to wedge something in the crack and pry it open wide.

"I don't want you to be afraid. You are going through a delicate time, and I don't want to break you," said Derreck, a smirk easing over his lips when Maddy's jaw ticked and he clenched his fists tight.

Almost there. Sometimes fucking with someone's mind could break them more than fucking with their body.

"Let me know if it's too much," said Derreck, slamming the final nail in the invisible coffin.

Maddy snarled, jerking in his chains and rubbing his wrists raw. The muscles on his back danced as he fought the restraints, which was exactly what Derreck had wanted. He wanted Maddy to deny his own weakness so he could understand how truly powerful he was.

"Did you want down? Are you safewording?" asked Derrek softly, waiting for Maddy to finally crack.

"Do your worst, fucker." Maddy's voice was so deep and dark that Derreck hardly recognized it. He reached into his pocket, touching the plastic handle of the only implement that he needed.

"Gladly." He pulled the modified knife from his pocket, clicking the blade once so the tip barely peeked from the guard. Similar to an X-Acto knife, he could adjust the blade to different lengths and lock it in place so it wouldn't slip, no matter how hard he hit something with it.

The setting he had it on would only be deep enough to match a papercut, but it was still razor sharp. Of all the blades he could have used, it was probably the most dangerous in the wrong hands, but it happened to be Derreck's favorite way to fuck up his subs.

Maddy stiffened at the noise, hopefully recognizing the sound. Derreck didn't know what he had used to decorate his skin, but there were signs of more than one kind of implement.

Derreck locked the handle, ensuring that he couldn't do any more damage than he wanted, before he pressed the tip of the sharp edge to Maddy's skin, dragging it down along his back. It was a tease more than anything — and a promise.

"Please," said Maddy, his breath rushing out of him as the chains jingled and his feet sagged.

One of the best parts about the blindfold was how easy it was for Derreck to fuck with Maddy's mind. The scratch that hadn't even broken the skin would be amplified by his mind, tricking him into thinking that Derreck had actually cut him. The sweat trickling down his back would feel like blood running from the wounds.

"Too much?" asked Derreck, tracing the same pattern again, but pushing until the blade cut through the first layer of skin. There was no blood, and hardly any redness, but to Maddy, it would feel so much deeper.

"More, please." Maddy's voice had pitched, his beg earnest as his defenses were driven away. They didn't belong in the room to begin with.

Derreck pulled the knife away, loosening the guard and clicking it twice—out once, and the second click when he moved it back into its original position. But Maddy would have imagined it going out twice, the blade getting longer to drive deeper. He tightened the guard again, double and triple checking it before he pressed it to Maddy's skin.

"Just wondering what I'm going to write," said Derreck, scratching back and forth with rapid strokes. A tiny drop of blood welled up, quickly clotting before it could even drip. He scraped over and over along the same line, until the area was bright pink. "You can't erase it yourself back here, so I can do what I want with the canvas, and you won't be able to change it."

He dipped down, pushing hard enough that the plastic guard scraped over Maddy's skin. He knew Maddy would feel it, and think Derreck was carving so much deeper.

"Whatever you want," said Maddy, his voice trembling. Derreck knew he was close—so fucking close to slipping into subspace.

"I know," said Derreck, scratching and reddening Maddy's skin with painful strokes that would sting like one-hundred papercuts.

He moved to the next space before doing the same, playing with Maddy's mind until he hopefully couldn't tell up from down. Clicking the blade in and out several times, he toyed with him, giving him agony while barely making a scratch.

Pulling back, he retracted the blade all the way, testing the guard to make sure it was locked in place. With a grunt of effort, he slammed the guarded blade into a safe spot on Maddy's back, the hidden point still pressing into his flesh. Maddy jerked and cried out.

What did Maddy feel? He must've thought that Derreck had ruined him — brutalized him.

Derreck continued until he was buzzing with energy and Maddy was floating, his back decorated with a haze of pink that looked more like rug burn than hundreds of tiny cuts.

He grasped Maddy's hair before tugging his head back to whisper in his ear. The blindfold was soaked in sweat and tears and Maddy's cock dripped a steady stream of pre-cum onto the floor. He hadn't collapsed into the supports yet, but he looked as if he were barely hanging on.

"Enough?" asked Derreck, keeping his voice low. "Because I'm not done yet. Safeword now, because in a minute, you'll wish you had." He waited three beats before Maddy shook his head, his lips shaping into 'more', even though he made no sound.

Derreck let out a chuckle that was low and deep before letting his eyes drift shut. He had never flown so high before, and his sub was safely in subspace. Derreck's control was still absolute, as it always was, basking in the light of his sub.

He strolled to the cupboard, keeping his steps light before grabbing the bottle of isopropyl alcohol from the first-aid kit inside. Clint kept everything well stocked so Doms and subs could attend to their wounds as part of aftercare. Derreck distantly wondered if Clint had ever imagined his kits being used in a scene when he had purchased the super-economy size of alcohol.

"Last chance," said Derreck, slowly opening the lid to give Maddy time to safeword if he needed to. "What's your color?" he asked when Maddy didn't answer. They'd gone over the stoplight system as well as Maddy's specific safewords, just to make sure that they had a back-up system.

"Green. Please, Der." It was barely a whisper, but it was there.

Derreck tossed the lid toward the couch before he stepped closer to Maddy, pressing the mouth of the bottle to his skin. A tiny drop of liquid dripped out of the bottle, drawing a line down Maddy's back. He flinched harshly, sucking in a breath. Derreck throbbed, his entire being on fire.

"Scream for me." Derreck upended the bottle, pouring the alcohol down Maddy's back in a torrent that seeped into every little slice and dice. He could imagine one sting turning into thousands in every place that the blade had chafed raw.

Maddy screamed, his voice so loud that Derreck had to take a step back as his ears started to ring. He kept his hand steady, though, still pouring, even as alcohol splashed onto the floor. His eyes watered and he crinkled his nose as the fumes struck him in the face, but the circulating fan was quickly taking care of it and sucking the harshness away.

Writhing, and kicking, Maddy took every drop, screaming until his voice abruptly cut off and he went limp in the chains. He sagged, the manacles cutting deep bruises in his wrists.

Derreck dropped the bottle, not caring if the rest chugged down the drain or not. Blisters on his palms singing, he lifted Maddy before his shoulders could be damaged from the weight of his own body. Maddy was trembling harshly, his breathing low and slow. He was deep—so fucking deep that he would be there for a long time.

Derreck peeled the blindfold from Maddy's face, chucking it to the side before freeing Maddy's wrists from the manacles with the safety latch. Maddy clutched at him, his hands slipping over Derreck's skin. He was still conscious, but probably too overwhelmed to stand on his own.

Derreck had them on the couch with water pressed to Maddy's lips before the alcohol had dried. Tears streamed down Maddy's face, his stomach covered with cum from the orgasm that had struck the moment Derreck had broken him.

"Perfect," said Derreck, drawing his fingers through Maddy's hair as their heartbeats slowly evened out and their sweat began to cool. He was hard again, but it was easily ignored with the utter perfection of the scene behind them. He had never pushed someone so far, and if he had, they certainly wouldn't have writhed like Maddy had, or come untouched as they'd been overwhelmed.

Maddy snuggled close to him, sucking a spot on Derreck's neck as his trembling slowed and his breathing returned to normal. He was probably still floating, and his back had to be stinging, but it was so fucking perfect.

It was the first time that Derreck had ever considered filming a scene, so he could watch it over and over again and study Maddy's every reaction. Maybe he would bring it up with his sub in a few days.

"How bad is it?" asked Maddy after a long stretch of time where Derreck simply held him close, kissing the top of his head whenever he felt the need. "Will I need stitches?" He didn't sound upset or angry at all, the practicality of his questions soothing Derreck's worry.

"There are no marks," said Derreck, grinning at Maddy's wide-eyed surprise. His jaw ached from every smile Maddy had dragged out of him. "Come see." He lifted Maddy from the couch, heading for a mirror along one side of the room. He hadn't used it, but maybe he would next time so he could watch Maddy's face as he fell apart. He turned Maddy in his arms, lowering his feet to the ground with their chests together.

"Look for yourself."

Chapter Fifteen

Maddy

It had to be a trick or a play of the light. His back should have been in ribbons. He clutched Derreck, breathing in the scent of his sweat and the burning bite of alcohol. His eyes watered, but he blinked away the tears.

He'd felt every drag of the blade as it pierced him over and over, sending him higher than ever before. When the alcohol had touched him, there had been a second when he had thought his heart might explode, it had been beating so hard and fast.

Blinking in the mirror, he squinted against the bright light reflected back at him from the overhead lights. He glared at the reflection of his back, searching for anything. But there was nothing. *Nothing.*

He blinked again, his mind taking longer than usual to process everything he was seeing — or not seeing. His lips and jaw ached from sucking the spot on Derreck's neck, but he wanted it in his mouth again, so he could taste his Dom. He wanted Derreck's cock in his mouth, too, but only to hold it there. He couldn't fathom dragging up any desire for sex. His body and mind were completely astonished and blank.

And there was *nothing*.

"I felt it," he said, reaching back to touch the plain of his back. Derreck moved them closer to the mirror, supporting him with every step. His knees wobbled at the movement, barely able to hold half of his weight.

"You felt what I wanted you to feel," said Derreck, drawing his fingers down Maddy's spine. The touch sent fire along his nerves, pushing an unexpected groan through his lips.

On closer inspection, his back *was* red, almost like a rash that extended from his shoulders to his lower back. There was no blood, but it throbbed and ached as if there should have been.

He tucked his head under Derreck's chin, taking a deep breath before he found the same spot with his mouth. It was reddened through the natural tint of Derreck's skin, and the sight of it did something to Maddy — something possessive and dark.

The moment the alcohol had touched him, sinking into every slice that his mind had created, the strangest surge of fear had consumed his thoughts. Derreck could have left him hanging from his wrists, and there would have been nothing Maddy could have done about it.

He should have. Everyone else in Maddy's life had. Even when his parents tried to understand, they still backed away from him, looking at him like he was some sort of demon when they caught a glimpse of his designs. They pulled away from what they didn't understand.

But Derreck…? Derreck had released him from the chains, cradling him like he was the most precious thing. The fear had sizzled away to nothing the moment they were on the couch, and Maddy had latched onto Derreck's neck because…he still wasn't sure why.

He'd just needed to leave his mark. Derreck was *his*.

"Things were intense," said Derreck, lifting Maddy and carrying him back to the couch. He was so gentle, making sure not to tug too hard at where Maddy was latched onto him. That in itself filled his belly with something warm.

Maddy nodded, sucking Derreck's skin back into his mouth when it tugged free. He couldn't let go yet. The high was fading, leaving him lost in a way that he hadn't expected. Where was he supposed to go from here? Not home. Not to an empty house that was filled with nothing but childhood memories of hiding.

He didn't want to hide anymore. This was who he was, and no one else was ever going to tell him otherwise again. He had tried so hard to fit inside the tiny box that his family and job had built for him. When the box had first burst, he'd been lost without the walls to keep him sane. But things were finally starting to make sense again.

"You okay?" asked Maddy, slowly releasing Derreck's neck. He stared at the spot that was flushed deep purple from his attentions. It was the only mark on Derreck's body, and it was *his*.

Derreck nodded, letting out a low grunt that Maddy was only able to interpret because of the time they had spent together. He had a feeling that most people were afraid of Derreck, whether it was because of his height, his obvious strength or his gloomy expression. Maddy had been one of those people until he'd learned how to pay attention.

Derreck's lips could say a lot about his thoughts from the way they went tight when he was stressed or upset or the brief uptick when he was pleased. After Maddy had tasted his lips, he could hardly bring himself to look away.

"Did you want to stay here for a bit, or can I buy you a drink?" asked Maddy, grinning at Derreck's surprise.

"You asking me out?"

From Derreck's tone, it was probably supposed to have been a joke, but Maddy frowned as the words sank in. What they had wasn't labeled, and he didn't really want a label, either. No more boxes for the foreseeable future.

"You know you're mine," said Maddy, biting at his lip as he stared at Derreck's purpling bruise. It wasn't a question — not really.

He tried to ignore Derreck's flinch, but it cut him all the way to his core. "I'm sorry. I thought… I don't what I thought." Maddy scrambled to mentally recover as the floor dropped out from under his feet and his chest went tight.

Why did I have to ruin the best thing I've ever had?

"Maddy." Derreck gripped his chin, tilting it up from where his gaze had dropped. "I feel the same, but sometimes after scenes our feelings can get messed up. I don't want you saying anything you'll regret later."

"Oh, that's a relief," said Maddy, letting out a laugh as he eased off Derreck's lap. Derreck reached for him, and Maddy threaded their hands together, breathing deep as his legs wobbled. "I thought maybe you didn't want me anymore. But you're wrong. I won't regret this. I've felt this way since the first time you touched me, and it's been getting stronger ever since. It just took me a while to figure it out."

Maddy leveled Derreck with a stare, gazing into his almond eyes. "You're mine, Derreck."

Derreck gripped his hand, tugging Maddy until he was back in his lap, his naked thighs stretched over Derreck's clothed ones. His eyes were searching, probably trying to find any hint of doubt or insincerity in Maddy's eyes. *Derreck is just as broken as I am, and just as easily shattered.*

"I won't run. You're mine from now until you kick me to the curb." He placed a single kiss to Derreck's lips, leaning back before it could become more. He wanted to take his time before he had sex with Derreck again and give him everything he deserved.

"Buy me that drink," said Derreck, a smile curving the edge of his lips. "But just to warn you, I'm a Jäger man."

"Uh, gross." Maddy stuck out his tongue, twisting his face. He could barely tolerate most hard liquors, and usually preferred a sweet fruit wine. He was even hoping to make some homemade wine from his elderberries if the birds didn't get to them first.

He grabbed his shirt from the arm of the couch, pausing to feel the weight of it in his hands. It was heavy, just like all the shirts he possessed. He could have gone with something thinner, but he hated the way they hugged his body. He hadn't wanted to be seen.

He took a deep breath, pulling at the sleeve until a thread started to unravel. *No more boxes.* He tossed it back to the couch, tugging his pants on instead. He didn't think anyone would be cool if he went completely naked, and he had no desire to be *that* exposed.

The bare flesh of his arms tingled, so unprotected that even the movement of the fan had him breaking out in a shiver. He ran a hand down his arm, skimming over the bumps and ridges of his designs as his stomach started to twist. *I can do this.*

Derreck gave him a blank look that lasted a few seconds before he turned and headed for the door. He was either oblivious to Maddy's lack of clothing or he had been telling the truth when he'd said that Maddy's marks didn't matter. "I'll clean up the room later. Clint won't let anyone else in here tonight, anyway."

Keeping from wrapping his arms around his body was a practice in stubbornness as well as perseverance. He glanced back at the door a few times as they slowly moved from the hall toward the bar. At the edge of the seating area he paused, taking a deep breath that refused to fill his lungs.

"Whatever you're thinking...don't," said Derreck, running a hand down Maddy's spine and lighting up his nerves as the invisible cuts stung from the sweat on Derreck's palm. The sensation edged the fear further to the outskirts of his mind. "I may be yours, but you're mine, too, and I take care of my things." Derreck's voice dropped into a growl.

Maddy got the message loud and clear. He wasn't doing this alone. He was with someone so much stronger than him.

He'd held onto the small hope that the club had cleared out while they'd been playing in the *Wet* room, but it was smashed to bits when he picked up the murmur of conversation. The club never seemed to be empty, and the people that came and went seemed to keep the strangest hours. Maddy was starting to wonder if Clint ever slept.

He reached for Derreck's hand, squeezing it tight as they rounded into the main bar area. The lights were lower than he remembered, probably a direct result of the hour. Every step toward darkness had them fading lower, giving the appearance that it was far from five in the afternoon.

The hub of conversation didn't pause, and neither did the clink of glasses as a group of couples at one booth made a toast. No one looked their way until they passed under one of the few spotlights, and even then, it was only to glance at Derreck and give a quick nod. Maddy's heart pounded, his palms slicker than the condensation on their glasses.

Eventually, a few people glanced his way, their gazes curious. There was none of the shock, horror or judgment that he'd expected. It was like opening the stopper in a tub and watching a lifetime of self-doubt wash away. He squeezed Derreck's hand, shooting him a smile.

All the booths were taken, so they gravitated back to the bar. Clint didn't even look up at them as they approached, rushing back and forth to try to get drinks out faster than his two hands could handle. The man was running off his feet, and there was no sign of any help.

"You smell like a pharmacy, Derreck." A man in the next stool grumbled as he curled over his glass. There were a few watery inches in the glass, the ice cubes long since melted and the condensation dried.

"Henley." Derreck grunted, turning a light glare on the man. "Still no luck?"

Maddy stiffened, his nose scrunching. All the alcohol had evaporated, but the smell remained. He sniffed his shoulder, his eyes burning as he coughed. He really did smell like a pharmacy.

Henley grumbled, slouching lower in his chair until his chin touched the bar top. His gaze flickered Maddy's way, his eyes going wide as they swept up and down his naked chest.

No more boxes. They don't matter. Squeezing Derreck's hand, he steadied his breathing. His heart pounded away, oblivious to his mantra.

"Are you sure you're taken, gorgeous?" asked Henley, leaning across Derreck and tipping his stool until only a single leg remained on the ground. "I'm looking for a mutt, but you are fucking beautiful."

Derreck grabbed Henley by the back of the neck with his free hand, slamming his face down into the bar top. A few glasses jingled and the conversation next to them went quiet. It hopefully wasn't hard enough to break Henley's nose, but it probably smarted something fierce.

"Ow, fuck, Der, I didn't mean anything by it," said Henley, flailing his arms as Derreck rubbed his face into the wood like he was rubbing a dog's face in its accidental mess.

"He's mine," said Derreck, his voice a deep growl. He jerked Henley upright before lowering him back onto his stool. The hovering stool legs slammed back onto the hardwood floor. Henley rubbed the back of his freed neck, a scowl on his lips.

"Any chance you'd share?" he asked, somehow oblivious to the murder in Derreck's eyes. Even Maddy was getting a little worried — worried and turned on.

"Not unless Maddy's interested," said Derreck, gripping Maddy's hand tight, which was the complete opposite of his nonchalant words.

"No, thank you," said Maddy, trying to flag Clint down and utterly failing. He wasn't doing a very good job of buying Derreck a drink.

"Fair enough," said Henley, giving them both one last look. "But I had to try. I'll be around if you ever change your mind." He slipped off his stool, heading toward the door.

Attempting to flag Clint down a second and third time was just as unsuccessful. Maddy bit back a growl, glaring at the empty glasses behind the bar as Derreck grinned.

"You sure you want to buy me a drink?" he teased, just as Clint swept past them again, balancing a tray with about ten drinks on it. "We might be here all night."

"Not if I have anything to say about it," said Maddy, slipping from his stool and rounding the bar. He would buy Derreck a drink, even if he had to make it himself.

Mixology was like riding a bike with thirty-seven finicky gears and brakes that didn't quite work. He knew the liquors and the recipes, but getting it right was the real trick.

Memories rushed back as he examined the stash of liquors, breathing deep until their scents hit him all at once. There was a stash of large glasses as well as small shots under the bar, and a chest of ice that had been left open and was slowly melting. He slid the lid shut, turning to wash his hands in the sink. His back flexed from the move, a hiss pushing its way through his lips.

When he turned back, Derreck was staring at him, a question in his eyes.

"I'll be right back," said Maddy, heading to the end of the bar where a very thirsty-looking woman sat twirling her straw. She took one glance at him, her gaze flitting over his designs before settling back on his face.

"What can I get you?" asked Maddy, still looking around the bar and cataloguing everything in sight. It was basic, but he could probably make a few of the fancier things from scratch. As long as no one ordered something ridiculous, he would be set.

"I was just about to give up," she said, a laugh on her lips. "Clint's got his hands full, but can you make me a Bloody Mary?"

"No problem." He ducked down to where he'd spied a tiny fridge, cursing when he only found the basic ingredients with nothing premade. Blood Mary's were a bitch to make from scratch.

Grabbing all the ingredients from memory, he tossed them into the blender, chewing on his lip as he tried to recall the amount of horseradish he used to use. Working in a bar on his way through college had been an eye-opening experience, but it had also been a long-ass time ago.

With his parent's money he could have had a free ride all the way through his education, but he had turned their offer down. His education was something that he'd had to earn for himself because it had been his first real chance at freedom. He hadn't let anyone take that away from him.

He circled the bar again. His memory bike was looking a bit rusty. *An old piece of shit with no celery salt. Oh, there it is.* He tossed some in, hitting the power button on the blender and preparing the glass. He fished out a pickled bean from the fridge, putting it in the glass instead of celery, before passing it over to the woman.

"I think I got it right," he said. "Let me know if it's not okay, and I'll buy you something else...on me."

He turned to the next person, a middle-aged guy who was with a lady who had hair so blonde it was nearly white. "What can I get you?"

He worked his way down the bar, doubling back once when someone new, and apparently desperate, pushed to the front. The majority of the drinks were virgin cocktails, probably for the couples that hoped to play later, but a few had actual liquor in them. Maddy made note of each of them, making sure he could inform Clint when he came back.

When he finally slid in front of Derreck again, the man was grinning, each of his white teeth on display as Maddy poured him his Jäger. "I still don't know how you can drink this stuff," he said, grabbing a wine bottle from the fridge for himself. He would pay for the whole bottle if Clint was upset with him for opening it.

He took a sniff of the dark liquid, swirling it in the glass once before he took a sip. *Dry. Really dry.* He swirled the glass a few more times, sliding the bottle back into the fridge.

Turning to exit from behind the bar, he stopped dead when he saw Clint standing there. He was taller up close, but not nearly as tall as Derreck. His arms were still thick, though, his biceps flexing as he crossed his arms and tapped his foot on the ground.

"What are you doing?" he asked, motioning up and down the bar to the line of prepared drinks. The lady was back for another Bloody Mary, but otherwise, everyone appeared to be happy.

"Uh, helping? Sorry," said Maddy, chewing his lip as he looked back to Derreck who was still grinning. *At least I'm not in trouble.* "They were thirsty, and you were busy, so I thought I could help. Sorry if I crossed a line." He went to slip past Clint, but the man blocked his path.

"I heard you are looking for a job," said Clint, eyeing him up at down. To his credit, he never paused on Maddy's marks. "Is this your job application?"

"Umm..." Maddy trailed off, looking around the place. He tried to remember why he'd left his bar job during college. Drunken frat boys, their puking girlfriends and the gay-bashers were three of the top reasons. Other than that, it had been a kind of fun social experiment, as he recalled.

"Maybe for now? I'm not sure about long-term, but it would come with one condition," said Maddy, looking back to Derreck. "Every member has to have a background check before they get their card, then on a yearly basis after that. One of your members—I don't know if he is one anymore—is a convicted sex offender and an ex-con. I wouldn't feel right working here knowing that the patrons could be taking advantage of their partners."

"What? Fucking who?" Clint growled, looking at Derreck for confirmation.

"Phil. I work— I mean, I worked with him. I did some digging as part of my job and was able to find that out pretty easily." Maddy twiddled with his wine glass, swirling the liquid around. "He lied on his application in a government office, so it's not a stretch to think he did the same here."

Clint took a step forward before he held out his hand. After a beat of hesitation Maddy took it, shaking once. "You're fucking hired."

Chapter Sixteen

Derreck

"My place or yours?" asked Derreck, as they stepped out into the late afternoon sun. It had finally, *finally* stopped raining after a solid week of river-bursting downpours. Derreck's work was postponed another few days because, surprisingly enough, people didn't want to bury their loved ones at the bottom of a puddle.

"Mine?" asked Maddy, squinting at Derreck as the sun caught his eyes. His nose scrunched up, and it was so fucking adorable that Derreck had to stop himself from ruffling Maddy's hair.

He'd put his shirt back on as Derreck had scrubbed the playroom, erasing their presence as well as their germs before they'd left. Sometimes, subs who wanted to volunteer would clean the rooms, but it was usually left up to the couple that had used it last.

It was just another thing that fell under consent, as well as a few health codes. The next couple to use the room hadn't consented to step in a pile of jizz that had crusted to the floor.

Maddy slipped into his car, which was parked a few spots ahead of Derreck's, giving him a quick wave before he pulled away from the curb. The car's paint caught the light, momentarily blinding Derreck as he stared after him.

He knew the way by heart, but he still checked every sign as he made his way to Maddy's, falling behind until his Mustang was slammed in the afternoon traffic. It wasn't that he was stalking Maddy, but he'd definitely made himself aware of his sub's area of town. It was so different from his own that it nearly made bile rise in his throat. The perfectly trimmed grass, that smelled of pesticides and fertilizer, longed to be fucked up with his shovel.

He tried not to have a problem with the neighborhood, but it was difficult.

He could depend on his neighbors for almost anything. A cup of sugar? No problem. An alibi? Sure. His frequent babysitting duties put a few people in his debt, even if he had no intentions of ever cashing in — except for the sugar, because drinking coffee black should have been illegal.

He pulled into Maddy's driveway, glancing at the neighbor's house as the curtains moved. People needed a fucking day job on this side of town. Luckily Maddy was waiting for him on the porch, rocking from his toes to his heels with a smile on his lips. His shirt cuffs had fallen down from when he had rolled them up before they had left, the fabric covering the designs on his pale skin.

Some people may have called them ugly or twisted, but Derreck wasn't some people. They were almost desperate in their beauty, and they were a mark of Maddy's strength. No matter how deep the wounds of his mind were, they always healed when Maddy laid them bare.

"Your neighbor's going to call the cops if I ever show up here when no one's around," said Derreck, stepping from the pristine cement sidewalk to the plush indoor-outdoor carpeting on the porch. His shoes weren't fancy enough for it.

"I don't think so," said Maddy, glancing up at the house in question, and apparently knowing exactly who Derreck was talking about. "She's friends with my mother, but she's harmless." He waved as the curtain moved again. The woman on the other side of the window balked, pulling the curtains shut and dropping the blinds.

Cupping Maddy's chin with his hand, Derreck moved in close until Maddy was pinned to the pillar of his own house. His eyes were alight, a smile on his lips as Derreck leaned down and pressed their lips together. Dragging his tongue over the seam of Maddy's mouth, he pushed his way inside, tasting every inch of him until they were both panting and hard. Maddy wrapped his arms around Derreck's neck, pulling him closer as their kiss pushed past the boundaries of acceptable for the public eye.

Derreck had no qualms about public affection because, as far as he was concerned, everyone should know that Maddy belonged to him.

"How about now?" asked Derreck, sucking a spot on Maddy's neck as his sub let out a gasp. "She gonna call the cops and report that someone is taking advantage of you? Or should I just keep going until she does?"

Maddy gripped Derreck's hair, pulling him down harder until Derreck grazed his teeth against Maddy's pulse, sucking the salty skin into his mouth. Maddy writhed beneath him, like they were in a bed and not on the front porch of his house.

"I want..." Maddy's eyes fluttered shut and he shook his head as if he were trying to clear his thoughts. "Can I have you Derreck? I mean, with me inside? I've been dreaming about what you would feel like wrapped around my cock and how tight you would be for me." His face flushed as he asked, his nails scratching against Derreck's scalp.

Derreck couldn't hold back his shudder or stop the way his cock throbbed in his pants, leaking pre-cum all over the inside of his zipper. It had been a long time since someone had been inside of him like that — almost long enough for him to forget the way he loved to be stretched open slow and soft, and so different from how he liked to give it.

He nodded, swallowing anything he might have said. Maddy would already be nervous enough without a list of likes and dislikes. And as much as it terrified him, he trusted Maddy more than the last person he'd been with like that, and he had willingly given in to *them*.

With one last look at the neighbor's house, Maddy took his hand, entwining their fingers before tugging him through the door. His stomach fluttered more than it probably should have. It was a fuck, not prom night.

But it was more than just a fuck. And it was their first time together without Derreck in complete control. Hopefully it was the first time of many, unless one of them fucked it up horribly.

If anyone would fuck it up, it would have been Derreck. He was the experienced one who should have been taking the lead, but it was Maddy leading him up into the bedroom.

Tugging his hand free, he grabbed the back of Maddy's neck, walking them the rest of the way to the bed before he pushed Maddy down to his knees. He went easily, trust and adoration in his gaze.

"You might be fucking me, but you won't be topping me. Are we clear?" Derreck growled, as he finally realized the source of his hesitation. He couldn't submit to anyone — not even Maddy.

"Like, I can't be on top of you?" asked Maddy, tilting his head in confusion. "That's okay. That would probably look a little strange anyway, like a Chihuahua humping a Great Dane or something."

"No, that's not what I meant," said Derreck, stifling his laugh. Maybe Henley had been onto something if Maddy's first thought was that they would look like a bunch of horny dogs. Besides, Maddy wasn't that vertically challenged. He was just seventy pounds or so short in the muscle department.

"You can fuck me however you like. You can even fuck my mouth if you want, but I will always be the one in control. Don't fight for it because you won't win. I'll have you pinned so fast that you won't even be able to scream, and once I do, I'll fucking destroy you." Taking Maddy's hair in his hand, he gripped it hard, forcing his face down into the bed sheets before releasing him.

Shuddering, Maddy let out a deep breath, his pupils blown wide as he turned to look at Derreck. "That is the hottest thing I've ever heard." He closed his eyes. "I still can't believe you...and this." He motioned to his cock that was obviously tenting his pants. "I didn't even realize that I was so broken until I met you."

"You weren't broken, and you still aren't," said Derreck, petting Maddy's hair and soothing his scalp. "You were just waiting for someone to finally understand you. Thank you for letting me be that person."

Derreck stepped away, circling to the other side of the bed to give himself a moment to breathe and think. Even though they lived on opposite sides of town, Maddy's bedroom was startlingly similar to his own. Maybe that was the reason he didn't care which place they went to. It was only Maddy's presence that mattered.

"Come here," said Derreck, pleased that Maddy was still on his knees. His sub was still new to his world, but he followed directions so well that Derreck didn't even have to ask him.

Easing down onto the bed, he waited until Maddy slowly rose, pulling his shirt over his head before he crawled across the bed. Maddy leaned over him, his gaze searching, before he finally brought their lips together. The touch was teasing and soft, and probably the opposite of what Maddy was craving.

Derreck pulled back, shaking his head. "You don't have to be afraid that you'll break me," he said, cupping Maddy's chin before biting his lower lip and soothing it with his tongue at Maddy's gasp.

"How do I know if I've gone too far?" asked Maddy, his forehead furrowing as he sat back on his heels, corralled by Derreck's legs on either side of him.

Derreck tilted his chin up, forcing Maddy to hold his gaze. "Part of the fun is pushing boundaries to see what will happen. I'm not asking you to be a brat, but I'm saying that if you push too far, you'll know — and I don't think you'll mind." Derreck brought their lips together, plunging into Maddy's mouth and tasting every bit of him.

Maddy let out a low groan, sliding his hands to the back of Derreck's head and threading through the short, curly strands. Maddy pressed his lips harder against him, tilting his head and moving over Derreck's body, taking the position of power.

Derreck gripped Maddy's ass, kneading the globes and spreading his cheeks wide. Maddy's pants were too tight to be able to trace his seam through the fabric, but the threat was there, all the same. He wanted to know how far his sub would push him. He wanted to know what Maddy really wanted.

Sometimes easy submission wasn't all that it was cracked up to be. Sometimes a little fight made the victory all-the-more worth it.

Maddy growled, grinding against him and pushing his hard cock along the plane of Derreck's six-pack. He was smaller than Derreck, but fucking mighty and throbbing, even through his pants as their passion ignited.

"Can I taste your cock, please?" asked Maddy, his eyes heavy and filled with need.

Derreck nodded, spreading his legs wide and leaning back against the pillow as Maddy when straight for his zipper. He had barely burst from the too-tight seam before Maddy's lips closed over the head of his cock, his cheeks hollowing out from the force of his suck.

"Fuck," said Derreck, losing control for a split second and jerking his hips. Maddy gagged as Derreck hit the back of his throat, convulsing around his cock exquisitely.

"Soon," said Maddy, drawing back for a deep breath and to clear his throat. "Soon I'll fuck you, baby."

Derreck's hand twitched against the bed at the endearment. If it had been anyone else except Maddy, they would have been face down, ass up, with a red handprint across their cheek. With Maddy, it was barely tolerable. *Barely.*

Revenge is sweet. He kept his hips still until Maddy dropped his mouth over his cock again, then he bucked up, sinking into Maddy's throat as he spluttered. He put one hand on the back of Maddy's head, holding him there with his cock just a touch too deep for comfort.

"If you need to safeword but your mouth is occupied, pinch me instead. It works the same way. You pinch me and I stop, *baby*." He growled the endearment, relishing it as Maddy's eyes went wide.

For three long beats, he held himself there, until he finally pulled back, allowing Maddy a quick breath before he pushed inside again, going just a hair deeper. Maddy's throat was just as tight as his ass, but Derreck knew that he could do a lot of damage if he wasn't careful. Maddy was still inexperienced, and although his ass was getting better at accepting him, his throat would take longer.

Derreck had never met a man who could take him to the base, and from the tears in Maddy's eyes, he wouldn't be that man, either. It didn't bother him. The effort Maddy put in made the shallow thrusts worth it.

Lying back on the bed, he sank his hands into Maddy's hair, using his grip as a handle to pull him up and down his cock. He moved slow enough that he would be able to last for a long time—long enough for Maddy's jaw to hopefully start to ache and his tears to spill over onto his cheeks.

Maddy blinked, his eyes watery and red as he stared up at Derreck.

"Too much?" Derreck pulled back until only the tip of his cock was between Maddy's lips.

"No." Maddy shook his head, his voice hoarse and fucked out. Derreck gripped his hair harder, until he saw Maddy's cock jerk within his pants.

"Get naked," said Derreck, lying back on the bed so he could watch the fabric slide from Maddy's skin. Each morsel was revealed, so perfect and pale, even with the writhing designs that marked Maddy's upper body. They really were beautiful, especially when they stood out pale as Maddy flushed pink.

"You're still dressed," said Maddy, dropping his gaze to Derreck's cock, which was the only thing that was exposed. Maddy opened and closed his hands a few times before reaching for Derreck. He blinked once before dropping his hands back to his sides.

"Go ahead," said Derreck, lifting his hips as Maddy immediately dove at his pants, stripping them from his legs with a few jerks. He paused, staring down at Derreck's exposed legs before running his hands up and down the limbs. The contrast of his pale fingertips against Derreck's legs only made him throb harder.

Maddy dipped his hands under Derreck's shirt, smoothing his palms over the plane of his abdomen. Even after all this time, Maddy was still hesitant, taking his time as stared at Derreck's face. *What is he thinking?*

"Push me," said Derreck, his infinite patience wearing thin. "Fucking try it." It was a dare as well as a command.

Maddy curled his hands into claws, raking his nails down Derreck's belly and carving into his skin. Hissing, Derreck, humped into the touch, his cock bobbing in the air as Maddy scratched him again.

He hadn't taken Maddy for a cougar—more of a biter if he had been a betting man. It was a good thing that he wasn't, because Maddy had proven him wrong at every turn.

"Come on, kitty cat. You can do better," said Derreck, spreading his legs as Maddy growled at him before raking his nails down his inner thighs. It smarted, but not enough that Derreck couldn't smother his grimace with a grin, humping so his cock bobbed again.

Dropping down, Maddy sucked Derreck's cock into his mouth again, but this time he dragged his teeth along the underside, sending a shot of real pain straight to Derreck's balls. Derreck growled, fisting his hands in the sheets to hold himself back.

Control. Control. He whispered over and over in his head until it became a reality. He needed to see how far Maddy would go.

Maddy popped off and turned his head into the cleft where Derreck's thigh met his groin, his breath tickling over the sensitive skin there. Derreck's hair stood on end, a shiver going through his body as Maddy tongued one of his most sensitive spots.

He had no problem with spreading his legs wide and bending his knees so Maddy would have access to anything that he wanted. As much as he wanted to reach out and take control, he let Maddy go, his tongue dragging over the nooks of his skin.

What is he tasting? It had been a long time since Derreck had let anyone get close enough that he wondered that. He'd showered before he'd scrambled to meet Maddy at the bar, but he'd fucked Maddy since and had sweat through the most epic scene of his life. His taste was bound to be strong.

Maddy hummed, mouthing over the bottom of one ass cheek before he spread Derreck wider, plastering himself to the bed as he dipped lower. When the moist pressure of his tongue swept over Derreck's hole, he let out a high gasp, a sound that was so foreign that at first, he'd doubted it had come from him.

He should have grabbed Maddy to return the favor, or simply to pin him to take back his control that was slowly slipping, but he couldn't. As Maddy probed deeper with his tongue, it opened a long-closed door of desire that filled him to the brim and beyond.

He grabbed the backs of his knees, bringing his legs to his chest to give Maddy better access. Maddy spread him, his tongue pushing deeper until it was joined by a probing finger.

Maddy had been inside him before with more than one finger, but it had never felt so good. Maddy had never pushed his tongue inside along with his finger, licking and sucking as if Derreck were a delicious treat. He rolled his eyes back and Derreck felt himself slip a little deeper as he gave in to the pleasure, whimpering as his prostate was teased.

He'd always been sensitive, and luckily, he had long enough fingers that he could play with himself, but it was always better with someone else. It was the same way that Maddy's pain apparently felt better when it was Derreck's hand providing it instead of his own.

When Maddy slipped in a second finger and the ache of the stretch hit him, Derreck cried out. He'd been topped before, but not with such a gentle persuasion that his entire being wanted to unravel.

Maddy would take care of him. He just knew it. And if he didn't, then Derreck would shatter, like he'd always known he would have eventually.

"I've got you, baby," said Maddy as he tongued at Derreck's entrance, slipping in a third finger so he was stretched so wide that he could hardly bare it. Maddy moved slow, never pushing him beyond what he could handle. *How does he know exactly what I can take?*

"Nnngh." Derreck arched into the touch, gripping the sheets so hard that they would probably start ripping soon. He wanted to ask for more, but he bit down on his tongue. He would *not* beg.

His cock leaked onto his abdomen, a pool of pre-cum dripping slowly into his belly button. When Maddy peeked up from between Derreck's thighs, he must've caught sight of it because he dove at Derreck's navel and licked his pre-cum into his mouth like it was a second course of dessert.

"You taste good," said Maddy, sucking a line down Derreck's cock before tonguing at his balls. He sucked one into his mouth and Derreck let out a groan as wet heat surrounded him. His hole ached around the three fingers inside him, but he tightened himself, just to feel it.

"You feel good, too," said Maddy, slipping from Derreck's entrance and leaving him open and empty. He'd never ached to be filled, but he could no longer deny it, not when he could barely keep the plea behind his lips.

Maddy scrambled from the bed, rummaging through his bedside drawer as Derreck struggled to control his breathing. His legs slipped from his grasp until his feet were planted on the bed. His skin prickled from the chill as Maddy's heat slowly dissipated, the drying trail from his tongue like ice.

"Derreck."

Derreck snapped his eyes back open. *When did I close them?* Maddy was staring at him with concern, a strip of condoms and a bottle of lube in his grasp. The lube was completely full, the plastic seal still wrapped around the mouth of the bottle.

"You're shivering," said Maddy, his hand like molten lava against Derreck's skin as another shudder racked his body. He fought his urge to close his legs, knowing it was ridiculous. He wasn't a virgin — or even close to one — so what the fuck was wrong with him?

You've never let your sub fuck you before. He hadn't even come close. His subs had always been under his full control. They had never been inside of him, not that he would have denied them if their relationships had been remotely sexual. He had no problem being the giver or the taker, as long as he had control.

And that was it. He had no control. It had slipped through his grasp, despite his threats and warnings to Maddy.

"I need..." He trailed off, looking to the lube and condoms in Maddy's hands. "You bought those just for us."

Maddy nodded with a soft smile, dropping the lube to the bed and moving up Derreck's body until their chests were pressed together. Every touch sent a shock up Derreck's nerve endings, until he was no longer freezing but sweating on the bed, his cock hard and dripping.

He could picture Maddy at the drug store, staring at an aisle that he'd never bothered to look down before.

Had he stood there reading the back of every bottle to make sure he got the right kind? And how did he know which box of condoms to get? It was certainly not one size fits all.

"I got them online, from one of the stores that my online friend recommended. The lube had a whole bunch of reviews that said it lasted a long time and it's extra slippery, which is apparently the best for anal sex." Maddy grabbed the lube, turning the bottle around to read the tiny printing on the back.

"It's warming, too, which is supposed to help with any aches. I didn't want you to hurt after. And the condoms? Well, they had a size guide because it's been fifteen years since I've had to even look at condoms, and at that time, I still had the ones my mom gave me after she figured I would start having sex." He shuddered, before reaching for the strip of condoms.

"I think I'll be able to get it on okay. I've never actually worn one, though, but I watched a video." Maddy flushed, as if he'd just realized that he'd been rambling on about lube and condoms seconds before he was about to get laid.

Derreck snorted out a laugh, grabbing the lube and reading the label. It was the good kind—the one he'd splurged on when he'd realized that Maddy and him might become more than Dom and sub. The condoms? Well, he was pretty sure that Maddy had accidentally gotten the cherry-flavored ones, but there was only one way to find out.

"Lie back," said Derreck, easing Maddy down to the bed. His cock had softened as he spoke, but a few quick tugs had it coming back to life. Derreck gripped the base hard, waiting until he could feel the pulse in his hand before he slapped Maddy's hip.

Maddy squirmed, his hips coming off the bed when Derreck pinched him, digging his nails into Maddy's soft skin that was already blooming red. Derreck poked the spot right next to Maddy's cock, where it was bound to be as sensitive as Derreck was. Grabbing a bit of tense flesh, he pinched, twisting it until Maddy went rock hard under his hand, his breath a pleading moan.

Releasing Maddy's cock, he grabbed the condoms, tugging one off the strip and opening the foil packet. The tang of sweet cherries layered over the scent of latex, making it slightly more tolerable than spermicidal lube.

"It smells funny," said Maddy, leaning up on his elbows to stare at Derreck as he carefully rolled the condom down Maddy's cock. It was a good fit for him, but how had Maddy managed to measure himself?

"It's flavored," said Derreck, grinning as Maddy's tilted his head to the side in confusion.

"Why would they flavor a condom? I'm not going to eat it," said Maddy, the cutest dimple appearing between his eyebrows as his confusion deepened.

"I might." Derreck slid his lips down Maddy's covered cock, taking him to the base and sucking as hard as he could. The head tickled the back of his throat uncomfortably, but he lifted the corner of his lips to suppress the gag. Cherry flavor was only good for two things, and condoms was one of those. Cough syrup was not.

"Oh." Maddy bucked his hips, pushing himself a touch past Derreck's comfort zone. "I didn't think of that, but *oh*."

"Hmm-m." Derreck pulled back, licking his lips to get the rest of the sweetness. He would have rather eaten the saltiness of Maddy's cock. "My mouth or my ass? It's your choice."

"Oh...shit." Instead of answering, Maddy cupped Derreck's chin, pulling him up until their lips slid together. He pushed his tongue into Derreck's mouth as he hooked his leg over his hip, using his newfound agility to flip them.

Derreck sank into the cool sheets as Maddy settled on top of him. His weight was easier to take than he had expected. It wasn't the weight—*not really*. It was the idea of being pinned beneath his lover that had him shivering again.

"I'll take care of you, baby," said Maddy, as if sensing the resurgence of Derreck's unease. He slid his hands along Derreck's arms until he could entangle their fingers. Moving Derreck's hands over his head, he pinned them to the bed, his meager grip the only thing keeping Derreck stationary.

What am I doing? Derreck should have broken the grip. Hell, he should have stopped Maddy the moment that he'd pinned him. He took a deep breath, his heart pounding.

When Maddy released him, Derreck kept his hands above his head as if they were still bound. Even as Maddy peeled the plastic off the lube bottle and slathered a generous dollop over Derreck's hole and his own cock, he stayed still. He sank deeper, letting himself enjoy something he never thought would be possible.

"Tell me to stop and I'll stop," said Maddy, offering Derreck one last out.

He couldn't hold back his whimper as Maddy breached him, sliding slowly inside and glancing over his prostate that was even more sensitive than usual.

M.C. Roth

Derreck had taken bigger cocks before, but not for a long time. He didn't even know how it had been possible, when he felt so close to breaking.

"Wow, baby," said Maddy, finally settling his hips against Derreck's ass. "You feel so good, and I'm going to come way too fast." His hips were already jerking, as if he couldn't even help himself. "You're so tight around me, so hot and so good." Maddy's eyes rolled back as his grip went fierce.

"Ah." Derreck whimpered as Maddy slipped past his prostate again, lighting up his nerves and bringing tears to his eyes. He wasn't crying — definitely not — but his cheeks were damp all the same.

Maddy moved so slowly, so carefully, as if he could break Derreck if he thrust too hard, shattering the delicate china of his body. But his inexperience showed in the way that he pushed in just a bit faster than he pulled out, rushing to bury himself deep as instinct warred with his other emotions.

"Oh, baby, are you close?" asked Maddy, his breath shuddering as his pace picked up, gentle and soft none the less.

Derreck shook his head, biting his lip. It would take him a long time to get off, but that didn't mean that his cock wasn't drooling and twitching with every slow thrust, and his toes weren't curling as pleasure overrode everything else.

"Ah, I can't hold back," said Maddy, his hips jerking unevenly as he curled over Derreck's body, bringing their lips together. "Derreck, please." Maddy let out a deep groan, slamming himself inside one last time, his cock hitting Derreck's prostate hard enough to push the air from his lungs.

Maddy collapsed onto his chest, and Derreck pulled him close in a bear hug, pushing Maddy's cock from his body before the condom could leak. One day — when Maddy could last longer than thirty seconds — he wanted Maddy to keep his cock inside of him until his cum dripped down over his cock, and he was hard enough to start all over again.

But there was a lot of trust involved with fucking someone without a condom. It was more than just testing negative. It was feeling full of your partner's spend for the rest of the day, and feeling it slide from you, even as you clenched your aching rim.

Maddy's breath fluttered against his chest, cooling the sweat on his skin as his heart pounded hard enough for Derreck to feel. Derreck grinned, his cock twitching as he bucked against Maddy's belly. He curled up to bring his lips to Maddy's ear, his abdomen straining as he whispered.

"My turn."

With a jerk of his hips and one muscle spasm, he had Maddy pinned on his belly, his ass in the air and his face pressed into the covers. Grabbing Maddy's wrists, Derreck folded his arms behind his back before gripping them both with one hand.

Maddy didn't struggle. He just turned his head to the side, watching Derreck's every move with heavy eyes and a grin on his face. "Did I do good?" he asked, his voice still giddy from his orgasm. "Do I get a reward?"

Derreck grunted, reaching for the nightstand and pulling the drawer open. The drawer came free of its housing as he tugged too hard, a pile of sex toys, condoms and lube flipping out onto the ground.

A bit of Internet shopping had not been entirely accurate, apparently. There were at least a dozen toys and all of them were still in their packaging.

"Don't look," said Maddy, weakly struggling in Derreck's grip. "They were supposed to be a birthday surprise for you, even though I don't know when your birthday is."

Best. Birthday. Gift. *Ever.*

"July seventh," said Derreck, scooping up another unopened box of condoms, and glancing at the size to make sure they would fit. One of the downfalls of having a massive cock was how difficult it was to find stores that carried his size in stock. He disliked talking to people to begin with, so placing a special order for jumbos with a teenage cashier was always a hoot.

"Oh no, I missed it," said Maddy, turning his face into the bed.

Maddy probably didn't realize that the day they'd stumbled upon each other had been Derreck's birthday. There was nothing that pushed him closer to the edge of his sanity than the reminder of another year blown away at his life's expense. Another year alone, with nothing to show but a bruised heart and a few battered memories.

"So, what are you...forty now?" Maddy snarked, wiggling in Derreck's hold, his hands opening and closing as he counted off forty on his fingers.

Derreck ripped the condom packet with his teeth, rolling it on one-handed. He used his left hand, too, which was pretty fucking impressive, if he said so himself.

"Just for that, I'm not prepping you," said Derreck, growling even as he fought back a grin. People always mistook him for someone much older than he was. It had gotten him into a lot of bars when he was underage — Unkinked included. Although he'd waited to engage in anything sexual until he was of age.

"Forty-five then. You're still pretty spry, old man," said Maddy, struggling harder as Derreck dripped lube over his cock and Maddy's hole. Dropping the tube, Derreck brought his palm down on Maddy's back, slapping the reddened rash of cuts there.

Maddy yelped, his body going tight and his hole winking at Derreck as he lined up his cock. Derreck braced himself and pushed into Maddy in one long thrust.

His sub was still stretched from their scene, but fuck he was tight, as if it had been days and not a few hours. Maybe it had something to do with the fact that Derreck only fit into jumbo-sized condoms, because Maddy always clamped down on him like the tightest virgin.

"Ah, Derreck," Maddy cried out, his voice pitching as his body spasmed from the unexpected intrusion.

Reaching around Maddy's hip, Derreck found what he suspected. Maddy's cock was rock hard again, the condom still partially clinging to his dick. He pulled the latex sheath from him, tossing it to the ground before gripping Maddy's cock in his hand.

"I'm thirty-two, brat," growled Derreck, slamming himself deep, "and that's how many minutes I'm going to last before I come in your ass." He punctuated each word with a brutal thrust and Maddy's cock throbbed in his hand, leaking onto the sheets.

Thirty-two minutes was definitely an exaggeration, but Derreck managed to keep his pace for a solid ten before he had to slow down or risk coming. Maddy had already emptied himself onto the sheets, his cock still swollen. He groaned and whimpered with each thrust, writing when Derreck raked his nails down his back — just enough to hurt, but not enough to bleed. Maddy would heal well and easily with how shallow and clean the cuts were, and Derreck didn't want to open them and risk infection.

Gripping the base of his condom, Derreck pulled out, watching as Maddy's reddened hole winked at him and attempted to close. He rolled Maddy onto his back, pushing his knees up to his chest before covering his cock with lube again and sliding home.

And it was *home*. Everything about it felt like a place that he never wanted to leave. If he could have fucked Maddy forever, with their gazes locked and Maddy's pupils blown wide, then he would have.

"It's too much," said Maddy, whimpering as Derreck rocked his hips, glancing over his prostate with every thrust. Maddy's cock leaked a few drops of clear liquid, more spent than he'd probably ever been before.

Derreck leaned in, bringing their lips together into a possessive kiss that stripped the last meager glimpses of Maddy's dominance. Maddy went pliant, sinking into the sheets and molding to Derreck's body as if he'd finally figured out where they both belonged.

It was right there.

"You want this old man to give you a break? I'm close, Maddy, but I gotta make you hurt before I can come. Can I do that?" He pushed Maddy's knees firmer against his chest, spreading them wide so he could get even deeper inside.

"Yes, oh God please, come in me, Derreck."

Derreck shuddered as his groin started to tingle. If porn ever aspired to be better than real life, then that was the moment that it had to beat.

Derreck's toes curled and his abdomen flexed as he let loose, slamming into Maddy with all his strength and leaving his mark inside and out. Maddy would be sore for a week, if not longer, but that was exactly what both of them wanted — no, needed.

Letting out a low sigh, he jerked his hips one last time before he started to shoot. Maddy convulsed around his cock, his body clamping down as he probably experienced another orgasm of his own, and it pushed Derreck even higher — until he was floating, then collapsing, his full weight settling on Maddy.

They found each other's lips between lungfuls of air, twining their legs and fingers together as they came down. Derreck pulled away long enough to take care of the condom before he had Maddy back in his arms, settling on a dry patch of sheets.

"I'm older than you," said Maddy, chuckling as he rested his cheek on Derreck's chest. Derreck hummed, skimming his hand over Maddy's ass, but avoiding his back. He wanted them to come down with nothing more than the mutual aches in their asses.

"It's okay, old timer. We'll work on your stamina," said Derreck, drawing his lips back over his teeth as Maddy sent him a glare.

"I'll show you stamina," said Maddy, pouncing on Derreck and bringing their lips together again.

Chapter Seventeen

Maddy

Maddy knocked on the door to the bar with three sharp raps, his knuckles throbbing as they struck the rigid surface. It was only eight o'clock in the morning and his ass was aching tremendously, along with his back that felt like he'd rolled in fiberglass insulation.

Shifting, he looked over his shoulder. His car was the only one on the street, its tinted windows reflecting the early morning light. Maybe Clint hadn't made it in yet?

He tried again, knocking hard enough that his bones shook, but it barely made a sound. He grumbled at the door, grabbing his phone, and double-checking the instructions that Clint had sent him late the night before when Derreck had still been in his arms.

Eight a.m. sharp. Knock three times and I'll let you in.

It *was* five minutes to eight, but there was no way that Maddy was going to show up just on time. One of his biggest pet peeves in the world were workers that clocked in at the exact time their shift started. It was beyond rude.

He rapped on the door again, shaking his hand out to try to get feeling back into his fingers. Derreck had put him through the ringer, and most of his body was still aching in some sort of way, including his wrists. His hand had been okay, up until the last knock.

With a single beep, Maddy's watch announced as seven bled away to eight o'clock. He glanced at his watch, startling as the door flung open. Maddy's mouth dropped open as he looked up.

Clint was nearly naked in only a flimsy pair of pajama pants that were covered in animated dalmatians. His short blonde hair was askew, and his eyes were half-open with sleep clinging to his eyelashes. It would have been moderately adorable if Clint's torso hadn't been on display. Maddy caught the gasp in his throat, forcing himself not to look.

Burns stretched from Clint's left hip up to his right shoulder, the skin marred and pocked in a swirling pattern that made Maddy's heart thud. It was as beautiful as it was desolate, and beneath the irregular design was solid muscle.

The muscle was something that Maddy probably wouldn't have noticed a month before, but since he'd started looking at Derreck—really looking—he had started to notice a few others, too. He'd always assumed he was gay, since he'd never been drawn to women. But Derreck had lifted the veil from his eyes and Maddy's dick directed his sight more than ever before, pointing directly at men.

"Sorry... Slept in," Clint mumbled, turning away as he rubbed his hand over his face. His pajamas sagged lower as he walked, the top edge of his pubic hair on display. The curtains matched the drapes.

Eyes up. Maddy grumbled as he reminded himself for a third time. There were times when he wished he could go back to before delicious skin and the size of a cock mattered. Okay, there was no way he wanted to go back, but he really didn't want to embarrass himself on his first day.

A boner probably wouldn't get him fired, but it could make his time much more uncomfortable...in more ways than one. He'd seen the beauty of Clint's skin, and he would never be able to unsee it.

How? The question was on the tip of his tongue, but he clamped down on it. Clint didn't need his curiosity, especially since he was technically his boss.

"You sleep here?" asked Maddy, looking around the dim bar. It was so different without the music, people and lights...almost dead. It was just a room with wooden chairs and smooth fabric booths that were waterproof and easy to clean. The bar was just a bar without the crowd of Doms and subs.

But where the hell did Clint even sleep? Was there a bedroom tucked along with all of the other rooms down the narrow hall? The thought was extremely uncomfortable. Sleeping where other people had fucked would give Maddy nightmares. The intimacy of their play would seep into his dreams, their scents still strong on his pillow.

Different strokes. He tried not to judge. He really couldn't judge if he was going to be working at Unkinked. Even if it wasn't his thing, that didn't mean that it wasn't someone else's.

"I have an apartment across town, but by the time I close, I usually just want to crash, so I keep a cot in the office." Clint scratched his scalp, his hair sticking up a little taller as he ran his hand through it and let out a large yawn. "I used to be good at this waking up at crack of dawn shit, but I guess I'm getting too old."

Clint slipped behind the bar, filling a glass with water before downing it in three swallows. The counters were clean, and the dirty glasses had all been washed and stacked away from the night before. From what Maddy understood, the bar opened around eleven in the morning and stayed open until two. For Clint to have everything cleaned up and away, he would have had to have been up until after three at least.

"I would die on that little sleep," said Maddy, shaking his head as he followed Clint behind the bar and through a door to a tiny, cramped office. Eight hours was his bare minimum, and he usually required an afternoon nap to catch up on the weekends.

Clint grunted, grabbing a blanket from the ground before tossing it over his shoulders. "I have a shirt around here somewhere. Sorry. Sometimes I forget that it bothers some people."

Maddy tilted his head as he looked around the office. *Oh boy.* There were scattered stacks of paperwork...well, everywhere. In fact, there wasn't a spot, including the floor, that didn't have some sort of paper, crumpled or otherwise. There were a few bookshelves, which were stacked to the brim, and a small television screen along with a few electronic boxes.

"It doesn't bother me," said Maddy, looking everywhere but Clint's torso and trying to make some sense of the disorder. "I wish mine were so beautiful." Maddy flushed. Was he flirting? The words made his mouth feel fuzzy. He would have to ask Derreck.

Clint hadn't exactly told him what his job was supposed to be, so Maddy had assumed bartending or cleaning. The monstrosity of the office would have to be tackled first, though. The disorder was already starting to give him chills.

Clint grunted again, pulling his blanket tighter as he eyed the cot, his eyelids slipping lower. He swayed, his mouth going slack as his eyes slid all the way shut. A hint of drool creeped past the corner of his lips.

"Go to sleep, and I'll start to tackle this, uh, stuff," said Maddy, eyeing up a desk and the chair that he hadn't seen at first because of the amount of stuff piled on them.

"Nah, this is my mess," said Clint, his eyes opening into slitted cracks as he spoke. "I'm going to have you on bar duty so I can get caught up." His pants slipped a little farther on his hips, and Maddy almost got an eyeful before Clint grabbed the drawstring and hauled them up again.

"Un-huh," said Maddy, crossing his arms. "You want the businessman and best auditor slash investigator in this country behind a bar, while you crash on a stack of—" He leaned over and picked up the top sheet on the nearest teetering stack, his eyebrows nearly hitting the roof. "—donation forms? Why do you have these?"

He grabbed the second one in the stack, which was the same form but for a different charity. The third one down was identical. Each deposit form was nearly identical, except for the name, and they were completely filled out with the inputted amounts nearly mind-boggling. There had to have been at least thirty or so in the stack.

"Yeah." Clint scratched the back of his neck, blinking slowly. "The club actually makes quite a bit of money from the membership fees, but I don't need it, so I just donate it. Once I have the monthly nets calculated, I send them off to the charities anonymously. We've been so busy that I've gotten a few months behind."

Maddy bit his lip. A *few months* looked more like a few years' worth.

"You should donate it under the club's name so it would be tax deductible," said Maddy, grabbing the entire stack. They were signed and complete. They just needed to go to the bank. Or he could save time and do it all online.

"Nah," said Clint, turning away and sitting on the edge of the cot. His shoulders slumped under the blanket as his head dangled down. "They wouldn't take the money if they knew where it was coming from. Most people don't understand the world of kink, and I'm not going to try to make them. I just want to have a safe place for kinksters here and try to make a better world out there for everyone else."

I think I'm gonna cry. Maddy cleared his throat, setting the forms at the edge of the desk where they teetered dangerously. He'd never heard something quite so selfless before.

"I'll take care of this stuff, Clint," said Maddy, looking down at the slip for the children's hospital with a check for more than twenty thousand dollars attached. "I'll make sure that these all get sent before the end of the day, and I'll take care of the rest, too. You get some sleep, and I'll show myself around.

Everything here will stay confidential, so you don't have to worry about that."

Clint looked at him, the puffy bags under his eyes appearing almost black in the dim office. He was clearly exhausted, but it couldn't have been from a single night of missing sleep. Clint looked like a man that had been running on empty for a decade and hadn't even begun to realize it.

"I don't know," said Clint, looking around. "I don't want to bog you down on your first day, Maddy. Most of this stuff means a lot to me. This club is our—I mean, *my*—life. I don't think I can let go of that." He shook his head, flexing his hands even as his eyelids started to slide shut again.

"I'll take care of it," said Maddy, starting to clear the desk chair so he would have somewhere to sit. "I won't hurt your baby."

He wasn't sure who the other part of *our* was, but it was pretty obvious that Clint had lost someone and was struggling to hold on to things by himself. Maddy couldn't imagine building something like Unkinked and running every aspect of it solo.

It must've been enough reassurance, because, with one last grumble, Clint slid down onto the cot. Wrapping himself in the blanket, he started to snore almost immediately.

Maddy clicked on the lamp next to the desk, wiping off the thin layer of dust on the first stack of papers. His own name stared back at him from the top of the stack, along with all the other information that he had filled out weeks before when he'd entered the club for the first time. Below his non-disclosure agreement and waiver were another hundred pages of people just like him, their information on display for anyone who had cared to peek into the office.

Well, at least he knew now how Derreck had managed to track him down. He grumbled, looking around the room. Hidden in plain sight there was a printer, a massive filing cabinet, as well as a shredder. Beneath the stack on the desk was an ancient laptop. It was everything he needed.

* * * *

By the time Clint's snores had become a distant background noise, Maddy had started to question his determination. Clint had slept through two hours of data entry and shredding, and another fifteen minutes of cursing when the laptop's battery went dead because the cord had been unplugged the whole time.

He had made a dent—a ridiculously tiny dent—in the chaos of the room that probably would have taken Clint a literal eon to clean up. It might take Maddy just a few days short of that eon.

The filing cabinet had been divested, and any records older than ten years had been shredded, bagged and piled out behind the club in an alley that smelled less like sex than Maddy had expected. The shredder had already overheated three times and was flashing red, which probably wasn't a good thing. But the shredding had cleared up enough space to start filing member info.

The sheer number of members was startling, and his fingers were aching from filling out the template he'd created on the laptop. There was no point in having all the info if it wasn't organized, so he'd started entering it before filing it all alphabetically.

The checks had been taken care of and three more were filled out and awaiting Clint's signatures before he walked them all to the bank. The monthly bills for the place were surprisingly up to date, despite the chaos. Thank goodness for automatic billing.

Maddy shook his head as he shot a look at sleeping Clint. He looked younger when he was snoring, without the weight of a business on his shoulders. Clint was way too trusting to be running a business that was floating in financial heaven, with all the proceeds going to charity or being put back into improving the club itself.

Drink sales made for a pathetically low portion of that money, where the real saving grace were the monthly membership fees. They were reasonable, at only fifty dollars per month, which included use of any of the playrooms for someone who had been a member for more than one year, as well as viewing of any events on the main stage.

Apparently, there were over a thousand members and counting, which was honestly astonishing. It was a big city, but Maddy had never realized how big it really was.

But, a thousand members were bound to have a few bad eggs, a few of which he already knew about. He'd forcibly kept himself from ripping up Phil's member file when he'd come across it, growling as he read down the list of some of the questions. He wasn't even sure why it was there and how come Clint hadn't shredded it himself when they'd taken Phil's membership card away from him.

Personal Designation – Dom
Partner(s) Preference – Sub, female
Allergies and health conditions – None

Criminal convictions or arrests – None
Are you a sex offender? – No
Do you understand the meaning of consent and agree to
all terms and conditions of membership? – Yes

Maddy grumbled to himself as he typed in the responses, flagging the file before he saved it. The questions didn't matter if the fucker filling them out was just going to lie.

"What time's it?" asked Clint, rolling over and squinting at the lamp light before turning toward the clock. "Ah fuck, I've only got ten minutes."

Maddy glanced up at the clock in confusion. "The bar doesn't open for another forty-five minutes. I'll open up if you want me to so you can catch a few more minutes of sleep." Maddy finished typing up another membership file, signing off on it before moving onto the next.

He glanced up when Clint didn't respond. The man was staring at him with his mouth open and his pants resting way too low on his hips. If Maddy wasn't mistaken, there was a hint of a tattoo on his groin.

"What are you doing?" asked Clint, slowly standing and tugging at his pants as he circled around the desk and looked over Maddy's shoulder. Maddy smothered the urge to snap the laptop shut, finishing up the next file instead.

"Fixing," he said. He'd only started fixing the epic chaos, stroking it into a more semi-controlled storm instead. He was only one man, after all.

"Those all the member files? What are you doing with them?" Clint moved closer, the spicy scent of his deodorant tickling Maddy's nose. Clint's burns were inches from him, the mottled swirls drawing Maddy's gaze away from the laptop.

"Entering them into a master system, then filing them alphabetically. I'm almost done, then I'll move onto whatever the hell that is." He pointed off to the teetering stack on the other side of the desk that looked something like liquor orders. "And there are a few forms here for you to sign before I get them off to the bank. I wasn't able to access your bank account to confirm that the balances would all clear."

"They'll clear," said Clint, his eyebrows creeping up his face as he rubbed the last bit of sleep from his eyes. "Holy fuck, I know you said you were an accountant or something, but this is unreal." He thumbed the stack of completed files and Maddy held back the urge to swat him away. He had just gotten things sorted, and he would be pissed if he had to start over.

"I was an auditor. Actually, I was the auditor of the auditors. It was my job to make sure that guys weren't accepting under-the-table deals or fudging results to give unsafe workplaces a pass. I know how things are *supposed* to be organized, and I have my work cut out for me here." He glanced around the room and at the minuscule dent he had created.

"Oh, you can help me today, then," said Clint, scratching at the tiny patch of hair on the mostly smooth skin of his belly before he glanced at the clock. "Shit, now I only have three minutes." He scrambled for the door where a gym bag hung from the hook at the back. He tugged a T-shirt from the bag, as well as a pair of pants, dropping his drawers and pulling them on, despite Maddy's presence.

Dropping his gaze back to the laptop, Maddy stifled a groan. This had to be some sort of sexual harassment or something. "I'm here to help," he said, spotting another burn that curved over Clint's back to his hip.

Whatever had happened to him had definitely threatened his life.

"Fucking auditor bastard is coming today," said Clint, grumbling under his breath. "No offense. It did not go well last time—not at all. They always seemed to have it out for clubs like this. It's like they think I'm running a brothel here or something."

Maddy's blood ran cold. An auditor was coming here? Now? To this fucking disaster of a place? There were fifteen violations in front of his eyes and probably enough paperwork discrepancies to shut the place down if he looked hard enough. It could all be fixed with *time* of course, not that he had any now.

"Fold up the cot," said Maddy, jumping from his seat and slamming the laptop shut. "I'll take care of the paperwork, just get that out of here. Put it on the roof if you have to." He grabbed his carefully organized stack and jammed it into the file cabinet, returning for another seconds later. A beer order from eleven years ago. *Seriously?*

"What? Why?" Clint watched him, staring down at his cot and kicking the leg. "I just use it when I have to sleep over at the club when I'm too tired to drive home."

"Exactly. You are using this room as a bedroom. That window"—he pointed at the tiny circular thing that definitely didn't open—"is not up to code for a bedroom. I could also claim that you were using the cot for ulterior and unsavory purposes." Maddy growled, and Clint scrambled to comply, tugging the cot up one-handed and hefting it from the room.

"Crap," said Maddy, running his hand through his hair. The members he had seen treated this place like it was their heaven, and even Derreck had confessed that he relied on this place like nothing else in the world. He couldn't have that torn away from him — not on his watch.

He scrambled out to the bar. The liquor license was up to date, *thank God*, and everything else there was in order. But what about the finances? Was there even a fire escape? There were so many types of inspectors that could bury them.

An alarming buzz sounded behind the bar and Maddy whirled toward the sound. A doorbell mechanism that Maddy hadn't noticed before was tucked along the wall. *Well, that would have been useful.* His knuckles ached in sympathy.

Clint appeared at the crest of the hallway, scurrying toward the door as the buzzer sounded again. He looked like he had combed his hair a bit.

"Why did you have me knock on the door if there was a doorbell there all along?" asked Maddy, rubbing his knuckles.

"It's a motion sensor I activate when the bar is closed." Clint disappeared through the curtain and the click of the door opening sounded. The distant murmur of voices sounded through the curtain and Maddy's stomach dropped between his feet as his heart started to pound.

The voice was from his nightmares.

"I'm sure this won't take long. Like I said, I know the place — and the owner." Phil's voice carried through the curtain, along with his greasy chuckle that made Maddy want to puke. Of all the people in all the places, it had to be Phil? They didn't have a chance. Phil was a crook, but he was also very good at shutting places down if they didn't *appease* him. Maddy had seen it time and time again during his investigation.

"Yeah, it's good to see you again, man," said Clint, pulling the curtain aside to invite Phil in. He rubbed the back of his head, a strained smile on his lips and the bags under his eyes looking darker than ever. "I just hope this doesn't take too long. I need to open in half an hour."

"Of course," said Phil, his surprise turning into a smirk when he spotted Maddy. "I wouldn't want to inconvenience any of your paying members." He chuckled again, and Clint laughed nervously in response. Maddy cracked his fingers on the bar top. He wasn't a fighter, but he was not going down today.

"Exactly," said Maddy. "We have our set hours, and they have to be complied with for both city and permit regulations." It wasn't complete bullshit, but it certainly tested the waters. Phil's smirk dropped away.

"Madison," said Phil, sliding up to the bar and tapping the shining surface. "You the newest whore — I mean...member?"

"No and no," said Maddy, struggling to keep his voice even. He was not going to react to Phil.

To his credit, Phil managed to keep the surprise from his face, but his frown deepened. "Let's get this over with. I need your financial records, licenses and member lists now. And a tour, if those all check out."

Thank God Maddy had stumbled on a detailed financial report on the not-password-protected-because-Clint-was-way-too-trusting laptop, which he pulled up, along with the member list documents that he had just typed. It was short by a few, but Phil didn't have to know any of that.

"All my licensing is up to date, and we always check ID of any guests, and as well, members must be of legal drinking age," said Clint, his professionalism hitting the room out of nowhere. Maddy blinked with surprise. "Learned that one the hard way from your boy." He winked at Maddy, a smile flitting on his lips before it disappeared.

"There are massive discrepancies here each month," said Phil, the glee obvious in his voice. He swept a hand over his greasy head, his fingers staining the keys as he started to type again. "All of your profits seem to just disappear into thin air. Looks like money laundering to me."

Maddy rolled his eyes. If only money laundering was so easy to detect. There was a reason that crime organizations used it—because it was sneaky and it worked nine times out of ten.

"There's a detailed report and a list of donations to non-profit charity organizations here," said Maddy, clinking another document that he'd just made an hour before. "I think you'll see that everything adds up."

Phil grumbled, a weak pathetic sound that made Maddy want to smash his face in. He tightened his fist instead, his nails cutting into his palms. He was winning so far, but one slip-up and they would be done for.

"Give me a tour, then," said Phil, lifting out of his seat with an arthritic grunt.

"You've already seen the facility," said Maddy, cutting Clint off with a look. "You must've seen every room when you were a member here, or could you not get anyone to agree to go back there with you?" Maddy lowered his voice. "It would be a conflict of interest for you to tour a place where you may or may not have fucked someone before."

"Yes, but that's my place to decide now, not yours," said Phil, taking a few short steps until he was inches away from Maddy's face. Of course, Phil had to be taller than him, too.

Maddy paled, his gaze flickering to Clint. Phil could fine the club into bankruptcy, and no one would question him. Maddy could make an anonymous phone call, but who would respond to it?

"It's interesting that they put a rapist in charge of a decision like that—or did they not know?" As soon as Maddy said it, he wanted to take it back. Phil's eyes narrowed into black slits, his mouth going hard.

"And a club like this that knowingly invites a sex offender into their fold? Something like that could be dangerous if it continued." He looked to Clint, his smirk reappearing. "I don't think that tour will be needed after all. I think I've seen enough."

"Phil, wait," said Clint as Phil turned toward the curtain. Clint turned a glare on Maddy, clenching his hands into fists. "Maddy, get out."

Chapter Eighteen

Maddy

That had to be some kind of a record. *Three — no — three-and-a-half hours?*

Maddy hit the street, the thin layer of air conditioning stripping from his skin in a matter of seconds. He'd worn a sweater — because of course he had, and the morning sun had him instantly regretting it.

The rain had given them a quick reprieve, but the humidity had set in with full force as everything struggled to dry. Somehow, the intensity of the humidity was worse.

Things had been different after the last scene and with Derreck. He had thought that maybe he would have had the courage to go with short sleeves, but nervousness had set in as he'd prepared to leave. Clint, along with a host of other members, had seen him shirtless after all, but without Derreck there with him, the idea had put him on edge.

The T-shirt was out of the forecast permanently now. *Three-and-a-half hours.* He'd held down a job for ten years, and he'd maybe developed a bit of a working attitude, but he hadn't expected to get fired so instantaneously. Not when he'd finally started to do some good work for a place his boyfriend — *Dom, lover, whatever* — loved.

Why had he pushed Phil like that? Maddy shook his head, blinking against the light as his stomach rumbled. He should have retreated back to the office and let Clint take lead. It was Clint's bar, not *his*, and Clint had managed to keep it running so far.

It was just that…Clint had looked a bit desperate, and his office had been a maze of the past, where things from fifteen years ago were collecting dust. He seemed like a good man, but he'd been exhausted and in no shape to face something of such importance.

Maddy leaned against the brick of the building, soaking up the heat from the stone. He longed to reach for his phone to call Derreck, but he was probably dead asleep.

Derreck's boss had texted them while they were lying in bed to let Derreck know that digging was resuming as soon as the sun set. It still gave Maddy the jitters when he thought about tunneling at a graveyard in the middle of night. Derreck said the silence was calming, but maybe he wasn't afraid of ghosts?

Hey, so the club is probably getting shut down and I got fired. Maddy could imagine how a text like that would go over. He'd seen Derreck rage at Phil before and he didn't want to go down that path again.

He glared at the Buick parked behind his trusty companion, knowing instantly that it was Phil's. The exterior was spotless, presumably from going through the car wash every day, and it had all the extras. Peering into the passenger window, Maddy touched the keys in his pocket, more tempted than he had ever been to mess up someone's paint job.

Even with the spotless exterior, there were wrappers and tissues jammed into every available orifice of the interior that Maddy could see. It was as if Phil couldn't be bothered to clean something if it wasn't automatic.

Huffing out a laugh, Maddy gently tapped his key against the window, so tempted to leave a mark that his hands shook from the force of holding back. Maybe if he popped the hood, he could leave a nasty message on the inside? Phil would probably never see it. There was no way he changed his own oil.

Looking back to the club door, Maddy gritted his teeth and slid his keys back into his pocket. He could work at a coffee shop? But he'd probably get fired the first time he served a rude customer.

Anything related to manual labor was out, or he'd probably lose an arm. Other bars were out, too. People always asked the most uncomfortable questions when he had no desire to give them the answers.

He phone vibrated in his pocket, and he nearly sank to his knees. *Please let it be Derreck. Please.* He pulled it from his pocket, unlocking the screen and squinting down at it.

Unknown caller.

Not Derreck then. With nothing to lose, he accepted the call, bringing the phone to his ear. "Yeah."

"Where the fuck are you?" a voice growled into his ear.

He pulled the phone away from his ear, staring at the screen. He didn't recognize the number, either.

Whatever. He did not need anything else on top of his *wonderful* day. His give-a-shits had officially expired.

"Wrong number, asshole," he imitated the same growl, probably failing pathetically before he ended the call.

The time shone back at him in giant glowing numbers on his screen. It wasn't even lunch time, and he was already hopeless. He should have stayed in bed with Derreck, and maybe poked him until he got fucked again.

His ass ached at the thought. *Or not.* There was only so much his body could take, even if he did like to push it. Even his dick was a bit chafed and his balls were a whole different story.

His phone rang again, the same number appearing on the screen. Whoever it was, they were persistent. *What do I have to lose?* Laughing, he accepted the call and put the phone to his ear.

"House of the Lord, God speaking," he answered, almost making it through without laughing again. It was the same way that his dad had used to answer the phone when he had been younger, at least, until a priest had called one day. *Oops.*

"What the fuck?" The angry stranger now sounded closer to enraged. "Okay, that was actually a bit funny, but seriously, where did you go?" Their voice softened. "I hope you aren't walking out on me, 'cause I spent all morning training you."

Maddy paused, looking at the screen again. *Shit.* The number was a bit familiar. And the voice was too, once he thought about it. "Clint?"

"Yeah, of course," said Clint. "Who else were you expecting? Baby Jesus?" He snickered, the sound sending another wave of confusion through Maddy's day.

"I left. You told me to leave, so I did. I'm just by my car," said Maddy, kicking Phil's tire. His toes ached as his foot bounced off the surface.

"Shit, Maddy, seriously? I meant get out of the room, not the club. Get back in here!"

Maddy tilted his head, looking back at the club door. "I thought you fired me." He took the few steps back to the door. He knocked three times, just like he had that morning.

The door swung open seconds later, revealing Clint on the other side, who still had the phone pressed to his ear. The man's hair was in complete disarray, and he looked positively frantic. Snapping the phone shut, he gestured Maddy inside.

A flip phone? Do they even still make those? Maddy shot off another mental groan. With the money that went through the club, Clint should have had a proper phone.

"Come on in. I was just about to see Phil out of the door," said Clint, opening the door wider to let Maddy in. Sweet air conditioning greeted him like a cigarette after good sex, which was something he was going to have to try sometime. A sex bucket-list was definitely a thing.

"I can see myself out, thank you," said Phil. His beady gaze shifted around the floorboards, never looking up to Maddy or Clint. Even in the dim light of the bar, the guy looked like he'd seen a ghost.

"Take care of yourself, Phil," said Clint as he held the door wide for the guy, who slipped by without a word, his gaze never lifting from the ground. The moment he was outside, Clint let the door slam shut, locking them in cool silence.

Maddy looked around. There were no closed signs or caution tape that he could see — not that auditors worked that fast or had those things with them. And Clint didn't *look* upset. In fact, he was smiling.

Clint rubbed the back of his head. "Sorry about the misunderstanding, but yeah, I'm not going to fire you. I would end up six feet under, if you know what I mean."

Maddy did, and it didn't sit right with him. He wanted to be here on his own merits, not someone else's. "If it's not working out, just let me know. I'll take care of Derreck."

Clint's eyes widened and he shook his head. "You two are fucking made for each other." He turned away, strolling to the bar before flicking on several sets of lights. The lights alone gave the room new life. "Now, where did we leave off? Do you want to keep working in the office or did you want the down-low on the bar?"

Who says 'down-low' anymore? "How old are you?" asked Maddy before he could stop himself. Clint was a blond, which was a great way to hide gray, and his blue eyes were crystal clear. No age spots or even freckles, but that probably came with working inside for so many hours per day.

"Uh, I'm legal drinking age, if that's what you're asking. And you actually don't have to ask that. Everyone is vetted at the door and guests have to show ID and sign waivers and consent forms, which you already knew." Clint rambled on as he punched a few things into the till. The drawer slid open with a *ding*, only for Clint to snap it shut again.

"So, the club…it's okay?" asked Maddy, longing to relieve the pit in his stomach before it could get any worse.

"Fuck yeah, don't worry about it," said Clint, waving his hand like he was shooing away a fly.

"But, Phil," said Maddy, looking back to the curtain like Phil would suddenly appear and change his mind. Phil had been seconds away from tearing the place apart. What had changed in the few minutes that he was away?

"Like I said, don't worry about it," said Clint, leaning on the bar top and resting his chin in his hands with a grin on his face. "In this world, Phil might have one friend, but I have thousands, and all of them would put themselves on the line to save this place. This is a safe place and a home for members, and a little shit like Phil can't fight against that."

Maddy slid his hand over the countertop, feeling every ridge and bump in the surface. Clint was right. It really was like a *home*.

Chapter Nineteen

Derreck

Freezing-cold hands touched his back, breaking him from sleep and putting him on alert in seconds. His body went taut on its own as he lunged at his attacker, twisting in the sheets and grabbing them by the wrist. Using his momentum, he slammed them to the bed face-first.

His home was rich in community and unspoken laws of trust and reliance, but there was always a druggie or two thrown into the mix. No one was taking his fucking kidney that night.

Once he opened his eyes when he realized that they were still closed, the strangeness of his dream started to dissipate. A familiar groan cut the air, and he blinked in the semi-darkness. Dark hair splashed against the pale cloth of his pillow, and a wide, familiar eye looked back at him.

Maddy. He released his sub, flicking on the lamp before pulling Maddy's wrists to him to make sure he hadn't squeezed too tight. They were a touch red and there was a chance they might bruise, but it could have been worse. Derreck bit back the guilt that seeped in as Maddy looked at him with a grin on his lips and a sparkle in his eyes.

"I could have hurt you," said Derreck, looking over at the clock before shuffling back under his covers. They were all askew and Maddy's weight was pinning them to the bed in the wrong spot. It was too fucking early, and he still had another ten minutes before his alarm would go off.

"Did I scare you?" asked Maddy, poking Derreck's ribs with a freezing-cold finger. He was worse than his cat. "I didn't know you could even get scared. I just thought demons ran away from your glare or something." He laughed, the sound light and rich, before he slid his hand down Derreck's ribs again.

Derreck grunted, flexing under the touch. How could Maddy be so cold? It was hot as hell outside, and his air conditioner hadn't stopped running since he'd rolled into bed at a sparkly five a.m.

He peeked one eye open, taking in Maddy's grinning form. He was in a tank top with his arms on display, as well as his designs. That would probably explain the cold. Maddy was most likely used to sweaters, and the sudden lack of layers was bound to make anyone a little chilly.

"I think I freaked out those kids," said Maddy, apparently noticing Derreck's gaze on his marks. "They saw these and I think I've been upgraded from ice-cream cone to crazy psycho killer. We make a good match, Derreck. With my skills with pointy objects, and your killer glares, the world will fall at our feet." He let out a fake evil laugh and Derreck groaned, covering his ear with his arm.

Sleep.

"You shouldn't leave your doors unlocked when you are sleeping. That's just asking someone to steal your shit. You didn't even wake up when I said hi to Demon — who I fed, by the way. Apparently, she was starving."

Why is he still talking? He glanced at the clock. Down to five minutes. Five minutes of peaceful sleep where he could walk in his dreams instead of reality. Five minutes of...

"Did you fall asleep again?" asked Maddy, skimming his warming palm down Derreck's side to settle on his hip. He finger-walked over Derreck's hip and groin, getting closer and closer to Derreck's morning wood. "Because I need to ask you something."

The bed creaked as Maddy leaned in closer, his breath brushing over Derreck's ear. "I need you to hurt me."

Fuck sleep, wake up! Derreck growled, turning and grabbing Maddy by his shoulder and rolling so that he ended up on top with Maddy's face buried in his neck and their groins aligned. Derreck, braced himself on his hands, so he didn't completely squish his sub.

"Tell me what you need," said Derreck, grinding his hard cock against Maddy's awakening one. A flush colored Maddy's cheeks as he lowered his gaze, his inner brat receding to his more submissive nature.

"I crashed a bit at work yesterday. There was a misunderstanding, and I thought Clint fired me —"

"I'll kill him for ya. Just tell me how you want him to go," said Derreck, moving down Maddy's body so he could suck a spot on his neck. He slurped until the spot had to be aching before he bit down, pressing his teeth as hard as he dared. Maddy bucked against him, his cock suddenly rigid.

"Is it bad if I believe you would do that for me? And that it turns me on?" asked Maddy, bucking again when Dereck reached down to squeeze his cock harshly.

"It means that you're mine," said Derreck, "and you'll take anything I give you, even if it terrifies you." He moved his mouth to Maddy's nipple, pinching the bud between his teeth. It would sting like a motherfucker, and from Maddy's gasp, he was getting close already.

"Don't kill him, though. He didn't actually fire me, but I still went down a bit. I just need to level back out." He whimpered when Derreck bit into the soft skin of his ribs, his jaw aching from the effort of holding back. He would hurt Maddy any way he wanted, but he would never harm him.

"Turn over," said Derreck, leaning back to give Maddy just enough space to do as he was told. His sub scrambled to comply without question. "Put your ass in the air and your head down on the bed. Grab the headboard and don't let go. I'll fucking ruin you if you let go."

He reached for his bedside drawer to the few toys that he had purchased with Maddy in mind. After seeing Maddy's toy drawer, he'd popped over to an adult store and had grabbed anything that had caught his fancy. Most of the things he thought would look good on or in Maddy. He couldn't let his sub have more toys than him.

"Close your eyes, and don't open them, no matter what. I'll blindfold you if I have to." He watched the full-body shudder go through Maddy, presumably as he remembered the last time he'd been blindfolded.

With his patience thinned until it was nearly nonexistent, he brought his hand down on Maddy's ass, leaving a red print on his left cheek. Maddy let out a gasp, flinching in surprise before his body went taut as he presumably waited for the matching blow to the other cheek.

Derreck opened up the bottle of lube instead of doling out the second hit, pouring a few drops directly on Maddy's rim. "Gotta get you wet for my cock, brat. Gonna split you open so good."

Maddy groaned, but there was an edge of disappointment to the sound. Derreck bit back a grin. He had been spoiling his sub if a quick fuck was too disappointing for him.

He reached for two things in his bedside drawer. The first was a condom packet that he crinkled deliberately, hopefully throwing Maddy off. The second was a large dildo that was slightly smaller than his own cock and had bulbous sections instead of a straight shaft. It was bright purple, but Derreck wasn't picky. Anything would look good with Maddy stretched around it.

"You want my cock, brat?" asked Derreck, dripping lube along the toy and crinkling the condom wrapper again. He rubbed over Maddy's hole with his thumb, teasing his tight entrance into submission.

He waited for Maddy's nod before he pulled his hand away. "Too bad."

With one hand, he gripped Maddy by the balls, tugging them harshly at the same time he positioned the toy and started to slide it inside. Maddy writhed beneath him, but Derreck tugged harder, forcing him to go still. There really was nothing like a little cock and ball torture, and it was also what had paved the way for their sexual relationship.

Where would I be if I hadn't whipped his balls? Derreck knew the answer. He would have been in about the same spot—spending as much time as possible with Maddy, only with his hands tucked under his own ass so he didn't get carried away. It would have been difficult without a sexual aspect to their relationship, but nothing would have stopped him from being by Maddy's side.

Grinning at Maddy's whimper, the purple bulbs disappeared into Maddy's stretched hole one by one as Derreck pushed the toy all the way to its flared base. It would have hurt for sure, plus it came with bonus features.

He clicked the base of the dildo, turning the vibrations up as it hummed to life. Maddy flexed, his guttural scream music to Derreck's ears. One of Maddy's hands slipped from the headboard, gripping the sheets.

Derreck brought his palm down on Maddy's already-reddened cheek. *Once, twice, three times.* Maddy put his hand back on the headboard, gripping the wood until his knuckles blanched white.

"Good." Derreck smoothed over Maddy's ass before dialing the vibrations down to a tolerable level. One of the keys to Maddy was that nothing got him off better than surprises. If Derreck could have blindfolded him twenty-four-seven, he would have.

"You ready to hurt for me now? I won't go easy on you, so use your safewords if you need to," said Derreck.

Maddy shook his head, his eyes clenched shut. "I won't need to."

"We'll see."

A slap rang out, then another, before Derreck gently tapped the base of the toy, moving it around until Maddy arched his back. *That's the spot.* One day, Maddy would use his safeword and take back control, but Derreck would keep pushing him until then, always keeping him safe and hopefully just inside his limits.

To be truthful, Derreck wasn't even completely sure of the extent of Maddy's limits at this point, but they were far beyond his own.

He reached for the drawer again, pulling out two flexible cock rings. One went around Maddy's dripping cock, and the second went over his balls, settling at the base and making them flush instantly. It was a good look.

He reached for the crop that he had hidden beneath his bed when it hadn't fit in the drawer. He'd found one that had a firm shaft, almost resembling the sting of a cane, and a long, narrow tip that had a similar thud to a flog.

He tapped the leather tip against Maddy's balls before he pulled his arm back and slammed the length of it over Maddy's ass. Maddy grunted with surprise, his arms trembling as he presumably tried to keep his hands on the headboard.

Derreck aimed for Maddy's still-reddened back on the next hit, then his thighs, striping out a pattern that would take Maddy a bit to catch on to. And just as Maddy seemed to figure it out, tensing up before Derreck could hand out the next blow, Derreck brought the leather tip of the crop over the back of Maddy's hands.

"Ah, fuck," Maddy cursed, flexing his hands as they flushed pink. He was shaking, sweat dripping down his back and painting damp streaks through the red lines.

"Too much?" asked Derreck, gripping Maddy's ass and pushing the base of the toy. Maddy's cock flexed as he probably tried to come, but he was stopped by the restricting rings.

"Not enough." Maddy arched his back, pushing his ass into Derreck's touch. "Come on, Derreck. You know I won't break. Now fucking *hurt* me." His voice was a growl with the edge of dominance in it.

When he had first heard the defensive tone, Derreck had almost been afraid of it, although he would admit it to exactly no one. Maddy was a powerful man, with a brilliant mind and a politeness that made Derreck want to give him everything. Derreck had wondered once if Maddy would be too much for him.

Luckily, he was just as creative as Maddy was resilient.

"Hmm-m." He traced the base of the toy in Maddy's hole, the pucker deliciously stretched. "I'm not sure you deserve it." He tugged at the toy, pulling it from Maddy with one harsh tug. Shutting it off, he dropped it to the bed and walked from the room.

What a pretty picture. Derreck leaned against the door as he took the room in for a moment before he dragged himself away. He would have to remember to ask Maddy if photographs were on the table or not.

To his credit, Maddy hadn't moved by the time Derreck returned, but his entire body had gone tense with either nervousness or anticipation. Derreck hoped it was the latter.

"I have a treat for you, so make sure to thank me for it." Derreck shifted the ice cube that he had retrieved, wiping the moisture from his fingertips before he pressed it to Maddy's entrance, then easily inside.

Sensation play hadn't been on Maddy's list, but sometimes sensation went hand and hand with pain. The ice cube would definitely feel strange and would probably be right on the edge of pain, but it was small enough that it wouldn't do any damage. Maddy didn't have to know that, though.

Derreck pressed a small second item to Maddy's entrance, squinting at the strong smell of ginger. It was smaller than the ice cube, and he had sculpted it into a round knob. The freshly peeled root would feel as if an actual fire had lit itself inside Maddy, and it wouldn't do any damage, either. Derreck owed a lot to whoever had discovered that.

He slipped the piece of ginger inside Maddy, replacing the dildo and sliding it back to the base to seal the fire and ice inside. He rubbed his hand over Maddy's cock, coating him with the juice from the ginger. Paying special attention to the sensitive head, he pressed against the small slitted hole, spreading the liquid just inside.

Maddy shifted, probably not feeling the hit of sensation quite yet. Derreck took a breath of sweat and spice, licking his lips and leaning back so he could watch every moment.

Maddy's thighs tensed first, then the toy shifted as he clenched down on it. The tension would only spread the tingle of the ginger deeper. Maddy murmured with confusion as he shifted again, his back bowing as he looked at Derreck over his shoulder.

Grabbing the crop, Derreck brought it down on Maddy's ass and thighs, marking every spot that he already had and painting new ones on Maddy's pale flesh.

Maddy's voice pitched higher and higher until he was nearly sobbing, his head hanging low between his arms as he finally closed his eyes again.

There was no way that it *wasn't enough*. Every time Maddy moved and squeezed down on the toy, the juice from the ginger would only spread farther and deeper inside of him, the fire building until it was nearly unbearable. As the ice melted, the heat would only burn fiercer.

Derreck grabbed a condom, tearing open the packet and smoothing it down his cock before he tugged the toy from Maddy's body. A few drops of water followed the toy before Maddy tightened up, his skin breaking out in a humiliated flush.

"How far can I fuck that ginger into you before you break?" Lubing up his cock, Derreck pressed to Maddy's entrance, pushing all the way to the base in one long shove. Even with the prep from the toy, Maddy was still tight, and the heat from his body had burned away the chill from the ice cube.

He slammed inside, giving every thought to Maddy's pleasure as he nailed his prostate over and over. The poor gland had to be swollen and battered by now, but Derreck prodded it further into submission, until Maddy's cock was a purple, strangled mess beneath them.

It didn't take him long until he was shooting into the condom, gripping Maddy's hips and pulling him close as he emptied himself. Maddy sobbed in small, strangled gasps, the pillow beneath his face damp with tears and sweat.

"Did you like that, Maddy?" asked Derreck, stroking gently down Maddy's sides. Maddy clenched around him, letting out a full-body shudder as he trembled. "Do you need more?" He scraped his nails down Maddy's spine, until the scratchy skin streaked red.

Maddy nodded again as Derreck withdrew, discarding the condom and tossing it on the ground. "I need you to mark me. Please." He let out another shuddering breath.

Derreck's cock throbbed, and he went momentarily dizzy as his blood pooled south again. He was not twenty anymore, and no matter how much he firmed up again, he was not fucking anyone for a good half-hour.

"I don't want to mess up your designs. I'm no artist," said Derreck, tracing the winding marks down Maddy's ribs. He could dig a perfectly rectangular hole, but he struggled with stick figures most days.

"You see it, too? The designs?" asked Maddy. He shook his head, wiping his tears on his arm.

Of course I do. They're beautiful.

"I trust you, Derreck. I trust you because you see them—and because you understand."

Derreck had wondered if there was something more to the intricate designs when he had first seen them. A pattern, almost like a tattoo had emerged before his eyes. But the last thing he wanted to do was taint that somehow.

"I can't, Maddy," said Derreck, soothing the reddened skin whenever he found it. "Not today. I can cut you, if you like, but I won't scar you. I'll call it a hard limit until we can discuss it more."

"Fine," said Maddy, letting out a huff.

"Open your eyes," said Derreck gripping Maddy's chin and forcing him up to his knees. Maddy struggled to hold onto the headboard, but Derreck tore him away. "Look at me...*now*."

Maddy's watery gaze focused on him. His eyes were red-rimmed, with tears gathered at the corners that were just waiting to spill. He was beautiful, even in his dejected misery.

"Apologize," he said, holding firm when Maddy tried to pull away. His wet gaze dropped, his mouth going slack as a tear rolled down his cheek.

"I'm sorry, Derreck."

Derreck laughed, his body shaking from the force of it. If there was one thing in the world that his sub was, it was apologetic.

"You know," said Maddy, his voice going light as he looked to the side, an adorable flush on his cheeks. A small smile flitted on his lips that told Derreck that everything was okay. "Clint told me that we belonged together. I didn't really get what he meant by that until now. We are the only people who will put up with each other." He laughed as Derreck released him, turning and looping an arm around Derreck's neck.

"We're the only ones strong enough."

Want to see more from this author? Here's a taster for you to enjoy!

It's a Kink Thing: Kinks and Crosshairs
M.C. Roth

Coming November 2022

Excerpt

Henley

The only thing worse than undercover work was babysitting. At least when he was undercover, Henley could give himself a cool superhero name and occupation like 'Mr. Duncan Peters, high school superintendent and nighttime vigilante'.

But babysitting?

Some agents loved it, but they were the ones who called it 'bodyguard duty' and got thrills at the idea of taking a bullet for someone whose middle name was 'rich boy'. Sure, there were some good cases out there, but for the most part, it was that rich boy in front of him.

He cast his gaze around the club, trying to ignore the way the lights made his temples throb every time they caught his eyes. The entrances were clear, with the same bouncers who had been standing guard all night. Only one had slipped away briefly and had returned red-faced with a hickey on his neck and lipstick smeared against the corner of his lips. *Lucky guy.*

The ceiling was solid drywall, only interspersed with two vents and the constant flashing lights. No one was getting the jump on him from above. And luckily, there was a single door, which made his job a hell of a lot easier but had him worrying about fire hazards.

The gig wasn't *terrible,* but it got old fast when his charge was some spoiled brat who was high on blow and had fucked seven different chicks in the last three days.

He kinda envied the kid's stamina, though.

Somebody didn't. Someone had put a death threat out on the kid after Henley's boss had apparently fucked with the wrong people. *Didn't see that one coming.* Henley rolled his eyes. He'd never seen so much drama in his life.

The kid's father had enough money and pull to get three more bodyguards assigned, along with his regular squad of four goons. The other two additional bodyguards were nothing more than glorified mercs with a bit of a conscience, but Henley?

He chuckled, shaking his head as he spied his 'colleague' along the far wall. He was checking the exits, same as Henley was, with his beefy arms crossed and his tattoos on display, much to the ladies' delight.

Henley hadn't actually been a mercenary for a long time, even if almost nobody in the world knew that. But even while in that department, people treated him as a bit of a joke. He didn't have the size or the tattoos for anyone to take him seriously.

Nodding along with the beat, he did a little twirl, bumping hips with a lady who gave him a *whoop* and a smile. She was rocking six-inch heels like they didn't even hurt, dancing with him for a minute before he gave her a wink and melted away from the crowd.

The view was decent from where he leaned against the wall, the beat shivering against his back. Tattoo guy was pretty hot, but one dropped suggestion for a hookup in the bathroom and that ship had sailed. And as nice as the ladies were, they didn't exactly have the equipment Henley was after.

Sigh. Sometimes it was like guys didn't expect him to be gay. It wasn't his fault that he missed more than he hit when trying to spot a fellow nut fan.

He *tried*. There was a rainbow sticker on the butt of his gun and a matching pin on his fanny pack that gave him away, if anyone cared to be observant. As for the fanny pack, he was bringing the trend back, and it was a great place to store extra clips for his lethal baby.

His knife was pink — and fabulous, too — although it was tucked away where no one could see it. And he was drinking a strawberry daiquiri — a little more strawberry, a little less daiquiri…because he *was* working, after all.

How could I not be gay? The male body and all its intricacies was where the party was at. It was a true shame that some straight men never indulged in the pure wonder that was the prostate.

Sighing, he tried giving the goon one last look from across the room, standing on his tiptoes to see over the writhing mass. *I need a fucking stool.* It was like trying to spot someone in a corn field.

His phone buzzed from within his fanny pack, humming against his belly and sending the strange sensation of vibrating bullets against his skin. Tapping the line hooked over his ear, he turned away from his charge, marching to the exit and easing through the first layer of doors to where the music volume was more reasonable.

"Rosco." He used his mercenary name to answer.

"Is he safe?" asked Mr. Martinez, his kinda-sorta boss on the other end of the line. Henley let out a huffing breath as he peered at a few flyers that had been pinned to the wall separating the club entrance from the outside world. *Are' high' and 'drunk' still considered safe?*

"He has a full squad with him at all times. No one is getting to your son unless he goes through every one of us first." He pressed the speaker farther into his ear, trying to catch Martinez's reply over the music.

"My sources tell me that the hit will be taking place tomorrow. I don't think I need to tell you what will happen if you fail me."

Always such a chipper guy. There was a reason that his body count was nearly as high as Henley's—which happened to be the main reason for Henley's undercover assignment to the case.

"He's not making it easy. He should be underground, not in a club," said Henley, ripping the number off one of the advertisements for car cleaning and stuffing it into his pocket. He was between vehicles at the moment, but he never knew when he would need a bit of remains scrubbed out of his back seat.

The bar was packed, and of course, the little dipshit he was trying to protect had dragged them to the same club again for the third night in a row. One more night and he would have to look up to see if his benefits covered hearing damage.

The music was so loud that it couldn't have been legal, thrumming against his chest in a monotonous beat that made him feel way too old. He knew music and a good beat, but that shit coming out of the speakers? *Gah.* He'd heard the same whispered line after a siren over thirty times that night alone.

The lighting was the second issue. It was hard to tell a purse from a weapon, and he had to squint to try to catch a glimpse of his Romeo across the club. The swirling lights helped visibility a bit, unless they were shining directly into his eyes. If someone smuggled in a shotgun, he wouldn't know until it was pressed to the back of the kid's head.

It really didn't explain why Henley was looking at close to forty female booties without a single interesting dangly between them. The kid's father had cleared the bar of all male clientele after a quick phone call. They were certain that a man had sent the threat, so bring on the ladies, right?

"I've banned every possible assassin from that club, and, as you said, you have a full detail on him. How is that hard?" asked Mr. Martinez, his voice dropping into a growl. "Keep him safe, or you'll wish you were dead."

Because apparently chicks couldn't kill.

Henley begged to disagree. The woman who'd trained him was the most terrifying person he had ever met, and she could probably still kick his ass, even though she was in her late forties and had popped out three screaming munchkins in the last five years.

"Hello?" Henley tapped his ear, but the line had already gone dead. *Just what I need…another death threat.* Some people collected stamps or classic dinky cars, but Henley had always liked to stay on the wilder side of things.

But death threats weren't worth much, and he couldn't exactly leave them for his family if he did wind up getting shot.

He popped back through the club door, shaking his head as he eyed his charge, who had a different woman in his arms and another grinding against his back. Looking off to the windows that lined the entire side of the club, he stared into the night, letting the music roll over him.

"You gonna head out soon?" asked his sexy goon as he moved closer, shouting into Henley's ear over the music. His breath was tinted with bitter alcohol and his shirt reeked of cigarettes. Maybe Henley had dodged a cancerous bullet.

What time is it? Oh, shit. Henley glared at his watch, hoping that the numbers were wrong. There were so many exposed women on the dance floor that he must've retreated into himself to try to save his sexuality. Women could be beautiful, but not when they were stumbling drunk and groping the only guy on the dance floor as if he were the last dick on the planet. Henley had seen that dick unfortunately, and it was not worth the effort.

He shook out his hand, his watch shifting on his wrist but not resetting like it was supposed to. He'd been standing there for the last half hour, not even getting fucking paid. *Babysitting blows.*

"Yeah, and the offer still stands. Come by my place if you want a good time later," said Henley, pulling the bodyguard down to him to whisper into his ear. The guy went tense, jerking back with narrowed eyes.

Nope, no interest at all. Couldn't blame him for trying. He hadn't bothered to ask the goon's name, so his hopes hadn't been that high, anyway.

The bodyguard shouted something, but Henley didn't bother trying to decipher it over the thrumming beat. He'd struck out…nine times in the last week? Maybe it had been more. Either way, everyone must've gone straight or moved to Colorado, because it was a fucking desert out there right now.

Pushing his way through the sea of sweaty, horny and drugged bodies, he headed for the exit and the promise sweet night air. Sweat beaded over his temples as he nodded to one of the bouncers before pushing his way out of the door. The touch of fresh air was better than a power nap on a Sunday afternoon and twice as refreshing.

Taking a breath, he slammed the door behind him, cutting off the plaguing sound of yet another siren. Whoever was making club music these days needed a muse or something because that shit had been pathetic.

Or maybe it's because anything remotely pop-like gives me hives?

The club door led directly to the street, a few streetlamps spotted over the empty plane of asphalt and concrete. The closest one flickered, giving off the same sound as a humming cricket as the bulb flashed. The smooth road was barely three steps away, the thin sidewalk the only thing separating the club from the rest of the world.

Old brick buildings surrounded him on all sides, with so many spots to hide that it was nearly impossible to cover them all. Three were multi-leveled stores, some with apartments above. The one across the road with the pale brick and the flashing sign was where he'd set up his temporary apartment when he'd taken the assignment.

Usually he didn't like to eat so close to where he worked, but the apartment window offered a perfect view of the place, and he could see inside the club with the stretch of windows that surrounded it from floor to ceiling. He was technically on point for the assignment, so he didn't want to let the kid out of his sight for too long.

He'd chosen that particular apartment because he'd heard a rumor that the club was a kink club of sorts, too. He didn't care if it hosted a munch or a full-blown party, because some fresh faces were exactly what he needed, even if they weren't the feral pups he was looking for.

Unfortunately, he had yet to see a single hint of leather making its way through the doors as he'd watched from his perch on the couch.

Henley slowed his pace as the thump of the music started to dim, pulling the sleeves of his shirt down over his wrists. The air had started to grow crisper as winter approached, although the days were still somewhat warm. If he held his breath long enough, he could almost see the steam of it under the lamp light as he exhaled.

When he'd moved to Canada, he had done it because everything he'd known about the country had told him it was supposed to be cold, with igloo houses and dog sleds and shit.

Three years earlier, during his first summer near the southern tip of the country, the air had been so thick and hot that his ice-cream cone had melted in thirty seconds flat. He'd spent most of the summers half naked by a pool since, only venturing out when he could get away with his long-sleeved T.

He had half considered moving back to… No, he was never going back, no matter how hot it got.

Luckily, the winters were ball-freezing cold, which was exactly the way he wanted them. And the kink community was thriving, even if they were more on the down-low than where he was from.

Nonchalantly reaching for his gun, he clicked the safety off, dropping his hands a moment later. There was someone standing outside of his apartment building, leaning down and inspecting the lock. The place was a little run-down, but it had decent security, and the guy didn't look like anyone he'd seen in the video feeds he'd hacked.

He had an entire wall covered in labeled pictures with every person who had come and gone in the building since he'd set up there. He didn't bother with their actual names on the photographs because *'lady with nine cats'* and *'guy who is always high'* were way easier to remember.

But the guy at the door was nowhere on his wall. In fact, it looked like the guy was either unsuccessfully trying to pick the lock, or…

Henley slowed, flexing his biceps to make sure that his knife was still securely strapped there. He couldn't feel the one at his ankle through his sock, but he had checked on it the last time he'd taken a bathroom break. The one at his back along his waistband shifted with every move, comforting him with its weight.

Something caught the light as the man at the door dropped to his knees, leaning closer to the lock. His long hair looked nearly as dark as the night that wrapped around them, falling past his shoulders to hide most of his face from Henley's view.

"It works better with the right equipment," said Henley as he ducked into the security lights at the door, taking a quick glance at his ankle as he took another step. A tiny sliver of a pink handle looked back at him. It was a specialized ceramic that was sharp as fuck and tricked most metal detectors. Unfortunately, it came with the cost of single-use-only sometimes, as it would shatter if he slammed it into someone's spine.

He'd been eyeing up a baby blue one just like it online a few days prior, and he hadn't decided if it was going to be his birthday gift to himself or not. Then there was the gun with pink bullets, of course. *Do they make pink bullets? Nah, it doesn't matter.* He would just make them himself.

The guy at the door snapped up to his feet, looking over his shoulder in surprise. "What?"

Very nice. The lock picker was taller than Henley had thought, and probably around six-one, which was just the type of challenge he usually looked for. He was thinner than he had looked from afar, packed into a thick coat that was too warm for the weather and dark gloves that hid his presumably pale skin from view. His long hair scraped against his coat as he moved, whooshing as if a breeze had picked up in the middle of the city.

The way the security lights caught his eyes made them appear almost black, highlighting the pale skin of his cheek bones and accentuating his jaw that looked strong enough to be a nutcracker.

"I just..." The lock picker trailed off as he gave Henley a once-over, flickering his gaze from the toes of Henley's rainbow runners and pausing on his fanny pack for a moment.

One look spoke more than a thousand words. It was the same look that Henley had been seeking for weeks. *Yes! There are still gays out there. Play this right.*

"You were *just* trying to pick the lock. Let's see what you've got, because it obviously isn't working," said Henley, crossing his arms so he could touch the blade at his wrist. It was rigid under his fingertips as he slipped down his sleeve to the handle, ready to pull it from its holster. The gun at his waist seemed to throb, exposed and visible to anyone who cared to look.

It was on display for a reason. Bad guys always seemed to wait to act until he grabbed for his gun. Watching their surprise as he pulled a knife on them instead was half the fun.

"I'm not." The lock picker shook his head, his eyes going wide as he caught sight of Henley's gun. Taking a step back, he let one a whooshing breath, condensation steaming against his lips. "I just... My key won't work."

Ah shit. Henley blinked, squinting at the guy's hand in the low light. Maybe it was time for him to give up his stubbornness and wear the glasses his optometrist had insisted on. He hadn't missed a target yet, but it was only a matter of time.

The guy didn't have any equipment on him at all. No pins or picks—just a ring and a couple of funky-looking key chains attached to an array of colorful keys. If he wasn't mistaken, the guy had gone to three different Mexican resorts and had gotten a sandal keychain at each one.

I'm getting way too paranoid for my own good.

"Heh." Henley scrubbed the back of his head, widening his stance *just in case.* He'd been fooled before by guys that were half as cute. One had even managed to get a jump on him when he'd reached for his dick, leaving a scar the size of a nickel right next to the prize.

But this guy wasn't *cute,* he was beautiful, with a smooth face that looked like it had never had a five o'clock shadow. *Lucky bastard.* Henley had a shadow fifteen minutes after he shaved, and by the end of the day, he looked like he'd been roughing it in the woods for a week. It was too bad that a beard didn't suit him.

"I'm Henley," he said, holding out his hand like an absolute dork. He flushed, ready to draw his hand back, before the guy clasped it, shaking twice.

Taking a moment to enjoy, Henley smiled up at the stranger. His grip was good, his wrist relaxed, so he was probably a successful interview candidate and definitely didn't have any weapons concealed there. And his legs were too close together to have enough balance to start a fight that he would have any chance of winning.

That left two options—civilian or amateur.

"You're supposed to tell me your name, too," said Henley, sliding his thumb over the back of the amateur's gloved knuckles. The leather was soft, like it had just been dipped in body butter.

"Li."

Interesting. The guy didn't look like a 'Li'. He looked more like a 'Damien', or 'Grey', or 'Marius'—with a little less vampirism. There was a chance it was a fake name, though.

"Can you help me get in?" asked Li, handing his keys over to Henley. "I just moved in, and the key the superintendent gave me doesn't work. I've been trying for five minutes, but no luck."

"There is no superintendent, and you look like you could save your time and kick the door down instead," said Henley, playing with the keys in his hand. None of them felt heavier than they should have...or lighter. Companies were getting better, though, and things could be hidden in the most innocent of places. One of the keychains looked pretty suspect. No one actually kept a smiley face on their keychain, did they?

"Um, Mr. Richty? Does he have a different title? Landlord maybe? And I can't *kick* the door down. That just sounds painful and expensive." Li reached for his keys, and Henley dropped them into his outstretched palm.

"I'm just fucking with you, kid. Try the blue one, and wiggle it a little," said Henley, leaning up against the door and crossing his arms. Li's hand trembled as he searched for the right key, almost dropping the entire bundle before he found it at last. A flush bloomed across his cheeks, and he looked to Henley every few seconds.

Civilian it was. *Booooring*, unless they were kinky. Normally, Henley had no problem asking someone outright. It was a conversation starter.

"Can I put a collar around your throat and plug your ass with a tail before I chase you around my apartment?"

There could be a reason that he was striking out so often. The last goon had looked like he was about to pass out when Henley had run that by him.

"Oh," said Li, slipping the blue key into the lock. It turned on the first try, the door clicking open with a low clunk. "Thanks, but I'm not a kid."

Henley grinned to himself, shuddering in the cool air. Of *course*, Li wasn't a kid. He was definitely legal, hence fair game. He did look a bit skittish, though.

"Sorry, Li. You said you just moved in?" asked Henley, slipping through the door as Li held it open for him like a gentleman. "You know what? I can't call you Li. It just doesn't suit you, and it's just going to bother me all night." He grinned at Li, waiting for the telltale flush that would spark any second. *Fuck*, he loved being right.

Li looked good to begin with, but with the beginnings of a blush, he turned downright fuckable. Henley was going to climb him like a tree…then trip him and take him the fuck down.

On that thought, maybe there was more than one reason he was striking out.

"All night?" asked Li, his voice catching with an adorable stutter that would have been cute if it hadn't been so sexy. The breeze of the closing door caught his dark hair, throwing it over his shoulder until his pale neck was on display. It looked like it would hold his marks for days.

"Yeah," said Henley, pulling the door shut behind him and leaning against it. The night air hadn't done Li justice. His skin was flawless perfection, everything hard and soft in just the right way. He belonged in a penthouse suite, not a run-down apartment building with neglected flyers bursting out of the busted rectangular mailboxes.

"This is the part where you ask me to show you around, and I show you my favorite spot. I'm a gentleman like that." Henley eyed Li up, wishing that he could see right through his thick jacket. Was he soft there, too, or hard and thick like his long legs? "Then I'll show you *your* new favorite spot." Henley leaned in, rocking up on his toes so he could get close enough to whisper into Li's ear. It was a bigger stretch than he'd expected. "I'll give you a hint. It's your prostate."

About the Author

M.C. Roth lives in Canada and loves every season, even the dreaded Canadian winter. She graduated with honours from the Associate Diploma Program in Veterinary Technology at the University of Guelph before choosing a different career path.

Between caring for her young son, spending time with her husband, and feeding treats to her menagerie of animals, she still spends every spare second devoted to her passion for writing.

She loves growing peppers that are hot enough to make grown men cry, but she doesn't like spicy food herself. Her favourite thing, other than writing of course, is to find a quiet place in the wilderness and listen to the birds while dreaming about the gorgeous men in her head.

M.C. Roth loves to hear from readers. You can find her contact information, website details and author profile page at https://www.pride-publishing.com